Turn From Evil

By

Geoff Loftus

Saugatuck
Books

Books by Geoff Loftus

Double Blind (Published in 2012)

Engaged to Kill (2012)

The Dark Saint (2013)

and the Jack Tyrrell novels:

Murderous Spirit (2016)

Dark Mirage (2016)

The Last Thing (2017)

Dangerous Purpose (2018)

No Traveler Returns (2020)

Fracture of the Soul (2020)

Casual Slaughters (2022)

Turn From Evil

© 2023 by Geoff Loftus

ISBN: 978-1-7346558-9-6

Turn From Evil is a work of fiction. Any resemblance to actual people is unintentional and coincidental. A serious attempt has been made to portray the details and geography of London, East Sussex, and the New York metropolitan area accurately, but I may have exercised poetic license, including with some actual places and buildings. The addresses on Upper Grosvenor Street and Eaton Square are fictitious. I hope the reader will excuse this.

Cover design by Tom Galligan, Green Thumb Graphics.

Published by Saugatuck Books.

Forward

Geoff Loftus knows what it takes to write a superior thriller. He's published ten of them and has more on the way, including the latest in the Jack Tyrrell series, *Turn From Evil*. I've long been impressed by his skills as a novelist. He knows how to grab readers and hold them for a 300-plus page ride. That's a skill that doesn't come easily but is essential to any author of thrillers.

Equally essential is the ability to create interesting characters, like the protagonist in the Jack Tyrrell series. Tyrrell is a drunken former Deputy Marshal who feels guilt over his wife's death and now is determined to help people by righting wrongs. What leads Tyrrell to this change of heart? In a word: God. In the Tyrrell series, Loftus does something very risky—he makes GOD himself a main character. Some readers may be put off by the notion, but as Lisa Tschernkowitsch of WCBS Author Talks says "With God as a boss and a guardian angel as a partner, it's safe to say Jack Tyrrell isn't your average thriller protagonist."

Of course, thrillers are only as good as the stories they tell. Getting them right requires a great deal of research. Here's where Loftus truly excels. He knows his weapons, his cars, and the details of every location in his stories. He's a history buff, and that enables him to write with authority about the smallest historical detail, which enriches the plots. The major portion of his books are set in New York City, and he knows the city better than any cabdriver, cop, or Amazon delivery truck driver. Good luck to any villain confronting Tyrrell. Speaking of villains, the bad guys in the Tyrrell series are a terrific and terrifying collection of psychos, narcissists, neo-Nazis, Russian mafia, the old-fashioned Italian mob, international spies, mercenaries, and even a psychiatrist. They bring more than enough evil to the stories to ensure these thrillers don't lose their thrills.

Most intriguing to me throughout the Jack Tyrrell series is that I cannot help but think they are autobiographical. Loftus's first-person narrative is so seamless and personal that you can't escape the feeling that Tyrrell is based on his author. But as Loftus said in an interview: "We're exactly the same. Tyrrell is six-feet-two, a former Green Beret and former Deputy U.S. Marshal. I'm five-feet-seven and an English major." But the two share a common Irish Catholic heritage and an irreverent sense of humor. And Tyrrell reflects his author's hope that the truth will be found and justice will prevail.

— Tom Seligson
Author of *Kidd* and *King of Hearts*

Turn from evil and do good;
seek peace and pursue it.

Psalms 34:15

**The New American Bible
with Revised New Testament and Psalms**

1

Until the woman staggered in front of my SUV, it had been a magical night driving through gently falling snow.

The first hours of a late night snowfall were lovely in Manhattan. Everything was quiet, and the sidewalks and streets were covered by a clean, white coating about an inch thick. The Hudson River flowed by on my left, its black surface rippling with occasional reflected light from the Jersey side. I was driving north on West Street at 1:07 A.M. There was almost no traffic, but the snow slowed down what traffic there was. I couldn't speak for any other drivers, but I definitely didn't want to skid out and bang up my cousin's brand new Subaru Forester. I was headed to my fiancée's apartment after a late night of work, and in the morning Kim and I were driving in our borrowed vehicle to Bucks County for the weekend. All was right with my world.

At which point the woman ran, stumbling and sliding on the snowy road, about 20 feet directly in front of me.

I slammed on the brakes. The Forester skidded slightly, but the anti-lock braking system kicked in and quickly brought the vehicle to a stop. As soon as the car halted, the woman ran the last few steps toward me and ducked down behind the hood on my side of the SUV.

Bullets thudded into the passenger side of the car. So much for returning my cousin's brand new Subaru in pristine condition. I had some uncharitable thoughts about the shooter, whoever he or she was.

More bullets shattered the front and back windows on the passenger side. I could have sworn I felt the breeze of a bullet passing by my chin. I pushed my door open and dropped to the snowy roadway. I shut the door and looked at the woman, who was only a few feet to my left, crouched behind the front tire. At this point in the proceedings, it would have been a really good thing if I could have pulled out a gun and returned fire. Unfortunately, I only carry a gun when I'm pretty damn sure I will need one. How could I have foreseen my current predicament?

The gunfire had ceased.

"Are you all right?" I asked the woman.

"They're trying to kill me," she replied, her voice husky with fear.

"I got that. Are you okay?"

"Yes . . . yes."

"Good. Stay here." I poked my head up and peered through the Subaru's broken windows.

Two men were coming toward us from Bank Street. I saw they were carrying pistols and other than the fact that they were linebacker size, I couldn't tell anything else about them. One of them must have spotted me because I heard the burping sound of suppressed gunfire and the ping of a bullet bouncing off of the vehicle's roof rack. I dropped out of sight below the driver's side window sill.

A Mercedes sedan slowly rolled past us headed south, and a Chevy Suburban cruised at a slightly higher speed north. The Suburban slowed a tiny bit as he went by us but kept going. Guess the driver figured he should mind his own damn business.

"How do we get out of here?" the woman asked, her voice rising toward panic. Her question and her panicked reaction both seemed reasonable to me. But my fiancée thinks I'm a tough guy, which means I'm not supposed to panic in ugly situations like this one. That left me with no option but to launch a counter-attack.

I peeked through the blown-out windows one more time. The guys were on the sidewalk of West Street, maybe 20 feet away from us. They had spread out; they were going to go around the front and back of the Subaru. I crouched down on the street.

I leaned in close to the woman and whispered in her ear, "I'm going under the car. As soon as you can follow me, crawl under, just far enough to be out of sight."

"But they'll look for me there."

"No, they won't." I didn't wait for her answer but slithered under the Subaru toward the rear bumper. Thanks to the vehicle's high ground clearance, it was a lot easier to do this than under, say, a Ferrari 308 GTS. But it was still a tight fit and we didn't have a lot of time. I felt the woman brushing my right leg as she followed me.

As a pair of booted feet walked past my face, I shot my right arm out, grabbed the near ankle, and pulled hard. The man crashed heavily to the road. I grasped the bumper with my left hand in an underhanded grip and yanked my upper body out from under the car.

The other man shouted, but I ignored him. The man I had toppled was rolling away from the vehicle, which meant that he had to roll onto his left side, then his belly, and then onto his right side—with his gun hand— before coming to a position where he could shoot me. My legs were still under the Subaru; I planted both hands in the snow and thrust myself into a horizontal lunge. I grabbed the man's gun hand just as it came out from under his rolling body.

I jerked the gun gun up and away from me. In the same instant, the man pulled the trigger. Twice. Two harsh belching noises as the gun fired. And an almost simultaneous man's grunt. I heard the thud of a body against the Subaru followed immediately by the softer thud on the ground.

I had my hands full—literally—with the hands and gun of the very energetic man. Underneath his bulky winter parka, he was a big, strong man, and he was doing his absolute best to turn his gun on me. The nerve of this guy. He dropped his left hand from the gun and jabbed me in the gut. It wasn't an ideal way to throw a punch, for which I was thankful, because it still hurt plenty. And even though I now had him out-handed two to one, I still couldn't gain control of his pistol.

I kneed him in the groin. It wasn't the best knee to the balls I've ever delivered, but he grimaced in pain, and his eyes began watering. Then I head-butted him, catching him in the nose and snapping his head back. I wrenched the gun from his hand and stuck it under his chin.

"Stop," I said.

He stopped clutching for the gun and moving around.

"Now listen," I said. "I know what you're thinking. This gun under your chin would be awfully easy to grab. But given that I'm tough enough to have taken it away from you, you might want to consider that I'm tough enough and fast enough to blow your head clean off. So you need to ask yourself, do I feel lucky?"

"Really?" he growled. "You're doing fucking Clint Eastwood?"

I shoved the gun harder under his chin.

"Okay, okay," he said, his growl lessening in ferocity. "I won't move."

"No, you can move. You can roll away from me. But don't stand up."

As he rolled, I did, in fact, stand up. I glanced over quickly at the other man, who'd caught the two bullets fired by my wrestling buddy. He'd been shot in the chest and was

5

as dead as the proverbial doornail. I scooped up the dead man's gun and put it in one of my parka's large pockets.

I returned my attention to the first man. Not only was he big and strong, he was fast. He had a small pistol—maybe a Walther PPK?—in his right hand. Still lying on the ground, he had the gun aimed squarely at my chest. I had only looked away for the briefest instant, yet this guy had gotten the drop on me.

"Drop the guns," he said.

"You first." I resisted the almost overwhelming temptation to bring my gun up and fire.

"Drop your gu—" he repeated but stopped as a Ford Explorer drove by on the southbound side of the road. His eyes diverted for a second, and by the time they returned to focus on me, I had my gun aimed at him. Turns out that I'm not exactly slow either.

Police sirens cut through the night air. They sounded far away, but that might have been an acoustical trick of the snowfall.

We continued staring at each other; our guns never wavering.

The sirens were definitely getting louder.

Even in the darkness, I saw the man's eyes glitter and his jaw tighten.

We fired at the same time.

The bullet tore at my left side, a few inches above my hip. The force of the shot spun me around and smashed me against the side of the Subaru. Somehow my legs did not buckle. I was able to push myself erect and turned to face the gunman.

He was flat on his back in the road, eyes wide open to the falling snow. I walked to him very slowly, knelt, and felt for a pulse. Nothing. There was a hole in his coat over his upper left chest. I'd shot him through the heart.

The police sirens were very loud now. I looked up to see the colors of the emergency lights bouncing off the faces of the buildings on Bank Street.

I managed to stand and walk back over to the Subaru.

"You can come out now," I said, leaning over and extending my left hand.

The woman grabbed my hand, and I pulled her out from under the vehicle. She stood up. For the first time I took note of her appearance: She was a very tall, about five foot nine or ten, very pretty Black woman. That was about all that registered before I slumped against the SUV.

"You've been hurt," she said, grabbing my arms, tried to hold me up, but it was no use. I slid to the ground and passed out.

*   *   *

I woke up to the sound of a patient monitor. There were a couple of nicely undulating lines in bright green stretching across the screen. Still alive and well, as Johnny Winter used to sing.

"Hey there."

I turned my head slowly toward Kim's soft voice and smiled. "Hey there, yourself. Everyone who wakes up in a hospital should get to see you first thing."

"You say that to all your fiancées."

"Every last one of them."

Kim Gannon was, in fact, wondrous to behold even when I wasn't waking up in a hospital bed. Long red hair, sparkling blue eyes, a wide mouth—and a dazzling smile. And just to clear up any confusion, she was my one and only fiancée.

"Where am I? What time is it? What day? What kind of shape am I in?"

"Since I don't agree with the order of your questions, first I will tell you that you're not too bad. You were shot in the left love handle. The doctor said it looks as if you've been shot there before."

"I have. It was no fun the first time either."

"This time around you lost a lot of blood, but other than quite a few more stitches and a new, bigger, badder scar, you're fine."

"Place, day, and time?"

"Beth Israel. First Avenue and 16th Street. Wednesday afternoon. You were out for a little more than 12 hours."

"Have you been here long?

"A little more than 12 hours. The police found an emergency contact card in your wallet."

8

"With your name on it."

"Amazing how that works."

"When am I being released?"

"Probably today."

"Would you mind taking me back to your place and overwhelming me with tender loving care?"

"Can you lay it on any thicker?"

"I can try if you really want me to."

"No thanks. Yes, I'll take you home and make sure you are cared for."

"Cappuccino on demand all day long?"

"There'd better not be any demanding."

"I can see why you'd feel that way. Listen, on another topic, what happened to the young woman who was with me last night? And the two guys who attacked us? Are the police going to be stopping by before I'm released?"

"You sure have a lot of questions for a guy who just woke up from a 12-hour nap."

"A 12-hour, blood-loss-induced nap. And, of course, I have a lot of questions. Wouldn't you want to know about the guys who shot you? And the woman they were chasing?"

"Well, I'm sorry to disappoint you, but I don't know any of the details. I am, however, supposed to call Charlie Winfield at the 6th Precinct as soon as you're ready to talk. Which seems to be now." She pulled her phone and a business card from her purse and dialed.

"Hello, Detective Winfield—yes, sorry, Charlie."

She paused.

"He seems to be okay. But you know how hard that is to determine with Jack."

"*I can hear you*," I faux-whined.

"Yes," Kim said, ignoring me, "I think he'd be happy to see you. . . . That's fine . . . we'll see you in a little while."

She tucked her phone and Charlie's card back in her purse and treated me to that amazing smile as if that made everything okay. I have to admit: It made everything okay for me.

"Charlie will be over here in a few minutes. You can pester him with all your questions."

"I'm not pestering—I was shot for crying out loud."

"And now you're going to use that as the reason for getting every single thing you want."

"It's worth a shot."

"Pun intended."

"Of course."

"So . . . will getting shot get me my way on everything for the next few days?"

"It might not get you what you want for the next few minutes."

"You're so mean."

She deadpanned her reply: "Yes. I am."

"I think I'm going back to sleep now."

"You are such a baby."

Two hospital staffers appeared at the door of my room at that point. A short, freckled-face nurse in scrubs asked me how I felt, nodded when I said "fine," and then checked all my vitals quickly and efficiently. A thin white orderly set lunch on a plastic tray on the bed table that stretched over my legs.

"Are you hungry?" he asked.

"Starving."

"Too bad," he said, pointing at the tray and grimacing.

"Boy, you really know how to sell the cuisine," I replied.

The orderly shrugged and walked out the door. As the nurse finished jotting down numbers on my chart, she said, "Eat hearty." She followed the orderly out of the room.

I said to Kim, "Did you hire those two especially for me?"

"I wish I could take the credit. When the EMS team brought you here, Charlie Winfield was waiting. He told them you were law enforcement and should be given the best possible care."

"I guess I—"

"Was a bloody mess—" Kim interrupted unnecessarily.

"Charlie probably felt that it was pointless to state that I was *former* law-enforcement."

"Are you going to eat?"

"Yes," I grumbled.

Lunch was a bowl of tepid tomato soup—a poor color choice for a hospital meal in my opinion—some crackers that were as tasteless as Holy Communion wafers, and a glass of orange juice. There was also a small cup of what appeared to be chocolate pudding. At least, I told myself it was chocolate pudding and not some other mushy brown substance.

I inhaled the soup, tried one cracker and gave up, and all but sucked the pudding out of its cup. As the orderly had said when he served the meal, "Too bad." At least it gave me some calories to burn.

"I've seen dogs eat with greater delicacy than you do as you consume your lunch."

"Yeah, well, were the dogs—"

"Shot before they ate?" Kim finished my sentence.

"Exactly." I was triumphant. It was a short-lived victory.

"You're using a bullet wound as an excuse to behave worse than a dog?"

"Well . . . it sounds bad when you put it that way."

"Is there a way to put it that doesn't sound bad?"

"No, there isn't," interjected Detective First Class Charles Winfield of the NYPD. Winfield was around five feet eight, stocky, and Black. He had a well-trimmed mustache, and was wearing a dark suit with no tie under his winter coat. He walked into the room at just the right moment to halt Kim's mocking. "How are you feeling?"

"I'll be fine once I get a cup of coffee and some real food in me."

"Maybe later," Charlie said lackadaisically. This wasn't the first time he'd seen me in an emergency medical situation. He pulled a small digital recorder out of his pocket and turned it on.

"For the record, this is Detective Charles Winfield, and I'm speaking to John Tyrrell."

"It's Jack. No one calls me John."

"Sorry, *Jack*. Can you give me the details of what happened last night?"

"First, can you tell me the woman's name and if she is all right."

He nodded. "Her name is Courtney Wilson. And she is fine. According to her, you saved her life."

"Oh no," Kim sighed. "Another woman who thinks Jack is a life saver."

"Excuse me, but I *did* save her life. Who were the bozos chasing her?"

"No ID on their bodies. We're running fingerprints and DNA now. Hopefully, we'll get a hit. One of them had a cell phone, a burner, recently activated. Only had three calls to another burner. We're getting the records to see what cell towers the calls pinged, but for the moment we have nothing on these guys. Now, would you mind telling me what happened."

"I was driving north on West Street, driving very slowly thanks to the snow. This woman came running out

13

of one of the side streets—Bank Street, I think—"

"Yes," Charlie affirmed.

"So, she came running out of Bank Street, right in front of my car, actually my cousin's car . . . is it a total wreck?"

"No. But it's going to be a hell of a repair bill, and who knows when the car will be released from evidence."

"Ugh. My cousin is going to be very disappointed with me."

"Just buy him a new car," Kim said sweetly.

"You're no help."

"If you don't mind . . . " Charlie said. "I need to hear your story. Ms. Wilson was in front of your car. . . ."

"Right. She froze in the middle of the road, and, yes, the 'froze' pun was intended, and I skidded to a stop just before hitting her. She ducked down behind the hood on the driver's side. The side nearest the Hudson River and farthest from the bad guys.

"I heard bullets hitting the Subaru and got the hell out as quickly as I could. The goons came up Bank Street toward us. I slithered under the SUV—thank God for high ground clearance—and told Ms. Wilson to follow me."

"I gotta stop you," Charlie said. "Are you telling me you attacked two armed men from under a car?"

"It seemed like a good idea at the time."

"How?"

"One went to the front, the other to the rear. I went to the rear, tripped the guy who was there, and scrambled

14

out on top of him. We struggled for control of his weapon, and he shot the other guy when he attempted to shoot me—"

"That was a lucky break," Charlie commented.

"It *was* a lucky break. Anyway, Bad Guy No. 1 shot Bad Guy No. 2. I punched No. 1, took his gun away, he pulled a second gun—this guy was really fast—and then we had an old-fashioned shoot out. A quick-draw contest. He lost."

"Wow," Charlie sighed. "You are either incredibly lucky or incredibly good."

"Or both," Kim said.

"Or both," Charlie agreed. He snapped the recorder off and tucked it back into his suit jacket. "Ballistics is no doubt going to find the bad guys' bullets in your car, excuse me, your cousin's car, and the bad guys' bullets in each other."

"Did you find the bullet that went through my left side?"

"No. The crime-scene techs calculated the angles on all the shots. They determined that your bullet went through your side and carried out over the river."

"May I ask you something?"

"Sure."

"Do you have any idea why the bad guys were chasing Ms. Wilson? Why were they trying to kill her?"

2

"No idea," Charlie said. "She's the general manager for a big-time art dealer. Place called the Bargen-Meijer Gallery. Ms. Wilson oversees accounting, shipping, private sales, IT, security, and auctions—all the logistical stuff."

"No customer-facing duties?" Kim asked. Leave it to my fiancée the consultant to inquire about the customers.

"None," he turned to me, "and before you ask, no spouse, no boyfriends, no family issues. She works long hours, goes to the gym a couple of times a week, sees friends for meals and movies."

"Does she have any digital footprint?" I asked. "Social media? Dating app? Maybe she has a digital stalker."

"Doesn't look like it," Charlie shook his head. "She has a Facebook account that she doesn't use much. She was on a dating app but canceled her account a few months ago."

"Do her parents have money? Could the two guys have been trying to kidnap her?"

"Comfortably middle class, but nothing to suggest their daughter would be a profitable kidnap victim."

"Maybe it was a robbery gone bad?" Kim asked.

"Two professional bad guys randomly go after a lone woman on a snowy night?" I responded to her question with a question—bad form, I know.

Charlie was shaking his head again, "It's possible but not very likely." He directed the next question to me: "You sure they were pros?"

"Oh yeah. A very capable pair."

"Too bad they ran into someone more capable."

"That's my Jack," Kim grinned.

"Thank you." I let my mind wander for a second then asked, "Why Bank Street? Does she live there?"

"No, she was leaving the gallery, which is at the intersection of Greenwich and Bank Streets, noticed the guys following her, and ran. Bank Street was just her escape route."

"To summarize: Two unknown men, both professionals, chase and attempt to kill a young woman for no apparent motive."

"Yes, that's accurate."

"Are you providing protection for her?"

"She's staying with a friend tonight. A squad car will be outside the building all night. And with that," Charlie extended his hand to me, "I'm going to say goodbye." We shook, and Kim kissed him on the cheek.

"Tomorrow?" Charlie asked me, "6th Precinct to sign your statement?"

"Yup."

"Thanks. And you are one lucky son of a—"

"Stop right there," Kim said, smiling.

"Okay." He nodded again, walked to the door, looked at me and shook his head, and left.

Kim came and sat in a standard-issue visitors chair with a tiny bit of a seat cushion. At least it was right next to the bed. She held my hand. "Maybe you should call your cousin and tell him about his car."

"You're really looking forward to that, aren't you?"

"I hate to admit it but . . . yes, I am."

"Sadist." I shifted in the bed, trying and failing to get more comfortable. "I guess you had to cancel the reservations for our stay at the cozy B&B in Bucks County."

"Yes. But you heal up, and I'll take you later."

"Promises, promises."

She squeezed my hand, let go, and stood up. "What do you say to my seeing if I can get you sprung from this place?"

"Sprung? We're not breaking out of prison."

She pointed at my lunch. "Are you sure?"

"Yes, please get me sprung before dinner time," I said enthusiastically.

Three hours later, I was happily ensconced on the couch in Kim's living room with a cup of cappuccino in one hand and the TV remote in the other. I sipped my hot beverage and contemplated what to do—if anything—with the television. Despite the caffeine, I felt sleepy. If I read a book, I'd definitely conk out and wouldn't remember the

18

couple of pages I drowsily made my way through before nodding off. If I watched TV, I'd probably conk out, too, but it wouldn't matter what I was watching before I nodded off.

Kim walked into the room and saved me from the necessity of making a decision. "Why do you think those guys were going after Ms. Wilson?"

"I honestly don't have any idea. I guess she was in the wrong place at the wrong time."

"But wouldn't Charlie be able to figure that out from talking to her?"

"Maybe. The last few days or weeks might seem totally normal to her. She might not have a clue what she saw or heard that would make someone want to kill her."

"Really?"

"You got any better ideas?"

"No. But I'm not—"

I joined her in saying, "—a government-trained private detective cum troubleshooter."

I then added, "With all due respect to you as the creator of that wonderful tagline, I think it's time to retire it."

"It still captures the essence of what you do." She was standing in front of the couch, which I felt put me at a distinct disadvantage so I began to get up. Kim put out her hand as if to press me down back into the couch. "Don't stand up. You're too tall. It's better when I'm higher than you."

"Easier to talk down to me?" I grinned.

"Yes, actually."

That created an awkward pause.

Finally, I said, "You think your tagline is my essence? I think I am more than that tagline."

"Okay, it's not the sum total of who you are and what you do, but it's not a bad descriptor. Until . . ."

"Until what?"

"Until it's not."

"What does that mean?" A hard edge crept into my voice.

"Until you're not righting wrongs anymore. Until you retire from your work with Harry for the Chairman."

"And you're hoping that will be very soon?"

"I'm saying that using the government-trained private detective cum troubleshooter tagline is a hell of a lot easier than using your mission statement: You're a righter of wrongs who works in partnership with an angel named Harry and reports—through Harry—to the Chairman, also known as God."

"You didn't answer my question. Are you hoping that I will retire soon?"

"Come on, Jack," Kim pleaded sadly, "you know I want you to retire. You've done enough. You've saved lives. You've righted wrongs. Isn't it time for you to have a normal life with me? A life where all we worry about is how soon our kid's broken arm is going to heal? Or whether or not she'll get into the college she wants to go to?

No more fretting about getting killed by psychopathic bad guys."

"I wouldn't say I *fret* about getting killed—"

She interrupted me, "You're not as funny as you think you are. And you *know* what I *mean*. Don't you think you've done your fair share of good deeds? Is it wrong to want to be able to have a family? Keep all the future good-deed doing inside our home?"

"But . . . but I feel *called* to do this work. It's not just some job."

"I get that. I really do. But does the fact that it's a calling mean it's a lifelong thing? After all, you're not getting any younger. Assuming the next bullet or knife or bomb doesn't kill—"

"I get it, I get it," I said holding up my hands to ward off anymore talk of fatal possibilities.

Kim sighed, "Assuming you aren't stopped by death or injury, you still aren't going to be able to do this forever. At some point don't you think the Chairman expects you to leave this calling behind and answer a different call?"

"I suppose. . . ." It was pretty hard to argue with her logic. My shelf life as a righter of wrongs, even with all my Special Forces and U.S. Marshals Service training, was not likely to endure forever.

"Can I ask a question about another but closely related topic?"

"Of course."

"How do you feel about the two men that you killed?"

"Well, I only killed one of them, and I didn't really know him very well—"

"Don't!" she cut me off sharply. "Don't make a joke about it."

"Sorry."

Kim sat down next to me on the couch and took my hand. "I'm sorry. I didn't mean to snap at you, but . . ."

"Look, it makes perfect sense that you're still feeling raw after what happened with Cecilia St. John only a couple of weeks ago. Killing someone—even when you're saving a life, even when it's *my* life—leaves you hurt for a long time. Eventually you'll find it easier to live with the pain."

"Do you already feel 'easier' about the man you killed last night?"

"Actually, it was the wee hours of this morning."

Kim frowned at me.

"Uh, I haven't really processed it," I said. "I passed out from blood loss within minutes of shooting him. And I'm going to try to stay focused on the fact that I saved Courtney Wilson's life."

"And I should focus on the fact that I saved your life?"

"It'll probably help. A little."

"You've killed a lot of people, and I'm sure they all deserved it," she said with a bittersweet grin, "but how do you live with it?"

"Until recently, I didn't live with it all that well. Look, I came back from Afghanistan with PTSD. I didn't get any help and drank myself silly. Then my wife was killed, and I got even worse."

"And then Maggie appeared to you as a ghost and saved you."

"Yes. She showed me the way to a different life. Now I help people in trouble, see a shrink, go to AA meetings, and have a relationship with a wonderful woman."

"Do you think I should see a shrink?"

"It might help. Do you want me to ask mine if he would see you?"

"Is that a good idea? The two of us seeing the same therapist?"

"I don't know what the professional ethics of the situation are, but he's the only therapist who knows about my work with Harry for the Chairman. Harry referred me to him because he works for the Chairman, too. That might make it easier for you to talk to him about *everything*."

We sat in silence for a while, holding hands.

After a few moments Kim leaned over and kissed my cheek. "Please ask your doctor if he'll see me."

"I will."

She pulled my mug out of my hand, stood up, and asked if I wanted another cappuccino.

"Always."

She smiled, leaned over and kissed me again, and walked off to the kitchen.

I gazed up at the ceiling as if that was where the Chairman resided. "God, please help her. Please."

*   *   *

From Kim Gannon's Diary:

I had to shoot Cecilia St. John. She had a gun on Jack and was going to kill him. It was the only thing I could do.

But . . . oh my God . . . I've never felt this kind of pain before. Killing her was the worst thing I've ever done.

Jack's been so kind. He listens to me. He holds my hand. He makes gentle suggestions about my getting help. He tells me about his own struggles after killing someone. He tells me repeatedly, patiently.

And he does all this despite our sex life having died the same night Cecilia did. I just can't bring myself to . . . make love with him. Too much death.

And then he goes and gets shot. Two men come out of nowhere, guns blazing, and Jack rescues a damsel in distress and gets shot! His rescue of the woman is so Jack, and it's why I love him. But he could have been killed. Again. How much violence is a fiancée supposed to put up with?

I still want to marry him. And have a family with him. I think. I mean, I think I still do. Maybe this is just emotional inertia? A body in motion remains in motion until something stops it. A feeling—like the desire to marry and create a family—continues until something stops the feeling.

I'm terrified that I don't actually love Jack anymore. That I don't want to get married. But I just can't admit it to myself. Maybe all my doubts are symptoms of PTSD after killing Cecilia?

How could I not love Jack? If I don't really love him, why am I still pushing him to retire from his work with Harry? Is that just another case of emotional inertia?

And throughout all this, Jack has been understanding and patient. He hasn't pressed me to have sex. Or impatience anytime I bring up the subject of his retiring.

If Jack promised to retire now, would that make everything better? Would it wipe away all my doubts and jump-start our sex life?

I have this anxious feeling that it wouldn't. Our problems go deeper than his calling. My problems go deeper than that.

*   *   *

Most people who felt pretty damn good less than

24 hours after getting out of the hospital would be happy. But not me. My near-miraculous recovery had left me with a sense of foreboding. Two cups of cappuccino were not sufficient to wipe away the clouds of gloom and doom. So, when Kim began her work day by walking down the hall to her office, I made another cappuccino and called for Harry.

He appeared, as he always did, instantaneously. There was no sense of popping into place. No fade in. No beaming in a la the transporter in *Star Trek*. One second he wasn't there, and the next second, he was. Harry had been whooshing in and out of my life for almost 2 years, but I was far from blasé about his instantaneous comings and goings. Harry was Black, about six feet, slender, always well-dressed. His smooth skin had no wrinkles, and his hair had no gray. Despite his fortyish appearance, I guessed he was thousands of years old.

"Do you require my assistance with your third cappuccino?" he asked.

"Of course not. And you *do realize* how creepy it is that you know how much caffeine I've had this morning, don't you?"

"I am well aware that you find it creepy."

"Which you enjoy immensely."

"I think immensely is a strong word . . ."

I finished frothing my milk and poured it over the espresso in my mug. I kept trying to create a leaf pattern in the milk the way many baristas do but failed again. Oh well, it would taste good.

26

"What the hell happened the other night?" I asked.

"You are referring to the contretemps on West Street?"

"I got shot not quite 24 hours ago, and I feel fantastic today. Has the Chairman cured me so that I'm ready for my next client? Is Courtney Wilson that next client?"

"If you choose to help her."

"I think I'm way past *choosing*. I killed a man to save her life."

Harry shrugged.

"Do you think you could introduce me to my clients without bullets flying?"

"I could . . ."

I took a large sip of my cappuccino. Warm. Delicious. Soothing. "What's the deal with Ms. Wilson?"

"The deal?"

"Don't be obtuse for the sake of messing with me."

"I am not obtuse. I don't know what her *deal* is."

"You don't know why two professionals tried to kill her."

"No. I do know that the fact that two men attempted to murder her is a strong indicator that she needs the kind of aid only you can deliver."

"Only *me*? Oh, don't worry. *No pressure*, Tyrrell. *Free will*."

"As you say."

"Okay. Of course I'll take her case. But are you

telling me that you don't know any more about her than I do?"

"Exactly."

I sighed. Harry didn't react to my theatrical exhale.

"Would you mind taking me to my apartment after I finish my cuppa, then to the 6th Precinct? I know I don't *need* your help to get there, but . . . ," I gently rubbed my wounded side and frowned.

"You are pathetic."

"And you are an angel."

I finished my cappuccino, rinsed the mug, left it in the sink, and headed to Kim's office. I knocked softly on the door and entered when I heard, "Come in."

I leaned into the office. "I'm off to work—"

Kim looked up from her computer. "Are you going to help Courtney Wilson?"

"Well, first I'm going to the 6th Precinct."

"Don't be evasive. You're going to help her, right?"

"After the other night it seems like the thing to do."

"And all our talk about retirement?"

"I haven't forgotten. I promise, I'm thinking about it. Very seriously."

"Of course you are." She started to turn to her computer, stopped, returned her focus to me, and smiled. "Don't forget you need to tell your cousin Tom what you did to his car."

"Wait. I didn't do anything to his car. More accurately, I didn't do anything to his SUV."

"Oh? Does that mean you'll be returning it in pristine condition with a full tank of gas?"

"You're no fun."

"Tell Tom I said, 'Hi!'"

I knew when it was time to retreat from the field of battle. I stepped over to the desk, gave Kim a kiss on the cheek, murmured my goodbye, and closed the door behind me.

As I grabbed my parka from the closet near the front door, I said to Harry, "Change of plans—"

"We're going to your cousin's place first."

"Yes."

*   *   *

My cousins, Tom and Judy Corcoran, lived in a loft in the Meatpacking District, where they had moved long before the area gentrified and the prices had skyrocketed.

Judy was short and cute with bobbed, reddish-brown hair. She greeted me with a big hug and sang out, "Sweetheart! Back so soon! What happened to your trip?"

Tom was stocky, prematurely bald, and had a puckish grin that made him look younger than his bald pate suggested. Unlike Judy, he was not overjoyed to see me.

"Always good to see you, but since our last visit was 2 days ago . . . did something go wrong?" he said.

"Well . . ."

29

"How bad is it?"

"It's 'don't worry I'm going to get you a new Subaru' bad."

"Oh, honey, what went wrong?" Judy asked.

"This had better be good," said Tom.

"It kind of got . . . shot up."

"Shot up!"

"Tom, honey," Judy interjected, rubbing Tom's arm in an attempt to sooth him, "let's hear what happened."

Tom was in no mood to be soothed. Not that it was unreasonable for him to be upset. I would have been in his shoes. He exhaled loudly, "You got my brand new vehicle shot up?"

"Yeah. Bullets. A lot of bullets. Very bad for the windows and body and engine."

"Are you all right?" Judy asked, worried.

"Here I stand, right as rain."

"You look a little pale."

"Well, I did get shot, but only once. Not a serious wound, but a lot of bleeding, which probably accounts for my pallor."

"I'm glad you're okay," Tom said. "At least I will be when I have absorbed this little catastrophe. Do you know how many bullets hit the car?"

"Thirteen. The police have impounded it as evidence. God only knows for how long. That's why I'm going to get you a new one."

"Oh, sweetheart, can you afford that?" Judy had

taken my hand and given it a squeeze.

"I just signed a big, new client, so yes! I can afford to buy you a new car." I didn't mention that my spending plans for my new client's retainer included long luxurious trips to Hawaii and Europe. Oh well.

"Well, you certainly lead an interesting life," Tom said. "How did you get our car shot to pieces?"

"The long and the short of it is that I was driving up West Street, two guys came out of nowhere with guns blazing, and I . . . dealt with them."

"Dealt with them?" Judy was a little pale now.

"You killed them?" Tom asked.

"I only killed one of them. Look, it doesn't matter. I had no choice, I'm not in trouble with the police, and you should order yourselves a new Subaru."

"I'm glad I'm retired," Tom said. "Maybe that's something you should consider."

"Kim tells me that all the time."

3

Harry met me outside my cousins' apartment and whooshed me home without saying a word. I took a quick shower, dressed in blue jeans and a Black Watch flannel shirt courtesy of L.L. Bean, wool socks, and Timberland boots. I thought about slipping a Walther CCP into my parka, but decided the folks at the 6th Precinct wouldn't be happy about my carrying a loaded weapon into their house. In their position, I would have felt the same way.

I found Harry in my living room, waiting patiently. At least, I assumed he was being patient. With Harry it was always hard to know what he was feeling.

"Can I ask you a question?" I asked.

"You *may* ask me a question."

"Pardon me, Mr. Grammar. Is Kim going to be all right? Should I refer her to Dr. Hoffman—is that kosher?"

"That was three questions."

"But who's counting? Will you please answer me?"

"I will. Yes, you can refer her to Dr. Hoffman, and yes, it's . . . kosher. He's the only therapist in the New York area who knows what's going on with you—"

I interrupted, "And you. And the Chairman."

"Yes. Thank you for offering that immensely

helpful clarification. Will Kim recover? As you know from personal experience, the road to recovery from PTSD can be long and hard. But with your love and support, and with Dr. Hoffman's help, she has a good chance."

"What if . . . what if I'm not enough? What happens if I can't help her through this? After all, Maggie wasn't enough for me, and she was a therapist and wonderfully supportive and loved me. . . ."

Harry stepped close to me and put his hand on my shoulder, something I don't think he'd ever done before. "You're not in this alone."

"Thanks," I managed to grunt as I choked up.

Harry removed his hand and asked, "Are you ready to see the police?"

I grabbed my parka, checked for my phone, wallet, and keys, and replied, "Yes, I am."

And *poof*! We were on the sidewalk in front of the 6th Precinct. Poof is the wrong word. It implies a small cloud of smoke, and Harry's whooshings never had smoke, no flashes of light, nothing.

"Will you collect me when I'm done?" I asked.

"If you need me." He had disappeared the instant he finished his sentence.

No two police precincts are exactly the same, but there is a sameness nonetheless. A worn and weathered quality. The paint always seems to need refreshing. The furniture was threadbare. I wondered how long it took a new precinct house to get a lived-in quality. Probably about

10 minutes.

I asked for Charlie Winfield at the front desk and was shown to the detective squad room by a young officer, who was neither worn nor weathered.

"Detective," she said as we arrived at Charlie's desk. "I've got Mr. Tyrrell."

"Thanks." Charlie smiled at her, stood up, and offered me his hand. We shook, and he asked, "How are you feeling? You don't look too bad."

"I feel pretty good actually. I think the hospital gave me a couple of pints of high test."

Charlie settled back down behind his desk and pointed me to a steel chair with the faintest hint of a seat cushion. He drummed his fingers on a file folder, then opened it, pulled out a document, and handed it to me. "Read it, sign it. Please."

"You don't want to ask me more questions? Try to get a fuller picture of what happened?"

"Why? Have you remembered something you didn't know the other night?"

"No."

"Then read it and sign it."

I glanced through the document and signed it. Charlie tucked it back into the file folder, closed the folder, and began drumming his fingers on it again.

"Do you know who the two guys were?" I asked.

"Yes. A pair of thugs from Liverpool."

"Liverpool? As in the Beatles?"

"The very same."

"What are a pair of English gangsters doing here?"

"I don't know why they were here." He stopped fiddling with the folder. "But you said they were pros, and when we couldn't find their fingerprints in any of our domestic databases, we checked with Interpol. Bingo. Both had multiple arrests and had served time in English prisons."

"For what?"

"Assaults. Very rough pair. They obviously didn't care about killing someone," he shrugged, "maybe they've done it before but haven't been caught."

"Do you think they were brought over just to go after Courtney Wilson?"

"Haven't a clue. Maybe they were here for some other job and got redeployed to kill her."

"Huh," I said, more because I didn't have a ready response than because I was a deep thinker.

Charlie began drumming on the folder again. "Listen, Jack, I got a call from the Chief of Ds this morning. He told me to warn you off this case."

"Me? Specifically me?"

"Yes. He told me he didn't want some former Deputy Marshal 'F'ing up the works.' He told me to make sure you understood you are not welcome to stick your nose in this case. You got it?"

"I got it. I have to say the Chief of Ds' attitude doesn't make me feel warm and fuzzy."

"It's not supposed to. Would a cup of coffee help? Just made it."

"Yes, please."

He stood up and pushed the folder toward my side of his desk. "I gotta check something and then I'll be back with the coffee. You take it black, right?"

"Yes," I said, suppressing a grin.

Charlie walked away. As soon as he was out of sight, I flipped open the folder, found Courtney Wilson's contact info, and quickly entered it into my phone. I closed the folder and slid it back to its original location.

Charlie returned with two cups of coffee. Both black. It was fresh, and it was pretty good.

"I think Ms. Wilson needs a friend," he said.

"Don't we all?"

"So, we get by with a little help?"

"Exactly."

"Please be subtle."

"Subtle is my middle name."

"I bet you can't even spell 'subtle.'"

"I'll learn."

"If you can't be subtle, please keep the breakage to a minimum."

"I'll do what I can."

"Thanks, Jack."

*   *   *

Despite the cold, I walked east from the 6th Precinct until I came to Washington Square Park, where I chose a bench with a good view of the small-dog play area near the southwest corner of the park. Some of the dogs were very calm, just surveying their surroundings. Others were little whirlwinds, running and jumping and barking. They were all great. What's not to love about dogs?

I dug my phone out of an inner parka pocket and called Courtney Wilson. Listening to the ring tone, I realized I would appear as an Unknown Number on her phone and wondered if she would even bother to answer.

"Hello?" Very neutral.

"Hi, Ms. Wilson, this is Jack Tyrrell, the man—"

"Who saved me. I'm so glad you called. Are you all right? Detective Winfield told me you spent the night in the hospital. I asked him to ask you to call me—I hope that's okay."

"It's very okay. Did he give you a way for me to prove that I am who I say I am?"

"Yes. He told me you'd probably ask me to make you prove who you are. How did the two of you meet?"

"On a multi-jurisdictional task force. NYPD, U.S. Marshals, FBI. What else did Detective Winfield suggest you ask me?"

"He said I should ask for your fiancée's name and hair color."

"Her name is Kim Gannon, and she has long,

glorious red hair. Is that it?"

"Yes," she chuckled. "Are you all right? Were you badly hurt?"

"No, not too bad. All systems go. But if you're ever stuck in a hospital, don't eat the green Jello."

"Thank you so much for what you did for me. There's no way I can ever repay you."

"Please don't worry about it. I was hoping I could talk to you about what happened. Would you be okay with that?"

"Yes. Detective Winfield said I could trust you."

"How heartwarming. I'll have to send him an especially nice Christmas card this year."

More chuckling. She was a good audience. "I'm happy to talk to you, but what's the point? Aren't the police investigating?"

"Yes, they are. But . . . well, I work for a different authority with incredible resources. I can help you in ways that might be much more effective than what the police can do."

"Wow. Are you a spy or something?"

"Something. Are you free to talk now?"

"Yes. Can I meet you someplace? I feel like I'm in jail."

"Believe me, whatever your friend's apartment looks like, it's much better than jail."

"I just meant that I feel locked in."

"Okay. I'm guessing that since Detective Winfield

helped me to call you, that he'd be okay 'releasing' you to my custody. Tell me where you are. I'll call you from the building's front door. You call Charlie and tell him you're leaving with me. He'll make sure the patrol car on watch is alerted. Sound good?"

"It sounds great." She gave me an address in Brooklyn Heights.

"That's a very nice location for a jail," I said. "I'll be there soon."

"Thanks. See you soon."

We disconnected, and before I could utter his name, Harry appeared.

"Care to whoosh me to Brooklyn Heights?"

"Don't you think your appearing on her doorstep a few seconds after hanging up might be frightening?"

"I didn't, but now that you mention it—"

"Let's wait for a few minutes."

"Okay," I said slowly. "What's on your mind?"

"Excuse me?" Harry replied.

"There's something you want to talk about. What is it?"

"Actually, you need to do the talking."

"Oh?"

"You said there was something on my mind. But you were transferring."

"Ah," I said, loading that simple syllable with as much significance as I could. "I wanted to talk but I transferred my desire for conversation to you."

"Exactly."

"Holy mother of pearl," I muttered. "All right, regardless of whom transferred to whom, I would like to discuss the nature of my calling."

"You are referring to the conflict between your work for the Chairman and Kim's desire for you to retire and become a husband and father."

"Wow. You just cut right to it. My therapist would have taken a whole session to get me to that point."

"Yes, well, even though my lifespan is very long when compared to yours, I don't have an eternity to spend waiting for you to realize the obvious."

"Ouch."

"Now that we've established what you are conflicted about, what do you want to ask me?"

"You're plunging right in? Not even giving me a moment to dig deep into my soul and find a way to explain what my problem is?"

"You're being evasive. And I don't have eternity."

"Maybe it's time for you to try decaf."

Harry had been staring at the Washington Arch on the north side of the park but now turned and looked directly at me.

"Okay, sorry," I said. "Yes, you summed up my conflict quite well. I feel called to continue to right wrongs at the Chairman's direction. But I love Kim and want to make her happy, and she wants me to stop."

"Aren't marriage and fatherhood also callings?"

"Uh, yes. Yes, they are. But Kim feels I should make a choice on which callings I follow."

"Exactly."

"Is that acceptable to the Chairman?"

Harry glanced upward back at me. I often thought that when he looked up the gesture was for my benefit. This time I was certain it was for my benefit. "Yes, He is fine with your making such a choice."

"So it's okay if I abandon my calling?"

"You are being unreasonably binary about this."

"Excuse me?"

"You would not be abandoning your calling of righting wrongs. It's something you've done faithfully, and if you retire, you would be leaving for another calling that you cannot follow simultaneously."

"In other words, I would be exercising free will in making a choice about which calling to follow."

"Exactly."

"What is it with you guys and free will?"

Harry's glare became positively arctic. I was cold anyway, so his expression had no effect on me.

"*You guys*?" Harry asked.

"You know what . . . or whom I mean."

"I don't appreciate your dismissive tone."

"I don't appreciate the choice that's being foisted on me."

Harry gave me his Mona Lisa smile and said, "Poor Tyrrell. Being asked to spend the rest of his life with

41

the woman he loves."

"And raising kids with her."

"Yes. Who knows? That might be the best part."

"Are you implying that I'm afraid of getting married and becoming a father?"

"Who knows?"

And, before I could respond in any fashion whatsoever, he whooshed me to Brooklyn Heights. I was standing on Willow Street by myself, directly across from the Greek Revival townhouse where Truman Capote had lived while writing *Breakfast at Tiffany's*. Eventually, full of booze and literary success, Capote would have an apartment in the swanky United Nations Plaza in Turtle Bay. But it all started for him here on Willow Street, where a police patrol car was now parked in front of Truman's windows.

Courtney Wilson's friend lived in another Greek Revival, red-brick townhouse on the other side of the street. I gave a short wave to the cops, turned, and walked up the steps. I pressed the middle one of the four doorbells. The door speaker squawked in what I imagined a goblin would sound like. It might have been my imagination, but I could have sworn the goblin said, "I'll be right down."

Ms. Wilson appeared a few seconds later, and there was nothing goblin-like about her. Her short, dark hair framed a pretty oval-shaped face and strong, dark-brown eyes. Her skin was the color of milky coffee. And even in a Patagonia Puff Parka, it was easy to see she was tall and slender.

Before I could utter a "hello," she threw her arms around my neck and hugged me tightly. "Thank you so much." She kissed my cheek. "Thank you. I still can't believe what you did for me."

"Happy to do it."

She pulled away from me a little, her arms still around my neck. "How are you feeling? You look a little pale."

"You say that to all white people."

She hesitated for a split-second then smiled. "You're joking, right?"

"Right."

"Seriously, are you all right?"

"I am. Really and truly. I have been pampered continuously since I left the hospital."

She hugged me close again and whispered "Thank you.". Then she let go of me and began moving down the stairs. "Is it too cold to walk on the Promenade?"

"Never. But can we grab coffee first?"

"That sounds perfect. There's a Joe Coffee around the block. Does that work for you?"

"I love Joe Coffee."

The Joe Coffee location was literally around the block from our starting point. I went for a cappuccino, of course, while Ms. Wilson ordered a chai latte. She insisted on paying and held out her credit card to the barista.

"Let's make this cash," I said, digging in my parka

for my wallet.

"That's okay. I got it."

"Please. Cash. I'll explain."

"Cash it is," she said, pulling a $20 from her wallet. Once we had our hot drinks in our winter-gloved hands, we walked the couple of blocks to the Promenade.

The Brooklyn Heights Promenade, or Esplanade, stretches for about a third of a mile above the Brooklyn-Queens Expressway, better known as the BQE. While the expressway is a manic bit of highway running along the edge of Brooklyn, the promenade above it is a beautiful pedestrian walkway with the most stunning views in all New York. From the promenade, you can see from the Brooklyn Bridge just to the north through downtown Manhattan, including One World Trade Center, and then out in New York Harbor distant views of Ellis Island, the Statue of Liberty, and closer at hand, Castle Williams on the tip of Governors Island. Spectacular.

I took a deep breath of the cold, fresh air then a sip of my cappuccino, which was already cooling. Ms. Wilson took a substantial sip of her latte.

"Hot beverages on a cold day," I said. "Love it."

"Me too. Can you tell me why no credit card?"

"Oh, I'm probably being paranoid, but I don't want anyone tracking you through credit-card transactions."

"What? Do you think the guys who were after me are doing that? I mean, is someone after me? Wasn't that just a mugging?"

"I don't know. But I don't think the other night was just random bad luck. It wasn't a pair of muggers out looking for a victim and stumbling over you."

"But why would you think that? Why would someone want to hurt me?"

"That's what I want to talk about with you, Ms. Wilson."

"First, you have got to call me Courtney. No one who saves my life has to call me Ms. Wilson."

"Okay. Courtney."

"Second, the police asked me all those questions. Are you having trouble with a significant other or spouse? Trouble with a family member or friend? Do you owe anyone money? Do you gamble? Or use drugs? Are you having any problems at work?"

"And the answers to all those questions . . . ?"

"No, no, no, no. . . ."

"Let me ask those questions again but with a slight wrinkle: Is anyone you know having some kind of trouble? Maybe your parents or siblings or significant other or close friend? Maybe these bad guys are trying to get to somebody else by going through you."

"I don't think so. My parents live in the same apartment here in Brooklyn where they raised me and my sister. My dad's been working for the Transit Authority his whole life. My mom teaches second grade at a public school that's a ten-minute walk from their apartment. My sister followed my mother into teaching and works at

Stuyvesant High School."

"Good school."

"Yes, it is. But my family members are not the kind of people who run up gambling debt or become addicted to oxy."

"No, it doesn't sound like they are. What about friends, romantic or otherwise?"

"I've been single and unattached for a few years. I see my ex every once in a while; he's always pleasant. He's been with another woman for a year or so. And my other friends, well, I don't know . . . I don't think any of them has got a problem so big that gunmen would come after me."

We walked north on the Promenade, heading toward the Brooklyn Bridge. I steered us over to the railing. We arbitrarily picked a spot, leaned against the rail, and enjoyed the view. I knew that studies had been done to determine what made a flock of birds wheel and soar through the sky in a random but unified way. I wondered if anyone had ever studied the seemingly disconnected moments that led two people to select a spot on a scenic overview. Whatever the reason for our arrival at this specific, unpremeditated choice of location, it provided an amazing vista of the greatest city in the world.

I finished the last of my cappuccino. "Okay, you, your family, and friends have not run up some gigantic, murder-worthy tab with these unknown bad guys."

"That's right."

"That means something you did or something

you've seen has triggered this."

"I work in an art gallery."

"The Bargen-Meijer Gallery."

"Yes," she smiled. "The name is Dutch, an allusion to the great Dutch masters."

"Shades of Rembrandt and Vermeer."

"Exactly. But the gallery is owned by Raymond O'Malley."

"That has a nice Dutch ring to it."

"Mr. O'Malley made a fortune on Wall Street. He was always interested in art, and when he retired from the financial services industry, he bought the gallery."

"And kept the name for that touch of authenticity."

"I suppose so," her smile grew wider. "We're not in the same class as Sotheby's or Christie's, but we handle hundreds of millions in sales every year."

"*Hundreds* of millions?"

"Yes."

"And out of that hundreds, Bargen-Meijer keeps a percentage of the action."

"It's called a commission."

"And what do the buyers and sellers get for that commission?"

"We verify the provenance of the art, handle the shipping and insurance, auction costs if the piece isn't sold privately, act as a broker if the piece *is* sold privately—"

"Okay, I surrender. There's a lot involved. And you're the office manager?"

"General manager," she corrected me.

"I'm sorry. That's a much bigger job."

"Yes. Thank you. I oversee all the business and logistical aspects of the gallery."

"But you have nothing to do with the art itself?"

"Well, I know what I like . . . but no, I have nothing to do with the artwork. We could be selling widgets as far as my job goes."

"Doesn't sound very ominous."

Just then my internal radar pinged. Not a loud urgent ping. But enough to make me turn around and scan the promenade. About two hundred feet south, two big guys were walking slowly toward us. One white, one Black, both with short hair and aviator sunglasses.

"We should move along," I said.

"Oh, okay." Courtney took a step to the south, in the direction we had come from. I grasped her arm above the elbow and gently tugged her in the opposite direction.

"Let's try something new."

She was puzzled, glanced back over her shoulder, and spotted the gentlemen behind us. She gasped softly. "Are they after us?"

"Probably."

"Do you have a gun?"

"I wish."

4

We walked quickly along the Promenade as it curved away from its place above the BQE. It was early March, which meant there were no handy bushes or leafy trees to hide behind. We reached Columbia Heights. Still nowhere to hide. No handy bricks or cobblestones or soiled tissues to use as weapons. I spotted a garbage can across the street at the corner of Columbia Heights and Orange Street.

I grabbed Courtney's hand and said "Come on!" pulling her along at a run. When we reached the can, I yanked off the cover and began combing through the trash.

"What are you doing?" she asked. She sounded perplexed. And more than a little bit frightened. I know I was scared.

"Just looking. Want to make sure people are recycling—ah ha!" I pulled out two amber-colored, 12-ounce Coors Light bottles. Since I no longer consumed alcohol my opinion didn't matter, but I had never seen the point of a Coors Light beer. Coors itself was not a full-bodied brew, so what the hell was the point of a Light version? Anyway, I digress—I grabbed the two bottles, checked around, and saw a dark-gray van that was parked a few spaces away from us on Orange Street.

"Let's go," I said and began running.

Courtney followed me, and we ran to the rear of the GMC Savana Cargo van: about seven-feet tall so no need to crouch. The side panels were windowless, but the windows at the rear gave us a clear view through the body of the van to the windshield and beyond.

Our buddies showed up a few seconds later. They looked around, exchanged a few words, drew their guns, and split up. The Black guy headed down Columbia Heights away from Orange Street. The white guy continued toward us. He was walking slowly and methodically, checking all around him, staying near the buildings and away from the cars parked next to the sidewalk. His path was making it very difficult for a nasty man like me to surprise him.

I dug into one of my pockets for my keys, waited until he disappeared out of sight of the windshield, counted to three, and lobbed my keys like a hand grenade near the front of the van. I could hear his shoes crunching on the sidewalk ice, burst from my hiding space, and raced toward him.

White guy realized his mistake pretty damn fast, wheeled around, and fired. I felt the bullet tug at my parka but not penetrate me. A micro-second after the tug there was a metallic *thunk* as the bullet slammed into a parked car. At the same time, I was in front of him, whipping a beer bottle across his face. He staggered backward,

50

dropping his gun.

Before I could scoop up his weapon, he blinked, which was all he seemed to need to clear his thick head, and counter-attacked. I dodged his left-right combo, then stepped within an arm's reach, and whacked him on each side of his head with the beer bottles. The bottle in my right hand shattered on impact as he fell, his head thumping on the sidewalk. He was covered in amber-glass shards.

I picked up his weapon. A Beretta M9, a favorite of the American military, with a 17-round capacity, not including a single round in the chamber.

White guy was conscious but barely. He rolled onto his chest and tried to push himself up off the sidewalk. I hammered his head with the butt of his gun, and that knocked him out for good.

In all the excitement, I had forgotten the Black guy. I wished he had returned the favor, but when he heard the gun shot, he must have run back on Columbia Heights toward us. I knew this because he shot at me. I heard the whine of a bullet zip past me.

I dove toward the van, where Courtney was still hiding, hit the sidewalk at the curb, rolled on impact, and went over the curb into the snowy slush on Orange St. My parka was probably beyond saving. I hoped the same wasn't true for Courtney and me.

A bullet bounced off the sidewalk a couple of feet away from the two of us as the Black guy hustled toward us. He fired again, missing me by a mere inch or two.

I lined up the Beretta and fired three times, aiming center mass. I hit him with at least one shot. The Black guy stood still for a moment then collapsed. I climbed out of the slush-filled gutter and ran over to him. All three shots had hit him. He was dead. I secured his weapon and patted down his corpse. I took his wallet and cell phone.

Kneeling next to him, I spoke softly to his body, "I'm sorry about this. I really am."

I stood up, found my keys lying on the sidewalk, pocketed them, and ran back to Courtney, who hadn't moved from her hiding place behind the van.

"It's okay," I said. "You're safe." I patted down the white guy and took his wallet and phone. "Much as I'd love to stay and chat with this man, we gotta go."

The sound of police sirens was in the air, distant but growing louder fast.

"What?"

"Come on, we've gotta go. Now." I grabbed her hand and walked her back to Columbia Heights then headed south. Two police cars screamed past us on Columbia Heights.

"How did they find me?" Courtney asked.

"I was just wondering that. Do you leave your cell phone on your desk at work? Could someone have scooped it up and installed a tracker app?"

"My phone sits on my desk all day. The gallery issued it to me."

"Are you carrying it now?"

"Yes, of course."

"Please give it to me."

She dug it out of her purse and handed over a Samsung Galaxy. "I have my own phone, but I always keep that in my purse. And I keep my purse with me or in a locked drawer."

"You're a trusting soul."

She grinned.

"Okay, hang onto your personal phone for now. But we have to get rid of this thing," I said, shaking her work phone in my hand.

A private-carter garbage truck was idling just ahead of us on Columbia Heights. The two-man crew was hauling trash cans from a low-rise apartment building. I dropped the bad guys' phones on the ground, quickly stomped on them, and plucked two SIM cards from the detritus.

"Will that prevent people from tracking those phones?" Courtney asked.

"No," I said, scooping up the pieces of the shattered phones in my gloved hands. "The GPS chip is usually embedded on the phone's mother board. The SIM cards will allow us to look at their call history."

As the garbage men dragged large empty canisters back to the building, I stepped into the street to the rear of the truck and dumped the shattered phones and then Courtney's work phone into the truck's dumping bay. I was back next to Courtney on the sidewalk before the men returned to the truck. I glanced back over my shoulder and saw one of the guys pull the lever to activate the garbage smasher. Trash compactor. Whatever it was called. Within seconds, all the phones were smushed into the stinking, rotting compacted mass.

The sound of sirens was still in the air, but we reached Clark Street without any more patrol cars passing us. We turned left to go to the subway station at Clark and Henry a couple of blocks away. I pulled my phone from inside my slush-soaked parka and was relieved to discover that it hadn't suffered water damage. I dialed Stewart Budman, who was the forensic accounting specialist at Tyrrell Security Consultants. (Okay, maybe the name was a wee bit pretentious, but it sounded solid, and most people shopping for security want solid.)

"Hey, Jack," Stewart answered.

"Hey yourself. Listen, no time for pleasantries."

"The usual?"

"If you mean being chased by bad guys."

"Yes, that's the usual."

"Didn't I just tell you that I don't have time for pleasantries?"

"You did. Sorry. What can I do for you?"

"My client and I will be coming to you in about 15 to 20 minutes. Can you please check out the Bargen-Meijer Gallery? And it's owner, Raymond O'Malley?"

"Got it."

"Our new client is Courtney Wilson, the—" I

hesitated and asked Courtney, whispering "your title?"

"Director of Operations."

I repeated that for Stewart. "See you soon."

Courtney was confused. "You really think this has something to do with my work? You got rid of my phone and now you're checking up on Mr. O'Malley. He's a bit of a stiff but a gentleman. Never hits on his employees, seems to have been happily married for more than 30 years. Father of two daughters and a benefactor to multiple charities."

"I get it. O'Malley seems like a good guy. But . . . you're pretty sure there's nothing going on in your personal life. That kind of leaves work."

We walked five blocks and reached the subway station. Only minutes after our shootout on Orange Street, we were safe and secure on a Manhattan-bound 2 train.

The subway conductor was announcing that the next stop was Wall Street, the first stop in Manhattan if you came from Brooklyn.

"When I asked if you were a spy or something, you said 'something.' Where . . . how did you learn this . . . stuff?" she asked.

"The Army. Special Forces."

"That's Green Berets, right?"

"Right. Then I was a deputy in the Marshals Service."

"You were a marshal?"

"I was a *deputy*. There are ninety-something

55

marshals, one for each federal court district. But there are a heck of a lot more deputies. I was one of the heck of a lot more."

"And you're not a deputy anymore?"

"No."

"What are you?"

"My fiancée likes to call me a 'government-trained private detective cum troubleshooter.'"

"Catchy."

"She likes to think so."

"You still haven't told me who you work for. Is it one of those 'I'd tell you but then I'd have to kill you' kind of things?"

"That would be bad after all the effort I've expended keeping you alive. No, my backstory is very . . . very difficult to explain." A subway running between Wall Street and Fulton Street didn't seem like the place to explain that I was a righter of wrongs, working for the Chairman.

"Which is the reason your fiancée thinks that 'government-trained' thing is catchy."

"Compared to the complete, full-detail download, it's very catchy. Look, Charlie Winfield told you that you could trust me. I hope that will be enough for you."

Courtney nodded, "I guess it will have to be. For now."

"Great."

The train stopped at Fulton Street for a minute and

then rumbled on toward Park Place.

"Where are we going?" Courtney asked.

"We'll get off at 14th Street. Three more stops. I want to introduce you to my team. After that, we'll head to the Upper West Side. Are you all right with that?"

"As long as you keep saving my life, I'll go anywhere with you."

"You're easy to please."

She smirked. I was struck by her resilience. A lot of people would have wanted to go into hiding after what she had gone through in the past few days. Not Courtney.

The train stopped at Park Place, and passengers did the off-and-on dance. The subway resumed its journey, now headed toward Chambers Street.

"Let's think about what might have happened at your job that could have led to all this," I said. "Maybe it's not what you do, but what you've seen or overheard." Speaking of hearing, if you wanted to have a meaningful conversation about dark dealings and attempted murder, a moving subway was not the optimal place. "Have you noticed any strangers around the gallery lately?"

"I see strangers at the gallery all the time. First-time buyers or long-time clients who've never visited the gallery before. What does a stranger—the kind of person who would send people after me—look like?"

That was a good question that would remain unanswered, at least for a moment as the train pulled into Chambers Street. The passengers did their bit. The train pulled out. The conductor announced that our next stop was 14th Street.

What did a person who would order others to attack Courtney look like? Was there a visual clue to a person's capacity for violence? I knew from experience that there was no way to detect someone like that.

"What made you leave the Marshals?" Courtney asked, interrupting my deep thoughts on strangers.

"I had a drinking problem. I associated with the wrong people. Got myself shot and my wife killed."

"Oh, my God."

"I'm pretty sure that was all on me and not God."

"I'm sorry, I didn't mean—"

"I know. It's okay. Really."

"When . . . I'm sorry. Do you mind my asking these questions?"

"Not at all. I asked you to trust me—I should be willing to tell you *something* about myself."

"When was . . . your wife killed?"

"Almost 7 years ago in 2010."

"Do you still have a drinking problem?"

"Yes. But now I have a solution. I'm in AA."

"My Dad's in AA. He loves it."

"A lot of us do."

I smiled, and so did Courtney. She understood, as much as anyone who wasn't an alcoholic could understand.

Our train slowed and pulled into the 14th Street station. We exited and joined the crowd climbing the stairs out of the station to Seventh Avenue. I scanned in every direction, looking for evildoers.

"What's wrong?" Courtney asked. "What are you looking for?"

"Just making sure no one followed us."

"But my phone is in the back of a garbage truck."

"Someone might have been following us before I trashed your phone."

Courtney began looking around, anxious as a horror-movie teenager in a dark room.

"It's okay," I said as soothingly as if I were selling hot chocolate on a TV commercial. "There's very little chance anyone was able to catch up to us by the time we hopped on the subway. I'm just being extra cautious." I made an exaggerated sweep of our surroundings. "And I'm pretty darn sure we're not being followed."

We reached the street and walked uptown on Seventh.

"Are we almost there?"

"Yes. We'll be there in just a few minutes, and all will be revealed. Okay?"

"I guess so."

We turned left on West 17th Street and proceeded past Eighth Avenue, passing a playground on our left and reaching a long row of narrow, five-story townhouses. We stopped at 324 West 17th.

"I'm afraid our destination is on the 5th floor, all the way at the top and there's no elevator."

"Does this count as my workout for today?"

"You tell me once we get there."

After being buzzed in, we climbed slowly and steadily up the stairs. We reached the fifth floor breathing heavily but not panting. To be honest, I was breathing more heavily than Courtney. Then again, I was almost 20 years older and at least 80 pounds heavier.

Stewart was in the open doorway of a railroad flat, a narrow apartment that ran through five rooms—the length of the building from front to back. Lots of space if you didn't mind going from room to room like walking through train cars.

Stewart was white, and a solidly built five-feet-six, with thick brown hair that curled over his ears and the back of his neck.

"Coffee?" he asked as we trudged up the last of the steps.

"Yes, please," I said. "Courtney, this is Stewart. Stewart, this is Courtney."

"Hello," Courtney said and shook hands with Stewart.

"Hello. Would you like coffee? Or tea?" he asked.

"Tea, thanks."

We entered the apartment in the kitchen, which had a small square, wood table and four chairs. I folded my coat over a chair and Courtney did the same. Stewart put a tea kettle on to boil then stepped over to the drip coffee pot.

"You know the way to the office," he said to me.

The word "office" might lead you to assume that the middle room of the apartment had sleek yet functional furniture and was a glittering technological operation. But the truth was far from that: tables and chairs that possessed all of the fashion flare of Salvation Army hand-me-downs, multiple computers, monitors, and keyboards.

Naomi, as she always seemed to be, was sitting in front a monitor. Naomi was very pretty, petite, Asian, and had black hair streaked in neon blue. She stood up and shook hands with Courtney.

"I'm Naomi."

"Courtney."

"Welcome to our lair. Hey, Jack, was that your handiwork on West Street a mere 36 or 37 hours ago?"

"Yeah, afraid so. And Courtney is the woman they were trying to kill."

Naomi said, "The *Post* said the rescuer was shot, but the wound was not life-threatening. Are you okay?"

"Yup."

Naomi turned to Courtney, "Well, you have Tyrrell on your case. He'll keep you safe."

"Are you moonlighting as my publicist?"

She shook her head and asked, "What are we working on today? Am I hacking the NSA? Or the Federal Reserve? Or Stephen Colbert's secret files?"

"Does Colbert have secret files?"

"Maybe we should find out."

"Interesting but no," I said. "May I?" I asked

Courtney, gently pulling her purse from her hands and giving it to Naomi. "Please check this bag for tracking devices. Start with her phone."

"What's your phone password?" Naomi asked.

"V-W-V-G 1890," Courtney said. "Capital letters except for the second V."

Naomi looked at her quizzically.

"Van Gogh's initials?" I asked.

Courtney nodded, "And the year he died."

"Given that you work in an art gallery with a Dutch name," Naomi mused out loud, "maybe not a super-secure password."

"And as an added bonus," I dug out the SIM cards from the bad guys' phones and handed them over to Naomi. "I don't know the passwords."

"Should I assume these were surrendered involuntarily?'

"Correct."

"You work fast, Jack," Naomi said. She sat down at her desk, plugged Courtney's phone into one of the many cords leading to her computer and began doing her hacker thing. What Naomi could do with technology seemed like magic to me. I was very glad she was on my side.

Stewart returned with two mugs and handed one to Courtney and one to me. "I began a dive into the international art dealer—at first glance, pure as Mary's little lamb."

"Before we get to Bargen-Meijer, I have a little

bonus for you," I handed the wallets to Stewart. "Could you see what you can find out about these clowns?"

Stewart was confused, "These aren't from the other night, are they? Didn't the cops keep any wallets or whatever?"

"They did. This is a fresh batch."

"Like the SIM cards?" Naomi asked.

"These are a *fresh* batch?" Stewart was surprised. "Did you kill more bad guys?"

"I didn't have a choice. They were shooting at us."

"When did this happen?"

"About a half-hour ago."

Stewart shook his head and muttered, "Wow."

"Yeah, I wish it had gone differently. Anyway, what does Bargen-Meijer look like at second glance?" I asked.

"Well!" Stewart sounded triumphant. "It seems that the gallery is owned by a shell company that is owned by another shell company. The ultimate owner is Raymond O'Malley. Now there's a well-funded corporate checking account at a New York bank—"

"We use that for expenses and payroll," Courtney said.

"Yes. But there's a lot of money coming in from sales that doesn't go into that account."

"We have an offshore account with a bank in the Caymans. It's easier for our non-U.S. clients."

"I bet it is," Stewart said with a big grin. "But

Bargen-Meijer doesn't happen to have *an account* with *a bank* in the Caymans. It has *several accounts* with *several banks* in the Caymans."

"I've never seen any record—digital or paper—that shows we have more than a single account in the Caymans."

Stewart nodded. "Before your boss became an art dealer, he was a Wall Street wizard. Lots of experience with shell companies and offshore bank accounts. I'm pretty sure he knows how to hide money. If I were him, I'd want my gallery staff to think everything is on the up and up."

"Why? What's he's hiding?"

Naomi spun around in her chair and handed Courtney her phone. "This is clean. Give me a few minutes to check your purse."

"Of course," Courtney said. "Thank you."

"You're welcome." Naomi addressed Stewart, "Go on, what's her boss hiding?"

"Well . . . at a guess . . . ?" he focused on me as if wanting my approval to proceed.

"Go ahead, please tell us what your guess is."

"Okay. This is all conjecture, but I think your boss might be laundering money through his gallery."

"Are you kidding me?" Courtney was stunned.

"I wish. But millions of dollars—maybe billions of dollars—in art gets bought and sold every year around the world. And here's the kicker: There's virtually no scrutiny regarding the flow of money."

"I'm not sure it's accurate that there is *no* scrutiny," Courtney demurred.

"Oh. Do most buyers and sellers know each other? Do the sellers know that their art work is being bought with legitimately earned funds? Or is it possible that the buyers are paying with the funds that come from dealing massive quantities of illegal drugs? Or weapons? Do the sellers even care?"

"Many sellers and purchasers have no direct contact with each other," Courtney admitted. "A large number of our transactions are anonymous on both ends."

"Exactly. The art world prizes anonymity. Large amounts of cash flowing in all directions through anonymous transactions is a perfect way to launder money. And the dealers are very happy middlemen, receiving their commissions on each transaction. Everybody wins."

"Except law-abiding citizens all over the world," I pointed out.

"Details, details," Stewart muttered.

"But if it's all anonymous, I'm not in a position to know what's going on," Courtney said.

"And if you don't know," Naomi said, spinning around again and handing Courtney her purse. "There's no reason for anyone to kill you. Your purse is clean by the way."

"Thanks," Courtney replied and looked to me. "Naomi's right, why would anyone kill me?"

Stewart answered, "Your boss has a lot of offshore bank accounts and shell companies. He's probably helping people conceal and/or invest their freshly laundered cash."

"And you think that I somehow know one of his criminal clients?"

"I do," said Stewart.

"Me, too," chimed in Naomi.

"Sorry, but it makes the most sense," I said. "Your boss is a practitioner of financial magic with offshore accounts, shell companies, and a commodity that is bought and sold anonymously. It sounds ripe for abuse."

Courtney's response was barely more than a whisper, "And for killing me."

"I'm afraid so."

5

Courtney and I moved to the room at the front of the railroad flat. The view north to the Empire State Building was the best thing about the room. The couch and arm chair were covered in an old, vaguely floral pattern. Weathered but still comfy. We drank our coffee and tea in silence as Naomi and Stewart continued to dig into Bargen-Meijer and Raymond O'Malley.

After a half hour—long after I had finished my coffee, but while Courtney was still sipping her tea—Stewart walked into the room.

"We have some results. Wanna come look?"

Courtney and I followed him back to the office. I kept going through the office to the kitchen and poured myself a refill. Despite having sat on the warmer plate for a while, the coffee had not yet cooked to a bitter paste. I returned to the office, and Stewart launched into his report.

"I put aside trying to untangle all the offshore accounts and shell companies. I'll figure it out if you want me to, but I don't think it will provide any useful information beyond the fact that Raymond O'Malley sits at the top of this little enterprise."

"Makes sense," I agreed.

"I did verify that a hell of a lot more cash flows to the offshore accounts than goes into the gallery's checking account."

"What's a hell of a lot more cash mean?" I asked.

"Tens of millions of dollars."

"Whoa."

"Yeah. And I checked the identities of your two guys. Fake driver licenses. Good quality but fake."

"However," Naomi smiled, "they used their real faces for the photos. I used facial-rec software and a quick hack of Interpol. They're muscle out of England."

"Listen to you—'muscle,'" I said.

She smirked in response. "That's what they are. Both have a bunch of convictions for violent crime, all in England."

"What about the SIM cards?"

"Both from burner phones. And they only called other burners."

"In England?"

"No. All the calls were in New York. Manhattan, in fact."

"And that's it?"

"That's it for the SIM cards," Naomi said. "But I hacked into the Bargen-Meijer's security system, and searched for customers who visited the gallery in the 72 hours before the attack on Courtney."

"Did you find anyone?" Courtney asked.

"I think so," nodded Naomi.

She clicked a file and a screenshot of a security video popped up on the monitor. Two men were standing in front of a large painting in one of the gallery's display rooms. (I didn't recognize it and couldn't begin to tell you who painted it.) The man on the right appeared to be middled-aged, medium height, thinning brown hair, horn-rimmed glasses. He was talking to a tall slender man with blond hair in an impeccably tailored suit.

"Do you recognize him?" Naomi asked Courtney.

"The shorter man is my boss. The other man is a customer, I think. He was in on Wednesday. But I don't know his name."

"I used facial rec and a bit of hacking the TSA to identify him," Naomi continued. "A quick bit of research revealed that he's Nigel Sinclair, twice married, twice divorced, 47 years old. Five feet eleven. From his drivers license photo it looks like he's got blond hair, a mustache and goatee, and brown eyes.

"Mr. Sinclair now lives in London, but he grew up in a working class neighborhood in Manchester. He attended King's College at Cambridge on scholarship. He polished his act at Cambridge, leaving behind his working class roots. Self-made millionaire in a variety of businesses. Seems to have the Midas touch. Enjoys the London club scene, almost always with a young actress or model on his arm. Began collecting art about 10 years ago. Active as a buyer *and* a seller."

"Why do you think he's behind the attack on me?"

"He's the only guest that Raymond O'Malley showed into his private office, *and*—" Naomi clicked on a file and a video played.

O'Malley and Sinclair were walking down a hallway in the gallery. The only other person to appear in the video beside was Courtney, who smiled at Sinclair. He appeared to greet her with a simple "Hello."

"I smiled at him. That's all. You think he's trying to kill me for smiling at him?"

"There must have been something else," I said.

Naomi shook her head. "That's the only point of contact between Courtney and a customer for 72 hours. Everything else is Courtney and various gallery staff."

"That can't be it," Courtney protested. "Nothing happened."

"Are you sure?" I asked. "Let's break it down, moment-by-moment. Naomi, can you play that video again? In slow motion? Just a second," I turned to Stewart, "can you do a quick dive into Sinclair's financials? See if there are any signs of ill-gotten gains that he might want to hide?"

"On it."

Naomi re-ran the video in slow motion. When television police watched video at a frame-by-frame speed it's a focused intense moment as some tiny detail is discovered. That was not my experience watching the mind-numbingly slow moment between Courtney and Sinclair. Less than 30 seconds of real time became minutes of slow-mo replay.

We were in the middle of watching it for the second time when Naomi suddenly paused the video and sang out, "I see it!"

"Where?" I asked.

"It's not Sinclair, it's O'Malley. Look at his right hand."

"He's holding a piece of paper."

"That can't be what we're looking for," Courtney said. "He frequently walks around with pieces of paper. Bids on artwork, or bank information for the transfer of funds from a buyer or to a seller. He marks everything down in a log he keeps then hands it to one of my staffers to enter into our QuickBooks Desktop Enterprise, our management software."

I asked. "How often does O'Malley carry paper around?"

"It depends. Sometimes it's once or twice a month. Sometimes it's two or three times a day."

*   *   *

AFTERNOON – BARGEN-MEIJER GALLERY

NIGEL SINCLAIR relaxed in a leather-covered, thickly upholstered arm chair facing Raymond O'Malley's mahogany desk. O'Malley paced around the desk. He was a solidly built man, five feet ten, brown hair going to gray, blue eyes, crow's feet at the corners of his eyes.

"Raymond, please, sit down," Sinclair said in an artificially plummy British accent—the product of much hard work on his part. "You're going to wear a hole in this nice carpet."

"Pardon me for being a bit anxious. I've never been involved in something like this."

"Like this? Are you saying that you've never had to eliminate an obstacle in your business dealings? Really?"

"I've never tried to have someone killed."

"Well," Sinclair smiled mirthlessly, "now you'll be able to cross that off your bucket list."

"That's not funny."

"Humor depends upon your perspective."

"I don't understand your perspective."

"Oh? Sorry. As you pointed out to me, you were holding an invoice detailing one of our purchases. You thought she glanced at it and might have noticed some of the details. Unfortunately, that made her a threat. And I always eliminate threats as soon as possible. You might say it's the secret to my success."

"This is crazy. There's no way Courtney knows anything. I didn't introduce you by name. She couldn't have read the invoice. You're overreacting."

"Maybe I am. But I find that I feel much safer when reacting swiftly and severely to anything that even faintly resembles a threat."

O'Malley shook his head and repeated, "This is

crazy."

"Fine. Let's agree that the situation is crazy. But we are engaged in business dealings with large sums of money at stake. I do not want our financial success jeopardized by one young woman who may or may not know what we're doing. Besides, it's too late now. My men are already in motion."

"Again. They're in motion again. Don't you think you're playing a little too fast and loose? The more your people behave wildly, the more vulnerable you and I become."

"I am not at all concerned. There is no direct connection between me and my teams in the field. As you know—since you established them—I have multiple companies held by other companies and my banking is handled through multiple off-shore accounts. The men cleaning up the Courtney issue have never met me, never communicated with me."

"But they come from England."

"They are far from the only Englishmen in New York." Sinclair smiled a tight, thin-lipped smile, more like a grimace than a grin. "I suggest you relax, Raymond. It won't be long before this conversation is moot."

*   *   *

"Why does O'Malley even use paper?" Naomi

asked. "Can't all the information be sent electronically?"

"It can. But Mr. O'Malley is a self-described troglodyte. He says that writing things down helps him remember the details."

"So that piece of paper he's holding is probably the details of an offer from Nigel Sinclair to buy a piece of art," I said. "Price and banking info, right?"

"Yes, but I didn't see any of the details."

"Naomi, could you please replay that few seconds where O'Malley's piece of paper is visible?" I asked.

Naomi reran the video at what must have been super slow-motion. The video rolled forward at an agonizingly unhurried pace.

"Wait! There," I said pointing at the monitor. "Look at O'Malley's hand. His wrist is turned up toward the ceiling so the piece of paper is clearly displayed."

"But only for a few seconds," Courtney said. "I still didn't see anything."

"You know that, and I know that, but that flash of paper might be what's driving someone to come after you."

"But I didn't see anything," Courtney said, frustrated. "I don't even know if the information was input to QuickBooks."

Naomi spoke up, "I'll see if I can get into the software and find transactions for Sinclair." She asked Courtney, "What's your login to the system?"

"My user ID is my company e-mail—"

Naomi interjected, "cwilson@bargen-meijer.com."

"Yes. And the password is—"

"Please, let me guess," Naomi grinned, "It's 'vermeer1675.' Right?"

"Close. It's 'pearlearring1675.' You're good."

"Thanks. Most people have habits when it comes to their passwords."

"Won't they have disabled my login?"

Naomi's fingers flew over her keyboard, "Depends on how many things Mr. O'Malley is juggling right now. Disabling your login and access to office software might not be top of mind at the moment. *Annnnd*—we're in!" She stood up and indicated that Courtney should sit in her chair. "You can probably find the transaction much quicker than I can."

"Thanks." Courtney took the seat, clicked and typed, and turned to us and said, "Sorry. Nothing. No new transactions for Sinclair."

"How fast do offers usually get entered into the system?" I asked.

"Within hours."

"So . . . no transaction?" Naomi asked.

"Nope." I answered. "A transaction so important that O'Malley would kill for it is important enough to be handled off the books."

"But there's no proof there was a transaction," Courtney said. "Never mind proof that it might have been illegal and that Mr. O'Malley might be trying to have me killed."

"Maybe O'Malley isn't behind the killing," I said. "My bet is that Sinclair sent the bad guys after you."

"But Mr. O'Malley would have to know."

"Yes, he would."

"But there's no proof . . . ," she repeated, having a hard time believing the secret-transaction theory. I would have had a hard time believing it in her place. How could catching a glimpse of a piece of paper be enough to put you on someone's death list?

"I know this is hard to accept," I said softly. "But what else could it be? You've been over all the possible personal motivations with the police and with me. You've never witnessed any overt criminal behavior. You didn't know about O'Malley's offshore accounts and shell companies. And you never met Sinclair except for a brief moment in the office at the gallery."

"What else could it be?" Courtney asked in a husky whisper, still struggling to accept what she had heard.

"Hey," Stewart broke into our conversation, "I've been looking into the English *muscle* men, and they all have home addresses and bank accounts in London. And they all work for Mr. Nigel Sinclair. Or to be more accurate, for one of his London-based construction companies."

"Which means it's Sinclair who's coming after you," I said to Courtney.

"Maybe Mr. O'Malley's not involved?" she said hopefully.

"Hey, I obviously don't know what kind of arrangement exists between Sinclair and O'Malley, but I doubt that one criminal would whack another criminal's employee without permission. Especially when the employee works in a legitimate business and the death would raise all kinds of questions about what's going on in that business."

"But . . . why . . . why are they trying to kill me?"

"I don't know. Maybe it's the first time they've done a transaction together." I asked Stewart to look into their mutual history. "Maybe there was more on that piece of paper than bank information."

"Maybe there was something about Sinclair," Naomi chimed in.

"If just being seen was dangerous for Sinclair's operation, he wouldn't have come to the gallery. After all, O'Malley does a lot of business remotely with anonymous buyers and sellers."

Courtney nodded, "There's no need for anyone to come in."

"Unless they want to see a painting in the flesh," Naomi said. "So to speak."

I shook my head. "If it's so dangerous Sinclair wouldn't take a chance by coming to the gallery. Whatever it is, it's on that piece of paper."

"And maybe in Mr. O'Malley's log," Courtney said.

"You mentioned that. And then the note goes to someone else to be entered into QuickBooks."

Courtney pointed to Naomi's computer, "But we already checked the gallery's system. There's no transaction from Sinclair in there."

"Could the piece of paper with O'Malley's note be sitting on someone's desk?"

Courtney shook her head, "Notes from Mr. O'Malley are entered into the system within minutes of receiving them. Then shredded."

"Okay. But O'Malley probably entered it into his log, right?"

"Right."

The four of us sat silently for a couple of minutes. I couldn't say what anyone else was thinking, but I had the beginning of an idea.

Naomi had been trying to read my expression and suddenly smiled. "You have a plan, don't you?"

"More like a very fuzzy concept," I admitted.

"Time for a caper?" Naomi loved assisting me on what she called "capers."

"Well, maybe."

"What have you got in mind?"

"Naomi, this may shock you, but your brain works a hell of a lot faster than mine. I'm still mulling my options."

Stewart said, "Maybe we should give the NYPD everything we have on the bad guys."

I nodded, "And everything we have on O'Malley and Sinclair. Everything so far."

"One anonymously sourced package of data on an untraceable flash drive coming up," he grinned. Like Naomi, Stewart enjoyed the stealth side of our cases.

"And I will ensure that it is delivered—in all confidence—to the desk of Detective First Class Charles Winfield," Harry said, appearing from nowhere. He made a show of slipping keys into his pocket, which I guessed was for Courtney's benefit.

"Courtney," I said, "this is my partner, Harry Mitchum." To Harry, I said "Courtney Wilson, our client."

"Client?" Courtney was confused. "I . . . uh, I probably can't afford whatever your fees are."

"Please don't worry about it," Harry replied. "You are a pro bono client. There is no charge to you."

"Thank you. That's very gracious of you."

"Being gracious is kind of our thing," I said.

Courtney didn't really understand that but decided to move onto another topic, "Why does the information you're sending to the NYPD have to be confidential? They know you saved me."

"They do. But since we don't have any proof of whatever Sinclair and O'Malley are up to, it's best to involve the cops through an anonymous tip."

"Oh. Well," she spread her hands out as if to include all of us, "you seem to know what you're doing."

"We do."

"I don't suppose you know where I'm going to stay. I don't think I can go back to Brooklyn Heights."

"No, you can't."

"You're welcome to stay here," Naomi said. "Although it's not exactly deluxe accommodations."

"Maybe at Kim's?" Harry asked. "She has a second bedroom and no obvious connection to Courtney."

"Yeah . . . uh . . ."

"Trouble in paradise?" Naomi asked.

I gave her my patented, steely-eyed glare. The look that had silenced numerous fugitives in my days with the Marshals. Naomi turned her back to me and concentrated on one of the monitors.

Harry asked, "Would you like me to check with Kim?"

"Very thoughtful of you," I said without a hint of sincerity. "I can handle my own difficult calls." To Courtney I said, "This will just take a minute."

I walked back through the railroad flat to the front room with a view of the Empire State Building. I soaked in the view for a few seconds. That was one beautiful building. Stop stalling, Tyrrell.

Kim answered right away. "Hey there. How's it going?"

"It's . . . uh, it's going."

She was alarmed. "Did you get in another fight?"

"Just a little one."

"What? No, really, was it little? Did you get shot?"

"No, no I did not."

"Did you shoot anyone?"

"The guy didn't give me a choice."

"Oh, my God," she sighed. "I don't think I can take any more of this. I really don't."

"I'm sorry."

There was a pause. Probably only 10 seconds, but it seemed like minutes to me.

Finally, Kim asked, "Did you call to tell me about the shooting? Or is there something else?"

"You know me too well." I tried to hit the conversation sweet spot between light-hearted affection and flippancy. I missed.

"What is it now, Jack? You need me to deliver more guns to you? Or rent a car so you can get another vehicle shot up? We were supposed to go away this weekend and spend time walking and talking—"

"And kissing and cuddling—"

"But instead you're spending your time with another woman being chased by bad guys. How are we going to build a life together when this is what you do?"

"I guess this is a bad time to point out that I feel—"

"You'd better not tell me that you are *called* to this life. I don't want to hear that."

"But it's true."

"And what I hear is that your calling to shoot bad guys is more important to you than your calling to make a life with me."

And with those words, Kim hung up.

Harry walked into the front room. "Your body

English tells me that your conversation with Kim did not go well."

"Nope."

"And she expressed no interest in sheltering Courtney."

"In so many words."

He put his hand on my shoulder and said, "I'm sorry, Jack."

"Aren't you going to tell me I need to trust in the Chairman?"

"Why tell you what you already know?"

"It might make me feel better."

He smiled, a full smile that remained on his face not like his usual came-and-went Mona Lisa expression. "Trust in the Chairman. It will be all right."

"Thanks."

"Do you feel better?"

"Microscopically."

"Better than nothing at all."

"It is."

"Will you take Courtney to a hotel?"

"I think off the grid is a better idea."

"Your apartment?"

"Why not? It's not possible Kim could get any angrier with me, right?"

Harry shrugged.

"That's very comforting," I said. "Could you collect Courtney's things from Brooklyn Heights?"

"Yes." He patted me on the shoulder again, and we returned to the office.

"We decided you should stay with me," I said to Courtney. She began to protest, but I held up my hand to stop her. "It's the most convenient. My place isn't far from here. Harry will get your things."

"But won't the men who are after me be on the lookout in there?"

"They've never seen Harry. And they never will."

Naomi jumped in to add reassurance, "Harry's the best. He helps us hack into any system, break into secure locations, deliver secrets secretly—"

"Thanks, Naomi," I interjected. "I'm sure Courtney understands."

"Feeling a little insecure?" Naomi asked without a hint of concern for my feelings. "Don't worry, you have talents, too."

"So kind." I said to Courtney, "If you're ready, we can go to my apartment."

"I'm ready."

We collected our coats off the kitchen chairs, and I helped Courtney on with hers.

"I bet the stairs seem much easier when you're going down," Courtney said.

"Ah, we can only hope."

Stewart walked with us to see us out. "We'll keep digging on Sinclair and O'Malley and call as soon as we have anything else."

"Thanks."

Harry was right behind Stewart. "I'll meet you at your place, Jack. With Courtney's things."

"That's so nice of you," she said. "I'm sorry but I'm not neatly packed."

"You didn't know you'd need to be," Harry spoke smoothly. He had one of those reassuring, TV-commercial voiceover voices.

We didn't talk much as we made the trek single file down five flights of stairs. Out on the street, we all deeply inhaled the cold air.

As we walked east toward Eighth Avenue, Courtney asked Harry, "How did you two meet?"

"I've known Jack for a long time. Seems like forever."

"Did you grow up together?"

"Yes," he replied.

"He's practically my guardian angel," I said.

"Wow. Does Jack require a lot of guarding?"

"Sometimes more than others," Harry said, treating her to a full smile.

We crossed Eighth and continued toward Seventh and the subway station with Harry and Courtney doing the talking. What I discovered by the simple act of listening was that Courtney had gone to NYU's Stern School of Business and minored in Art History at the College of Arts and Sciences. One of the advantages, she said, of going to a large university with diverse disciplines. Yes, she had always wanted to go into the art business. Until people had started trying to kill her, she had thought that working for the Bargen-Meijer Gallery was perfect.

"Hopefully," Harry said, stopping as we reached the corner of 17th Street and Seventh Avenue, "when this is all resolved you'll find another 'perfect' job. People with your skill set must be rare."

"So are the jobs."

Harry nodded. "Let's take this one problem at a time."

"Good idea."

"I'll see you in a while," he said and turned to head down the stairs into the subway station. Not that it mattered. Harry would whoosh himself to Brooklyn Heights the minute he was out of our sight.

"Are we walking?" Courtney asked.

"If you like. I'm on Grove Street, between Bleecker and Bedford. It's about a fifteen-minute walk."

"A walk would be nice."

We strolled down Seventh Avenue, huddled into our coats. I was extremely conscious of my parka's wear and tear. Especially the tear. I wondered if I could persuade Harry to give it an emergency makeover.

The sky had started to turn dark; sunset was in less than half an hour, just before 6:00 P.M. The brashly white streetlights contrasted with the warm glow of lights from apartments, stores, and restaurants.

"The day sure went fast," Courtney said.

"Well . . . starting things off with a chase and gunfight has a way of launching you through the day at an accelerated pace. All of a sudden, it's dinner time."

"Dinner sounds great. I don't remember having lunch. We didn't have lunch, did we?"

"No. Kind of slipped my mind. Sorry."

We crossed West 14th Street, heading south into Greenwich Village.

"What should we have for dinner?" Courtney asked. "And I'm buying. Seems the least I can do to say thank you for saving my life and all the help you're giving me."

"I hate to point this out to you, but you're unemployed. I'll buy dinner."

We debated who should pay, came to no firm conclusion, and moved to the topic of what type of food to eat. We hadn't settled on a cuisine as we crossed Greenwich Avenue. As we walked south of Greenwich, the streets shifted from a grid to a bunch of diagonal streets slanting away from Greenwich Avenue. This was where navigating the Village became tricky. But it was also where the charm of the neighborhood was still apparent. Some people might have thought the Village had lost its charm, but not me. As we approached Christopher Street, we seemed to be focusing on Chinese food.

We were partway across the intersection of Seventh and Christopher, with the Stonewall Monument to our right in tiny Christopher Park, when I heard an engine roaring behind us. A dark-gray Land Rover Discovery was barreling down Seventh Avenue.

I grabbed Courtney's hand and tried to yank her out of the way as the Discovery swerved out of its lane with its massive front grill aimed right at us.

6

From Kim Gannon's Diary:

I can't believe that Jack is with another woman—oh yeah, sure, I know that she's not the "other woman" as in somebody he's having an affair with. And, yes, I know that he saved her life and this whole thing is not his fault. It's never his fault. But it keeps happening. How can we possibly have any kind of normal life when Jack is in one fight after another? When he's running around shooting at bad guys and being shot at?

When—even though he works for the highest authority, for the Chairman—there's no guarantee that he's going to survive the craziness and violence?

How am I supposed to be his partner—in marriage, in parenting—if I'm terrified all the time?

This was supposed to be a weekend away for us. Away from all the insanity in our lives. Instead, a woman's in trouble, a gun goes off, and Jack has to ride to the rescue. Again.

But . . . but . . . am I being fair? I don't feel like I am. I feel guilty. Am I just being selfish? Jack is saving people's lives. He's helping them. He's righting wrongs.

I feel petty and stupid saying this but: Aren't marriage and family deeply satisfying? Maybe even joyous? To borrow a phrase of Jack's, 'in the grand, cosmic scheme' isn't it okay for him to answer a different calling?

The only answer I have for these questions is: I don't know.

I don't know. I don't know.

I'm so angry. And frightened.

I don't know . . . what I'm going to do?

* * *

The Discovery banged over the curb on the corner of Seventh Avenue and Christopher Street. The SUV's right side whipped past us, taking out a newspaper vending box and a wire-mesh trash can as it careened back into the street, tires screeching as the driver stomped on the brakes.

The front and back passenger-side doors were popping open. Not the time for gentlemanly behavior. I ran, kicked the front door with my right foot, and slammed the back door shut with both hands. The whomping sound of the doors crushing against the two men getting out was accompanied by pained yells. Then the doors swung open and the men spilled to the ground.

A bullet whined overhead. I saw that the driver was out of the car, firing multiple times over the roof. I ducked and yanked one of the Beretta M9s I had taken from the boys in Brooklyn Heights, tugged open the front passenger door, and fired. The driver fell backward into the road.

The man who came out of the back door on the driver's side of the Land Rover was the only one with any sense. While the others were busy getting smashed by doors or being shot, he went for Courtney. His back was to me as they struggled, his hands occupied as he tried to get hold of her. A couple of quick strides put me next to him, with a gun to the side of his neck.

"Let her go," I said.

He let her go and spun really fast toward me, one hand knocking my gun aside and the other punching straight for my chin. It was a good punch and sent me sprawling. I managed, however, to hold onto my gun. He was in the process of pulling his own weapon.

"Freeze," I said.

He froze but was clearly having second thoughts.

"Don't do it. Hands in the air. Kneel down."

He did as he was told. I stepped over to him and pistol-whipped him, knocking him senseless. If I had calculated the force of the blow correctly, he would be unable to fight for the moment but not be completely unconscious. I leaned over him and relieved him of his weapon. Another Beretta M9.

"Jack!" Courtney shouted. She was pointing behind me.

I whirled around and saw that the guy I had smushed in the front door was on his feet and moving toward us. Moving quite rapidly for a guy with blood dripping down the side of his face and covering his left hand. But his right hand seemed to be fine. I could tell because it was holding a pistol aimed at me.

I fired. Twice. Center mass, just as I had been taught. His body flew backward and bounced off the Discovery to the ground.

"God dammit!" I growled and looked to the sky. "Could I please not have to kill anyone else? Please?"

"Jack," Courtney said again, less urgently than the last time she had called me. "This one seems to be coming around."

I did a quick inspection of the guy I had pistol-whipped. He was moaning but didn't pose an imminent threat. I checked the guy who'd gotten crushed in the rear door. He wasn't moving either.

I told Courtney to keep alert as I crouched beside the moaning man. I gently slapped Mr. Moan's face and said, "Wake up. I have questions for you."

He responded with an anatomical instruction that was impossible to comply with. Nothing I hadn't heard before.

"Thank you for that suggestion. Now," I grabbed his crotch and gave a good squeeze. Just enough to pump his moaning to a slightly higher octave than his previous vocalizations. "Who sent you?"

"Fu—"

I squeezed really hard.

"I don't know," he gasped.

I relaxed my grip on his genitals and said, "Really? You think I buy that?"

"I get my orders from some guy on a burner phone. Never met him. But the money's good."

"How'd you find us?"

"Fu—"

If it were possible to castrate someone just by squeezing, this guy would have been a boy soprano. After about 20 seconds I relaxed my grip. He was panting and crying in pain.

"How did you find us?"

"There's a tracker on her coat," He gasped. "Short range . . . we've been driving all over . . . in a search grid . . . hoping to pick up the signal."

I let go of his gonads. He rolled over on his side.

I stood up, went to Courtney, and said, "There's a tracker on you. Probably under your coat collar." I turned up her collar, found a small plastic bulb the size of a beetle, and pulled it out. It was on a needle, like an old-fashioned ladies' hat pin. I dropped it on the sidewalk and ground it to dust under my heel.

"We're being watched," Courtney said.

She was right. About a dozen people, scattered around the intersection's sidewalks, were watching us. Most had phones up and recording. Oh, to live in a simpler time. As often happened to me after bullets and fisticuffs were exchanged, the sound of police sirens grew louder and louder.

"Nothing we can do about the watchers," I said. "But we need to get out of here. Come on." I grabbed her hand and pulled her to the Land Rover.

We climbed in, and I drove away, careful not to run over the driver lying in the middle of Seventh Avenue. Or any of the overly curious pedestrians. I saw in the rearview mirror that people were taking video of our getaway car.

"Shit," I grunted under my breath.

"What's the matter?"

"I freakin' hate shooting people."

"But . . . but you're so good at it."

"Yeah, it comes in handy sometimes. But I hate it."

I drove downtown on Seventh continuing on as Seventh turned into Varick Street.

"I know you're upset, but don't you live on Grove?"

"I do."

"Weren't we almost at your house?"

"We were. But it's probably best if we don't spend the night a couple of blocks away from our recent confrontation with the bad guys. What do you think?"

"Yes, I guess so. When you put it like that."

We reached Houston, and I stopped next to a hydrant.

"Come on," I said, and we both climbed out and began walking east on Houston.

Courtney didn't say anything but twisted to look

back at the Land Rover.

"The police are on the lookout for that SUV," I said. "People took video of us as we drove away. For that matter, the bad guys might be able to track its GPS."

"You're pretty good at this kind of . . ."

"Operation?"

"Yes, operation. You're pretty good at it, aren't you?"

We walked quickly and turned left, uptown, on Sixth Avenue. I pulled my phone out and dialed Harry. I didn't usually use a phone to contact him, but once in a while, like when I was with a client who didn't know Harry was an angel, I called him on a phone.

"This is an infrequent occurrence," he said by way of answering.

"Yes it is. Do you know what I need?"

"You would like me to take care of the videos shot at your brawl at the intersection of Seventh and Christopher."

"Yes, I would."

"Done. Anything else?"

I cupped my mouth to the phone and spoke softly so Courtney wouldn't overhear, "How many did I kill?"

"None."

"What? I hit one guy twice, center mass."

"No, you hit him in the shoulder and a flesh wound along his ribs."

"Oh, thank God."

"Yes."

"We're off to the New York Hilton Midtown. The bad guys don't know who I am, do they? They aren't looking for my credit card, right?"

"Right."

"Great. Could you please bring Courtney's things to the Hilton?"

"I'll meet you in an hour."

"Should I text you the room number?"

"Don't be ridiculous." Harry hung up.

We approached the West 4th Street subway station. We descended to the platform, used my metro card to go through the turnstiles, and waited for a train.

"Did I hear you say we're going to the Hilton?"

"Yes, you did."

"Do you mind if I ask why there?"

"Big hotel, lots of rooms, lots of entrances and exits, pretty nice. We'll take the next B, D, or F train that comes in, get off at Rockefeller Center, walk a couple of blocks to the Hilton, and check in."

"How do you . . . I mean, how do you think your fiancée will feel about this?"

"I will tell her we got a room with two beds and hope that is sufficient for her."

"If it's not?"

An uptown F train was coming into the station, and its noisy arrival saved me from having to respond. I had already spent some mental and emotional energy on the topic of what I was going to say to Kim about this. And so far, I hadn't a clue what or how I was going to tell her. Or what I would do if and when she reacted badly.

We boarded the train and found two seats.

"How are you going to tell your fiancée about our staying at a hotel?"

"Isn't that kind of a personal question?"

"I'm sorry. I thought at this point we might not have to worry about personal boundaries."

"You have a point. The answer to your question is that I haven't the faintest idea how I'm going to handle this."

We were stopping at 23rd Street; three more stops to Rockefeller Center. I leaned back in my seat and closed my eyes. I was exhausted. Way too much mayhem in a single day. Maybe I was too old and tired to even be thinking about becoming a father. Then again, maybe a day like today was not the best measure of my fitness as a father. Okay, Tyrrell, shut up.

I opened my eyes as the train pulled into 34th Street. No bad guys boarded. The same was true at 42nd Street. A few minutes later, we walked off the train at Rockefeller Center and climbed to street level. We emerged on the northwest corner of Sixth Avenue and West 50th Street, diagonally across from Radio City Music Hall, home of the Rockettes.

We quickly walked uptown three blocks to the Hilton, which occupies the entire block between Sixth and

Seventh Avenues and West 53rd and 54th Streets. A modern building with none of the charm of old hotels like the Sherry Netherland or the Plaza, but it was a big place; perfect for disappearing anonymously into the crowds. As we made our way across the enormous lobby, Harry appeared as if out of nowhere.

"How on earth did you find us?" Courtney said, pleasantly surprised. "Impressive timing."

"Just random good fortune," Harry replied. "I've already checked you in. Your luggage is in your room." Turning to me, he said, "And there's a brand-new, dark blue, L.L. Bean parka hanging in the closet."

"Thank you. That's great."

Courtney spoke with genuine appreciation in her voice, "What service. You would have made a great concierge."

"Maybe in a prior life," he replied dryly.

He escorted us to the elevators and then our room on the seventeenth floor, which had two queen-sized beds and overlooked West 53rd Street. A small blue duffle and a maroon overnight bag had been placed on the luggage racks near each bed.

"I don't mean to seem ungrateful," Courtney said, "but couldn't I have my own room?"

"It's easier for Jack to protect you if you're in the same room," Harry said.

I shrugged, "Sorry, but he's right. I won't snore."

"Are you expecting trouble?" she asked.

"No. But just in case," I replied.

She turned to me, then Harry, then back to me. "I guess it's a little late to be worried about whether or not I'm safe with you."

I nodded and smiled, hoping that was an adequate response because I had no idea what the appropriate words were to assure someone they were safe with you. Especially after you had fought off the population of a tiny medieval village for that someone's benefit.

"I'm going to take a shower, okay?"

"Sure. Of course," I said.

Courtney picked up her overnight bag, placed it on one of the beds, opened it, and pulled out a few items of clothing and a toiletries bag. She smiled as she went into the bathroom.

"I don't suppose you could stay with her," I said.

"I'm not the one who saved her from being killed."

"But you could."

"If needed."

"And you don't have a fiancée who might be more than a little annoyed by this situation."

"No, I do not. But Courtney already thinks you are going to stay. If you were in her position, would you accept a sudden substitution for a protector?"

"Probably not." I walked over to the window and gazed out onto West 53rd Street. Sorry, Tyrrell. No answers out there. "Did you drop off the information to Charlie Winfield?"

"Yes. Stewart had prepared a USB drive with a great deal of information on Sinclair and O'Malley's various shell companies and off-shore accounts, as well as names and faces of the men you tangled with today. There was a cover note—"

"A text file named 'Read Me First' suggested by Naomi?"

"Exactly."

"But you wrote the note itself."

"Of course."

"And you suggested that the NYPD reach out to the FBI, Scotland Yard, and Interpol with regard to the business activities of Messrs. Sinclair and O'Malley."

"Yes." Harry joined me at the window. "You might want to reach out to your friend at the FBI."

"Hmm."

"You might want to call while Courtney is in the shower. It would be a shame if she was frightened by what she might overhear in your conversation with Special Agent Agar."

"Ohhhhh-kay," I said. "I'm calling." I dialed Joanne's cell.

"Hey, Jack," she answered. "Nice to hear from you. What kind of trouble are you in now?"

"Is that any way to talk to an old Army buddy?"

"It's the only way to talk to you. Look, you saved my life in Afghanistan so we both know I'm going to help you. What's up?"

"You wouldn't happen to know anything about an Englishman named Nigel Sinclair, would you?"

All the light-heartedness left her voice. "Why the hell are you asking me about Nigel Sinclair?"

"I, uh, may have crossed paths with him."

"Uncross paths. ASAP."

"I can't do that."

"Don't tell me that. You need to stay the hell away from this guy."

"Let's assume just for a minute that I'm a professional," I said. "Someone you know you can trust. Someone who trusts you and would uncross paths with Sinclair if there were any way he could do that. Assume all of that. Now, please tell me: Who the hell is this guy?"

"Are you aware that the NYPD just reached out to us regarding some shootings that involved some men who work for Sinclair?"

"I can neither confirm nor deny that I might have been the anonymous tipster who was behind the NYPD's reaching out to you."

"Were you involved in the shootings?"

"I . . . kinda stumbled into the situation."

"Saving someone's life?"

"Yeah. You know how that goes."

"Oh, Jack," Joanne sighed. "Holy shit. You picked the wrong guy to get mixed up with."

"It's not like I had time to make an informed choice."

"Nigel Sinclair is a world-class bad guy. Working-class roots but Cambridge-educated. Made a fortune in London real estate and construction. Expanded into Europe and Asia. Into new businesses such as sex-trafficking, drugs, and, most recently, arms-dealing."

"He's a busy man. Disgusting but busy."

"Very, very busy. Word is he wants to open new businesses in the U.S. and is looking for someone to launder gigantic amounts of cash on this side of the Atlantic."

"Wow."

"The FBI, Scotland Yard, and Interpol have been investigating this guy long before the NYPD got in touch. We've been checking him out every which way. If there was any way we could give him a colonoscopy, we would."

"Thoroughness is your byword."

"You do not want to mess with him. You want to leave this to us."

"If only I could."

"Jack, we'll get him."

"Unfortunately, I don't have time to wait for that to happen."

"You need to understand: Sinclair is not just a bad man with a ton of resources. Our profilers believe he has narcissistic personality disorder that can lead to unreasonable rage."

"Huh. Like the new guy in the White House."

"I have no official comment on that observation,"

Joanne chuckled, "but yeah, like the new guy."

"What do your experts say about Sinclair's connection to violent activities?"

"Judging by his alleged activities over the years, our profilers believe that the signs of narcissistic rage mean that any setback or disappointment can smash his illusion of superiority and trigger a sense of vulnerability. One of the profilers emphasized that narcissistic rage differs from normal anger in that it is out of all proportion to the situation. And most important for you to remember: Narcissistic rage can be aggressive."

"Oh boy. To sum up: when Sinclair feels threatened it could lead to rage and extreme violence. Right?"

"Afraid so. If he feels vulnerable, he might do whatever he thinks he needs to do to protect himself. And with his resources, he can do a hell of a lot to protect himself."

"So you're saying I should be worried?"

"Take this seriously."

"As seriously as I can."

"Okay, your turn," Joanne said.

"As you may have already discovered Sinclair appears to be in the U.S. to do business with a guy named Raymond O'Malley. O'Malley made a fortune in financial services and then became an art dealer. I suspect that he's also into money laundering. The guy has more offshore bank accounts and shell companies than Lady Gaga has sequins on her costumes."

"I like Lady Gaga."

"So do I, but let's refocus on O'Malley."

"Fine art is a good way to launder money," she mused. "Especially if you have multiple bank accounts and shell companies."

"Absolutely. But . . . and I have no evidence of any kind, but I think that Sinclair might be here to acquire O'Malley's operation. He's looking to expand his operations into America, and he's doing it the old fashioned way—purchasing an existing business."

"Huh," Joanne grunted. "That is exactly what we think here at the Bureau. And our friends at Scotland Yard agree. But that probably doesn't help your immediate situation."

"No, it doesn't. Sinclair is trying to kill someone. I've already, uh, intervened on her behalf three times."

"Oh, Jack," she sighed. "Maybe you and the person you saved should come in. You know how good the Marshals Service is at protecting federal witnesses."

"No one is a bigger fan of the Marshals Service witness security than I am, but I really don't want to become a customer."

"That's your decision. Anything else I can help with?"

"Can't think of anything."

"Stay safe, Jack. I'm not kidding."

"I'll do my best."

"That's what worries me," she said.

*   *   *

EVENING – THE MARK HOTEL, NEW YORK

"CAN YOU GET TO GATWICK in an hour?" Nigel Sinclair asked, speaking into his phone.

"Of course," a woman replied crisply.

"There's a private jet waiting for you there. You'll leave immediately. You will arrive in New York around 3:00 A.M., a car will bring you here to The Mark, and I'll brief you on our problem."

"I'll see you tomorrow morning. Around 9:00 A.M. local time?"

"Yes. I suggest you get some sleep on the plane. And at the hotel once you get here. I need you to begin activities immediately."

"I can sleep anywhere."

Sinclair disconnected and accepted a martini from O'Malley, who took his own drink to a couch, sitting opposite Sinclair.

"This is a very nice suite," O'Malley commented.

"I am so glad you approve," Sinclair said dryly.

"Who are you bringing over? Don't we have enough people on the ground here?"

"Do we? Apparently not. I don't know who Ms. Wilson's savior is, but he seems to be rather competent.

Brute force isn't working for us, so I'm going to try finesse."

"And your new person uses finesse?"

"Yes. Amanda Rundle. Formerly with Scotland Yard and then Interpol. Now she handles a variety of security needs for a very select clientele."

"Just a guess," O'Malley grinned, "that you're her No. 1 customer?"

"Definitely."

"And you think she can handle Ms. Wilson's savior, whoever he is."

"What I think is that she can find him because Amanda can find anyone. And once we've found him, I'll find a suitable way to deal with him."

7

Narcissistic rage. What a lovely concept. I slipped my phone into a pocket and turned to Harry. "Did you get all that, or do I need to repeat it for you?"

"I know what Joanne told you."

"What now?"

Harry didn't answer. We heard the muffled drumming of the shower through the bathroom door.

"What the hell do we do now?" I repeated. "Sinclair obviously believes he's threatened by Courtney, and he's taking steps to eliminate her. But she never saw or heard anything. We have nothing to offer to get him to stop."

"There is no path to negotiations."

"And we have nothing to give law enforcement so they can stop him. This guy is scared of Courtney because of nonsense in his head."

"That is correct. I see no safe resolution to this problem."

"Yup," I nodded. "I hate to say this, but the only way to protect Courtney is to take down Sinclair."

"Are you going with your typical blunt-instrument approach to this situation?"

"You got any better ideas?"

He looked up for a moment before answering, "No."

"You consulted the Chairman in that micro-instant of prayer and all you have is *no*?"

"Yes. All I have is *no*. Were you hoping that I would convince you not to act as a blunt-instrument?"

"Of course I was hoping for that. Every time I go that way I get shot or stabbed or beat up. Not as much fun as you may think."

"I regret—in advance—the wounds that may be coming your way. Unfortunately, I have no alternatives to offer you."

The shower went silent. I glanced at the bathroom door as if Courtney were about to spring out of the shower like a dancer in a Broadway musical. Yeah right, Tyrrell. People always spring right from the shower without drying off, brushing and/or blow-drying their hair, and completing sundry other hygienic or cosmetic activities.

"Can you at least tell me what I'm up against?" I whispered to Harry, "Are more bad guys on the way from London or is O'Malley supplying local boys to join the fray?"

Harry again turned his eyes skyward (toward the ceiling actually, but skyward sounds more poetic) then to me, and said, "There are a dozen men here. All O'Malley's."

"Where the hell does an art dealer/money launderer

get his thugs?"

"They are employed, ostensibly, as security at the gallery."

"What about Sinclair's imported goons?"

"You've already taken care of the men Sinclair brought from London. Except for his two bodyguards."

"Okay, a dozen *plus* two bodyguards?"

"Yes."

"That's a lotta guys."

"There is also a woman coming from London. Amanda Rundle. Formerly Scotland Yard and Interpol."

"I'm going to assume she is not coming on behalf of one of those august law-enforcement agencies?"

"Your assumption is correct."

"Is she working for Sinclair?"

"Yes."

"Should I be worried?"

"Yes."

"This just gets better and better."

"Yes. Are you formulating a plan?"

"The word 'formulating' suggests more mental activity than I am capable of at this moment."

Courtney emerged from the bathroom looking relaxed and fresh in a cream-colored, cowl-necked sweater and dark brown slacks.

"Could I interest you in checking out the room-service menu?" I asked.

"Yes, please," she answered with a wide grin.

"Best idea of the day."

"Glad you approve."

Harry said, "I'll be going now. By the way, you are checked in as Ray Kinsella."

"Ray Kinsella? From *Field of Dreams*?"

"I know you like baseball." He treated me to his Mona Lisa smile, said goodbye to Courtney, and left the room.

"He didn't have to leave on my account," Courtney said.

"He didn't. He's always got someplace to go, someone to talk to."

I called room service to place our order; Courtney asked for a Cobb salad and a glass of Sauvignon Blanc, while I went for a burger and fries and water.

"What are we going to do about Mr. O'Malley and Nigel Sinclair?" she asked.

"I'm working on it."

"Have you done this sort of thing a lot?"

"I guess you could say 'a lot.' Army Special Forces in Afghanistan. Deputy Marshal. Now, I run a private security firm."

She hesitated then said in a concerned tone, "I know we talked about this, but I can't afford whatever you charge."

"Like Harry said, you're a pro bono client. Most of our work is pretty standard stuff: We check out the physical, financial, and cyber security of our clients. We get paid very well, which allows us to do some pro bono work."

"I'm very grateful. And lucky—what if you hadn't been driving by at that exact moment?"

"You've probably heard that coincidence is God's way of remaining anonymous."

"I have heard that. Do you believe in God?"

"Oh, yeah. You?"

"I'm not really religious."

"After all that's happened, maybe you should give God a try." I grinned.

There was a knock on the door. I hopped up and peered through the door's peephole. Room service.

I turned and whispered, "Hide in the bathroom."

Courtney quickly moved out of sight, and I opened the door to the young room-service waiter who pushed a trolley into the room and placed our meals on a small table by the window.

"That's great," I said, handing him $10.

"Thank you."

"You're welcome. You can leave the trays outside your door when you're finished."

"Thanks again." I gestured to the door, and he promptly exited.

I knocked on the bathroom door, "It's okay to come out now."

"Do I really have to hide from room service? Could Sinclair have infiltrated the hotel staff?"

110

"Well . . . I guess I'm being super-cautious. Sorry if I scared you."

She chuckled. "I wasn't scared. I was worried that I have an obsessive-compulsive bodyguard."

"I deserved that."

We sat down to dinner and ate in silence for a few minutes. From our window we could see the marquee of Radio City Music Hall.

"Whenever I'm high up and looking down, I always wonder what's going on in the lives of all the people I can see, " Courtney said. "I wonder how different their lives are from mine."

"And tonight you wish you were one of them instead of stuck here with me?"

"It's not you," she laughed softly. "It's being a target. Someone's trying to kill me, and as far as I know, I didn't do anything to deserve that."

"You didn't. I believe that Nigel Sinclair suffers from narcissistic personality disorder and has rage issues. Anything that threatens him—rational or not—makes him crazy with anger."

"Oh my God," she sighed. "I pass him in a hallway, he thinks I saw something important on a piece of paper, and now he wants me dead."

"That does seem to be the case."

"But I didn't see the paper."

"You know that. I know that. He doesn't."

"How am I going to get out of this?"

"Well . . . I think you and I should meet with Harry, Naomi, and Stewart tomorrow. We're going to come up with a plan to save you."

"What kind of plan can save me from a psycho like Sinclair?"

"Technically speaking, he's not a psycho, but I get your meaning."

"What kind of plan?" she repeated with a trace of impatience.

"I'm not sure. But it will probably involve a certain degree of mayhem. You know . . . just . . . standard operating procedure."

After dinner, I placed the trays with our dishes on the floor outside our door. I moved back into the room and said, "I need to make a personal call. I'm going to head down to the lobby and do that, okay?"

"I could go hide in the bathroom again."

"You're not going to let me forget that, are you?"

"Never."

"Well, thanks for that. Anyway, I don't want you cowering in the bathroom. I'll be back in 10 or 15 minutes."

"Okay. Do we need a *secret* knock so that I know it's you?"

I gave her my steely-eyed, U.S. Deputy Marshal's look, the one I had frozen fugitives with. It didn't bother her at all. Her grin was way too wide.

*   *   *

I roamed around the Hilton's massive lobby until I found a space at least 20 feet away from the nearest people. If I had been involved in an espionage operation, I probably would have wanted an even larger buffer between me and everyone else. But I was just your ordinary guy trying to smooth things over with his fiancée.

"Hello, Jack," Kim answered with all the warmth of the wind blowing over the Himalayas.

"Hey, Kim." I took a deep breath. This was going to be so much fun. "Listen, I have something to tell you that's a bit awkward. But I wanted you to hear it from me. And to reassure you that this is business."

"And nothing but business?"

"Yes, exactly. I'm in a hotel with the woman I saved the other night because—"

"What?"

"I said this would be awkward—"

"*Awkward*? Awkward is accidentally bumping into somebody and knocking them down. Staying in a hotel room goes way beyond *awkward*."

"Okay, sorry. I chose the wrong word. Anyway, you have nothing to worry about. Separate beds and all that."

"Why are you telling me this?"

"What if Harry mentioned it to you, and I hadn't already told you? What would you think then?"

It took Kim a few seconds to answer. Those few seconds seemed to last as long as the Great Ice Age, but maybe that was just my hyper-sensitivity to the emotional cold.

"I guess it's better that I heard it from you," she said.

"Thanks."

"Your admission doesn't fix everything."

"I didn't think it would."

"Does it strike you that your spending the night in a hotel room with another woman is exactly what's wrong with us? It's the perfect example of how your calling to right wrongs is going to keep us from having a family."

"I don't know how to respond to that."

"There is no response." She hung up.

"That went well," I muttered. "God, could you please help me out here?"

No answer. I didn't really expect an immediate reply. Hopefully, I would receive some kind of direction sometime soon. In the meantime, it was off to the elevators so that I could spend the night in a hotel room with another woman.

*   *   *

From Kim Gannon's Diary:

I don't know where we go from here. I just got off the phone with Jack, who told me he's spending the night in a hotel with another woman. He said it's business, which probably means he's doing it to protect her. I believe him. But I've made it as clear as I can that he needs to make a choice between his calling and our future together. And so far, his calling is winning.

When did this become so black and white for me? After we got engaged in Paris, and he went off and took on the bad guys, I thought I had worked my way through this issue. I thought I had resolved to trust God the way Jack does. Make a life with him.

Why do I now feel that he has to make a choice?

Because—before—I hadn't killed someone to save Jack's life.

I can't get past the fact that I'm a killer. I did it for Jack, but now I'm changed forever. I want to crawl out of my own skin.

I can't stand the way I feel.

But Jack . . . Jack wants to keep going, righting wrongs, helping people.

I love him. Part of what I love is that he wants to help other people. I want a future with him. But I don't see how we can get to any kind of future together.

* * *

Friday morning was cold and crisp according to the weather app on my phone. Well, the app didn't say it was "crisp," I inferred that from the combination of cool temperature and the sunny day. Courtney and I ordered a room-service breakfast of coffee (for me), tea (for her), scrambled eggs, bacon, and English muffins.

Snuggled into our winter coats, in my case was a brand-new parka—thank you, Harry—we exited the Hilton and walked to Seventh Avenue, where we caught a cab almost immediately. We got out of the cab at West 23rd Street and walked down Seventh toward 17th Street.

"Do you think maybe you're a little paranoid?" Courtney asked. "Getting out of a cab blocks away from your actual destination."

"Hey, just because you're paranoid doesn't mean they're not out to get you."

"And by they you mean—"

"They!" I said, waving my hands in a way that included the entire known universe. "They."

"You *are* paranoid."

"It pays to be paranoid in my line of work."

"Are you carrying the guns you took off the bad guys?"

"Yup. I have two Beretta M9s. With twenty-three rounds between them. And my knowing that doesn't prove I'm paranoid. It means I'm prepared."

Instead of going straight down Seventh and turning right on 17th, I had us go right on 19th and stopped at a coffee shop on Eighth Avenue.

"Hope you don't mind," I said. "We need to acquire supplies for our brainstorming session."

"Can I order what I want?"

"Of course."

A few minutes later, with enough caffeine for the team, we were on our way. The rest of our journey was safe and smooth. We even ran into Harry at the corner of West 17th and Eighth Avenue. We exchanged pleasantries until we arrived at Naomi and Stewart's place. Then we concentrated on making our ascent.

Once inside their apartment, with the beverages distributed, we gathered in the conference room, which was between the office with all the computers and the kitchen. When not functioning as a war room or conference room, it served the much pleasanter function of dining room. Not that Naomi and Stewart ate many meals there. The room had a rectangular, formica-topped table with six folding chairs around it. Bare bones. The kind of furniture even the Salvation Army would have sniffed at.

Harry sat at the head of the table, with Naomi and Stewart on his left, and Courtney and me on his right.

"What kind of plans do you have for us today?" Harry asked, looking at me.

"Uh, I was kinda hoping one of you might have been inspired. I have nothing."

"How 'bout a caper?" Naomi asked.

"Why did I know you were going to suggest that?"

117

"Cause they're fun?"

"For you. Not so much for me. Besides, we already penetrated the gallery's network using Courtney's login. All we have is offshore accounts and shell companies."

"We could go to London and pull a caper at Sinclair's place," Stewart said. He seemed as excited as Naomi at the prospect.

"Much as I like international travel, I think we should set aside that idea for the moment. And, sorry to disappoint you, but I don't think a caper is going to help us."

"Why not?"

"Well . . . Sinclair isn't afraid of one particular thing. He's just . . . *afraid*. He's tried to kill Courtney because he *thinks* she's a threat. It's not rational. No matter what we do, we won't find anything that we can use to negotiate with Sinclair. He's not rational."

"Are you sure about that?" Naomi asked.

"Yes, unfortunately," Harry interjected. "Sinclair suffers from narcissistic personality disorder. And as we've seen, has rage issues. He is not rational, so we have no way to persuade him that he should desist in his attempts to . . ."

"Kill me?" Courtney asked. "It's okay, you can say it."

"Yes. I'm sorry."

"You're saying that we can't offer him a deal?" Stewart asked. "You know, you leave Courtney alone, we won't expose your criminal enterprises."

"Exactly," Harry and I said in harmony. "Owe me a coke," I said immediately afterward. Harry's face displayed mild disgust at me, as if he had found something gooey on the bottom of his shoe.

"We have to go to war with this guy," I grunted.

Courtney, Naomi, and Stewart all blurted out some version of "*What?*"

"We have to make it so painful for Sinclair to keep on doing what he's doing that he stops. Even a non-rational being will stop doing something that causes pain."

"You're assuming that Sinclair will connect the pain you cause with his attempts on Ms. Wilson's life."

"I'll make the connection very plain to him."

Everyone was silent for a few moments until Stewart spoke up, "Are we sure that our problem is Sinclair? Maybe it's O'Malley?"

"Good question. Let's compare the two," I replied. "Sinclair has mental issues, he's been involved in violent crimes, and the guys who attacked Courtney are all in his employ."

"To be more precise," interjected Stewart, "in the employ of one of his shell companies."

"Yes, that's right. Thank you. Courtney has worked for O'Malley for 11 years without any problems, but the minute she passes Sinclair in a back passageway at O'Malley's gallery, she has people trying to kill her. As for O'Malley—have you found anything that proves he's a criminal."

119

"Nothing that proves anything," Stewart said. "Reading between the lines, the money coming and going from buyers and sellers, money headed off to multiple accounts and companies, well, it doesn't really pass the smell test, but it's not hard evidence of anything."

"And you haven't found anything to indicate O'Malley is committing any non-financial crimes. Nothing violent."

"No."

"Okay. Our problem is Nigel Sinclair," I wrapped up. "Although we can't ignore the possibility that he is receiving assistance from O'Malley."

"Excuse me," Courtney said. "But how do you go to war with Sinclair? And maybe Mr. O'Malley too."

We exchanged glances around the table, but no one said anything.

Stewart finally ventured a suggestion, "Maybe Jack breaks into O'Malley's gallery and does his blunt-instrument thing? You know, overpowers the guards, breaks things, steals stuff—"

"Excuse me?" I asked, heavily overemphasizing the syllable "cuse."

"I'm just . . . I mean . . ." Stewart shifted uncomfortably on his chair. "Just throwing stuff out there."

Naomi asked, "How 'bout a malware attack?"

"What?" I asked.

"We slip inside O'Malley's gallery, insert a Bluetooth dongle somewhere, set up a VPN connection

120

between O'Malley's and Sinclair's networks, encrypt all their data, and leave a ransom note."

"First off, slipping inside O'Malley's gallery sounds like your favorite plan: a caper," I commented. "Secondly, can't you just hack in from here? You did the other night. Thirdly, pardon my troglodytism, but what is a dongle?"

"First: I'm ignoring your comments about a caper," Naomi said. "Second: I could hack in from here, but it would be much better to do it from O'Malley's. If either Sinclair or O'Malley has a tech wizard, they might be able to trace the malware on Sinclair's network back to the computer that was the source of the attack. If the source is O'Malley's own computer network, we're safe. Third: A dongle is a small adapter that you can plug into a computer and access wireless broadband."

"Why is it called a dongle?"

"Who knows? I like it 'cause it's fun."

"So you get to use a 'fun' word and get a caper."

"Those are just a side benefits."

"And, once inside the gallery, it's possible that I end up doing my blunt-instrument thing."

Stewart smiled, "That's another benefit."

8

I turned to Courtney. "Let's humor my loyal teammates for a moment. What's the security like at Bargen-Meijer?"

"This is a really bad idea," Courtney said.

"That's our specialty," Naomi grinned. "Yesterday, when I logged into the gallery's network using your login, I created a new login for myself. Something the system administrator won't find, but now I can login whenever I want. I also downloaded all the technical specs on the alarm system. I have to double-check, but it looks like I can shutdown the entire alarm system through the network."

"I'm not a tech person, so I wouldn't know," Courtney said. "But since I signed all the contracts for our security system, I can tell you that the alarms are only part of what protects the gallery."

"I don't like the sound of that," I murmured.

"O'Malley hired a security geek—no offense, Jack—"

"None taken."

"He designed a system on the principle that no one should get close to the artwork inside the gallery. It would be expensive to set alarms on each and every piece of art, and the paintings on display constantly change, so the alarms would have to be updated all the time. Instead, the geek—"

"Hey, I resemble that remark. Could we please use the term security expert?"

"I'm sorry, the security expert designed the system to prevent *any* access. Alarms on all exterior access—"

"It's one hell of a system," Naomi nodded, "if you ignore the uniform point of failure: it's a single layer."

"True. But there's a fail safe: Four guards. Two roaming the floors; two watching the security cameras on monitors."

"It could be worse," I said. "There could be dogs."

"There is a dog," Courtney replied. "A four-year-old Doberman."

"Named Rembrandt, no doubt," I grunted.

"Named Kandinsky."

"I didn't know that O'Malley had an interest in abstract art."

"He has an interest in anything that he can sell," Courtney said. "And Kandinsky the Doberman only seems interested in protecting every single piece of art in the place."

"Do you know anything about the guards? Are they employees of the gallery or supplied by an agency?"

"Supplied by an agency. Even Kandinsky is from an agency. I've met them all briefly when I've worked late. They look pretty tough to me, but I don't really know.

Sorry."

"Probably all veterans and/or law enforcement."

"Don't look so glum, Jack," Stewart grinned. "Four guards and a dog? You can handle that."

"You're mighty cavalier about what I can handle."

Harry spoke up, looking at me, "Do you have any other ideas?"

I scrambled around the desolate wasteland of my mind and replied, "Nope."

"I assume that you would like to secure Courtney's safety as swiftly as you can," Harry said.

"Yup."

"Are we on to break into the gallery this evening?"

"Yup."

Harry turned to Naomi, "Can you be ready for tonight?"

"I'm ready now," she smirked. "Although we're going to need a van."

"Can I help you steal it?" Stewart asked eagerly.

"What the hell are you talking about?" I asked in return.

"Don't you usually steal the vehicle you are going to use in a crime?"

"Well," I said, "I don't know what your usual technique is, but I was thinking that Harry could rent one. With a phony ID and credit card."

"Regardless of the faux credit card, the rental car company will be paid," Harry insisted.

"I was kind of hoping we could steal a car," Stewart sighed. "I've never done that."

"Believe me, it's a life experience you can live without," I said. "But you can drive the van instead. No speeding, we don't want to attract any attention."

"Okay, I'll drive."

"Why do we need a van?" I asked Naomi.

"The Bluetooth dongle doesn't have the range for me to connect to it from here."

I nodded, "Makes sense. So, we're all set, right?"

Everyone said yes or nodded.

"Great. Stewart and Naomi, you should be parked outside Bargen-Meijer by midnight. Harry and I will get there by ourselves. I somehow get past the guards and Kandinsky then plant the dongle. Naomi, once you confirm that you've hacked in and set the malware, we pull the dongle, you drive away, and we depart. Got it?"

More agreement around the table.

"I have a question," Courtney said.

"Fire away," I responded.

"Where will I be?"

"Safe and sound in our hotel room."

"*Our* hotel room?" Naomi inquired with raised eyebrows.

"Don't start with me. Please."

Naomi grinned widely.

"Would everybody be okay if we do some prep for tonight's—"

"Escapade!" Naomi suggested gleefully.

"You seem to think that this is akin to waking up on Christmas morning and finding presents under the tree. I remind you that my ass will be on the line here. Literally."

"We wouldn't want anything to happen to your ass," Naomi said with a tiny hint of solemnity.

"I am forced to agree with Jack," Harry said. "We should review all of the gallery's floor plans and alarm specifications."

"Yup," I agreed. "And then you and I should take a walk around the building. There's nothing better than in-person reconnaissance."

We spent the next hour looking over blueprints and technical plans, all produced by Naomi's digital wizardry with an assist from Harry. Naomi was very fond of saying that there was nothing she couldn't hack as long as she had Harry's help. After that, we shared pizza and discussed the gallery's set-up.

"As I said before," Courtney repeated patiently, "there are four guards and one dog."

"Kandinsky. You also mentioned that two guards walk the floors and two watch the monitors," I said. "Do they have set routes through the building? What kind of weapons are they carrying? Does Kandinsky accompany one of the guards or move about freely?"

"Oh," Courtney said, pausing to think her way through my questions. "The two cover the entire building, randomly, no pattern, but mostly concentrate on the first floor where the gallery is. Kandinsky roams free but stays in the gallery. The guards carry Tasers but no guns."

"O'Malley doesn't want anyone shooting a painting by accident," I grinned. "Do the guards rotate? Take turns walking the floor and watching the monitors?"

"They do. I think they rotate every couple of hours. The security office with all the monitors is at the rear of the building on the second floor."

"Aside from all the valuable art work being in the gallery, why the concentration on the first floor? Is it the most vulnerable?"

"Far and away the easiest," interjected Naomi. "The front door is the best way into the building. Wait a minute."

She stood up, went into the office, returned with a laptop, and pointed to the screen. "Look at the plans: There are bars on all the windows. The steel door to access the building from the roof opens out and has no lock to pick or door handle. On the inside of the door, there are steel anti-pry bars set into all four sides of the steel frame."

She continued, "The top of the elevator shaft, which is next to the rooftop door, is locked with four different padlocks. You'd need a blowtorch to cut through the hasps. And there's a security camera over the rooftop access that covers the elevator shaft, so you'd never be able to burn through the locks without being discovered.

"If you managed to get inside, another steel door with anti-pry bars blocks entry to the third floor. And

127

another security camera.

"So . . . you can't get in through the roof and you can't get in through the windows."

"Which leaves the glass front doors," I observed. "Or the large display window."

"The glass is bullet-proof," Naomi was shaking her head. "Underwriters Laboratories-protection levels from 1 to 8. Should stop anything from a 9mm bullet to a blast from a 12-gauge shotgun."

"What about the front door locks?" I asked, despite my fading hopes.

"Top and bottom of each door, ultra high-quality. A real expert could pick them, but you . . . ?"

"Yeah. Ugh."

"*Annnd* . . . even if you get through the front doors, you have to deal with two guards and Kandinsky. That's assuming the guards didn't see you on camera and aren't waiting for you inside with their Tasers. But nothing you can't handle. Right?"

"I, uh . . . ," I looked at Harry, who shrugged then shook his head. I wished that just once Harry would whoosh me inside a place. But, by shaking his head he indicated that I didn't *need* such assistance. Harry was about as reassuring as Grumpy from the Seven Dwarves.

"What are you going to do?" Courtney asked.

"Look the place over. Pray for divine guidance."

Fifteen minutes later, Harry and I were walking down Eighth Avenue approaching Bleecker Street. Eighth merged into Hudson Street, and it was only a very short block to Bank Street. We turned right on Bank and walked another short block to the intersection of Greenwich and Bank. The Bargen-Meijer Gallery was on the southwest corner of the intersection. We strolled by it cautiously, taking a good long look at the building on both the Greenwich Street side and the Bank Street Side. The gallery's footprint was an irregular polygon; the building was three-stories tall. All of the windows that were visible as we walked past were barred and you couldn't see inside the gallery via any of the first-floor windows—sunlight was blocked to protect the artwork.

The front of the building, which faced north on Bank Street, consisted of a large display window and double-glass doors. Inside the window, posters featured works of art that were currently offered for sale inside the gallery.

I popped in my AirPods and called Naomi and Courtney. "Okay, it's just as bad in person as the security diagrams made it look. I don't see a way in without blowing up something."

Harry shook his head.

"Oh?" I said, exasperated. "No bright ideas from you?"

"Are you talking to us or to Harry?" Naomi asked.

"Harry," I replied disgustedly. In a much softer tone, "Do either of you have any ideas?"

"Sorry, no," Courtney said.

"I'm just a hacker," Naomi added.

Harry and I had passed the gallery and were continuing slowly west. On the southern sidewalk, headed east, were a couple of women out walking a beautiful little Bichon Frise. I watched as the dog stopped directly in front of the gallery, crouched, and urinated.

I glanced upward and whispered, "Thank you."

"Why are you thanking us?" Naomi asked.

"Not you. God," I responded. "Courtney, how do the guards handle Kandinsky's need to pee and poop?"

"He gets taken out in front of the gallery by one of the guards approximately every 3 hours, starting at 8:00 P.M."

"Where's the other roaming guard?"

"He waits at the front door."

"To make sure no one sneaks through," I said. "Well, it just goes to show you, one man's dog poop is another man's golden ticket inside the chocolate factory."

*   *   *

And that was how I came to be hiding in a dark doorway near the northeast corner of the intersection of Greenwich and Bank Streets, across from the Bargen-Meijer Gallery at 12:45 A.M. How I had gotten to my hiding space was quite simple. Harry whooshed me there. He wouldn't sneak me past all the security cameras, alarms, guards, and Kandinsky, but he was happy to do a simple transportation job. And then remain in hiding with me.

I was dressed in black from top to toes: balaclava, cargo pants, a heavy sweater, and crepe-soled shoes. Even my wool socks were black. I was carrying a Ruger SR9 with a suppressor in a shoulder holster that rested just below my left armpit. I also had a pair of Tasers in holsters on each hip. A Bluetooth dongle, wrapped in several layers of gauze to protect it in the event of roughhousing, was in my right cargo pocket. In my left cargo pocket was a multi-channel jammer to block all cellular and WiFi signals. The damn thing weighed almost four pounds, more than my fully loaded Ruger, but Naomi had assured me it would knock out all mobile phones in the building, and that was the only thing that mattered.

"Stewart and Naomi are arriving," Harry said. He was also dressed in black, however, he wasn't carrying any weapons or hardware.

I peered around the edge of the doorway to watch an ancient, battered, aquamarine Ford Econoline pull to a stop about 50 feet from the gallery on Greenwich Street.

"How old is that thing?" I asked Harry.

"Not quite as old as you. But it still runs."

"Just like me. Where the hell did you rent it?"

"Wrecks R Us," Harry deadpanned.

Stewart was behind the wheel, and Naomi had shifted out of the passenger seat and moved to the back of the van. I slipped an AirPod into my left ear and called

Naomi.

"Hey there," I spoke softly.

"Hey yourself," Naomi responded. "Are you all set?"

"We are. Are you ready?"

"Of course."

"Okay. When Kandinsky and the guard come out, we go. As soon as you see Harry and me making our move, you shut down the alarms and the video."

"Got it," Naomi agreed. "Activate the jammer to block all cell phones as soon as you can. Take the jammer with you."

"To ensure the best quality jamming?" I asked sardonically.

"Yes. Do what I tell you, Jack. I don't want you to get hurt."

"I appreciate your concern."

She ignored my sarcasm. "Remember, when the jammer is active, we can't talk. You're on your own. Once you've secured the guards—and more importantly their phones—you turn off the jammer, plug in the dongle, and let me know so I can access it and install the malware."

"I got it. Going silent until I'm not."

The four of us watched the gallery's front doors in silence for the next 5 minutes.

I spoke to Harry, "You need to handle the dog."

"You may believe you need me to handle the dog, but that's a feeling. It's not a fact."

"Here's a fact for you: I don't want to hurt this dog. I *really* don't want to kill him. Either you take care of Kandinsky or leave him to my not-so-tender mercies. And then you'll have to put up with all of my guilt and *agita* after I do whatever I do to the poor dog. Up to you."

Harry stared into my eyes for a moment, and when I didn't blink, he glanced skyward then back to me. "I will take responsibility for the dog."

"Thank you." I offered him the jammer, "Would you please hold onto this?"

"Why?"

"I need both hands free to deal with the guards."

"Don't you think I might need both hands free to deal with Kandinsky?"

"No."

Stewart broke into our dialogue, "I can see someone coming."

Harry and I focused intently on the front door. I pulled the Tasers from the holsters.

Stewart added, "Here comes Kandinsky and his escort."

One of the guards came down the gallery's two front steps with Kandinsky on a 8-feet-long leash. The dog was a sleek, muscled, and lethal creature. The leash didn't look anywhere near thick enough to control such a powerful animal. Oh well, that was Harry's problem.

As soon as dog and man reached the sidewalk, Harry and I pulled our balaclavas down over our faces and walked quickly across the intersection. The guard was—like all dog walkers everywhere—watching and talking to the pooch. I saw that the guard standing in the doorway was watching the two of them. These guys had done this way too many times before. It was routine. Boring. Tonight, it was cold. The biggest excitement would be having to scoop the poop assuming Kandinsky had a solidly productive outing. At the moment I thought about pooping, the dog obliged. He crouched, looking west on Bank Street, looking away from us.

I got within 10 feet of the dog-walking guard, raised the Taser in my right hand, and fired. The darts hit him in the back, and the poor guy positively vibrated for a few seconds then collapsed.

"Hey, freeze," came an angry voice to my left.

I fired the Taser in my left hand with the tiniest of glances toward the guard in the doorway. The darts caught the guard in the chest, and he gave the same vibration-and-collapse performance as his partner.

Harry was petting Kandinsky with his left hand and using a plastic bag to scoop the poop with his right.

Naomi's voice came into my ear, "Cameras and alarms are shut down."

Harry said, "The jammer is activated."

"Okay," I said, hopped up the steps, and dragged the guard at the door inside. A few seconds later, I had my hands under the armpits of Kandinsky's walker, and huffing and puffing, bumped him up the steps into the gallery.

Harry followed with Kandinsky who sniffed each of the guards.

"Sit," Harry commanded firmly but softly. The dog did as instructed.

I dragged both guards deeper into the gallery so their bodies wouldn't be visible from the street. I was crouched and securing them with plasticuffs when—

"Freeze!" a woman shouted hoarsely from further inside the gallery.

"Like clockwork," I whispered to Harry. "In the event of the alarms and cameras going down, they concentrate on the front door."

Harry nodded, "Exactly."

The woman got louder, "I said *FREEZE!*"

"You guys need to expand your vocabulary," I said, standing up and pulling my Ruger. "If you want to see how your Tasers stand up against my gun, you're welcome to try. Otherwise, drop the Tasers and come here."

In the soft light of the gallery I saw the shadows of the two guards trying to hide behind a freestanding wall, about a foot thick and 8-feet high, stopping short of the ceiling. I heard the Tasers hit the floor, and the guards stepped out of hiding and walked toward me.

Harry did the honors with the plasticuffs.

"What the hell do you think you're doing?" the woman asked.

"Don't worry, we're just here to window shop."

"*You* should be worried."

"*You* should shut up." I yanked off their black polyester clip-on ties, and shoved them into their mouths.

"Oh, Jack," Harry said, sounding disappointed. He shook his head and began searching the four guards, pulling phones and keys from their pockets.

"Safe to de-activate the jammer?" he asked.

"Yup. And please don't use my name when we're on a caper."

"They won't remember your name or face."

"So I didn't need to wear this damn balaclava?"

"But you look the perfect, professional cat burglar when you have it covering your face."

I tugged the balaclava above my face, muttering, "Freakin' angel humor."

"Hey! You made it inside," Naomi's voice came over the AirPods. "Everyone okay?"

"Yes. Thanks."

"Simple and smooth," Harry observed. "Jack didn't even have to scuff his knuckles."

"*Scuff my knuckles*? Have you been watching boxing movies from the 1940s?"

"No."

"It's time to get to work," Naomi interjected.

"Excuse me but what do you think we've been doing?"

"*Tempus fugit*, Jack. *Tempus fugit!*"

136

9

A minute later, I was sitting at Courtney's desk, installing the Bluetooth dongle in one of the computer's USB ports. The light on the antenna showed it was activated.

"How's it going?" I asked Naomi.

"It's fine, Jack," she replied patiently.

"Can I ask a question?"

"Is there any way to stop you?"

"No. Will O'Malley and/or Sinclair be able to trace back this digital incursion through the dongle back to your laptop? Can they find the originating IP address?"

"You're so cute when you talk tech. Yes, they can, but I'm using a VPN which hides the IP. Does that meet with your approval, Tech Sergeant Chen?"

"Oooh, nice *Galaxy Quest* reference. Always loved that movie."

"Me, too. Now please shut up and let me work."

"One more question . . ."

"*What?*" she did not sound happy.

"Doesn't the VPN slow down the connection?"

"Yes but not enough to matter for this operation. Unless you're telling me that we're running out of time. Are you telling me that, Jack?"

"Are we running out of time?" Stewart echoed.

"No, no, everything is fine," I said calmly.

"Good," Naomi responded. "Now please shut up."

After what seemed like an eternity, Naomi said, "Okay, the malware is installed. I've created a backdoor into Sinclair's network so we can pull out the data as soon as we're back at the office. Then we'll activate the malware and tell him to back the hell off of Courtney."

"Great," I said, meaning it. "So we're good to go?"

"We are."

"You sure you don't want a ride?" Stewart asked.

"No thanks. Remember to drop off Naomi then abandon the van at least ten blocks away from the office. Leave the keys in the ignition."

"Got it. Do I need to wipe down for fingerprints?"

"Good thinking, Stewart," I glanced at Harry, who shook his head. "But, no. Not necessary."

"Great, thanks."

I said to Harry, "Are we ready to depart?"

"I believe we are."

I shut down Courtney's computer, gathered up the dongle and the jammer, and walked downstairs to the gallery display floor.

"What are we going to do about the keys?" I asked. "We have to lock the doors from the outside, but then where do we leave the keys? 'Cause I really don't want to take them with us."

"Please leave that to me."

The guards, with Kandinsky sitting alertly next to them, were exactly where we had left them. The woman was looking at me with daggers, but I can't say that bothered me.

Harry placed the keys and phones in a pile on the floor at least 10-feet away from them. Given the way they were trussed up, it might as well have been a mile.

"Come on, Kandinsky," Harry said.

The dog stood and followed us to the small foyer area just inside the front doors.

"After you," Harry said, gesturing at the door.

I stepped outside, while he stopped in the open door and spoke a final time to the dog. "Stand guard, Kandinsky."

The dog snapped to attention, standing his ground inside the doors.

"Good dog," Harry said. He sounded more sincere complimenting the dog than he ever did when saying something nice to me.

"Anyone willing to take a chance on getting past that dog deserves whatever the hell happens to him," I said.

"Exactly."

*   *   *

Harry whooshed us to my apartment where I

restored my Tasers to my weapons cabinet, a secret compartment in my bedroom closet. You might wonder: How secret? Harry said it was undetectable, and that was good enough for me.

I grabbed two extra magazines of ammo for the Ruger and slipped them into my parka pockets. Then I went to the kitchen, made cappuccinos for everyone, and put the hot beverages into disposable travel cups.

Shrugging into my parka, I said, "I'm ready if you are."

Harry collected two of the cappuccinos off the counter, and I did likewise.

"Now," he said in my apartment, "we are ready." He finished his sentence in front of Stewart and Naomi's apartment door.

"Thank you for not making me climb five flights of steps," I said.

"You're very welcome," he smiled. "I thought you would appreciate the special treatment."

"I do. I *really* do. Guards with Tasers are nothing compared to the stairs in this building."

Harry ignored me and knocked on the door.

Stewart answered, "Come on in. Oh, you brought caffeine! Very thoughtful."

"It was Jack's idea," Harry admitted.

"Thanks, Jack."

"You're welcome."

Stewart led us to the office, where Harry handed a

cappuccino to Naomi, who was sitting in front of a keyboard and monitor, of course.

"Anything going on at the gallery?" I asked.

"Not a thing," Naomi replied. "From the time you you and Harry subdued the guards outside until you said goodbye to Kandinsky was less than 10 minutes. Nice work."

"The alarms, cameras, and whatever active again?"

"Yes they are. Did you bring back my dongle and jammer?"

I put both items on the desk near her keyboard. "They are returned in mint condition."

"I'll be the judge of that."

"What are you up to now?"

"I'm downloading as much data as I can from Sinclair's network in London."

"Using another VPN to hide your IP?"

"Oh, you were paying attention."

"Yes, I was." I sipped some cappuccino and leaned closer to the monitor to look at the progress bar on Naomi's monitor. "Looks like you're going to be a while."

"No problem. It's only 7:14 A.M. in London. My download will finish before Sinclair's legit business offices open in the morning."

"When are you sending the ransom demand?"

"9:30 A.M. New York time, 2:30 P.M. in London."

"Today? It's Saturday."

"Some of Sinclair's businesses operate on an

141

almost 24/7-basis. Besides, any senior exec who logs into their network will receive our ransomware demand."

"Why 9:30 here?"

"I thought it would be nice to give folks in New York enough time to have coffee before I start making demands."

"Very considerate of you."

"It was Stewart's idea," she turned and smiled at Stewart, who made a slight bow.

"Good thinking," I said. "Okay, I see you made it back from the caper safely and have things well in hand here, so I'm going to say, 'good night.'"

"I'll escort you to the Hilton," Harry said.

"Thank you."

Naomi and Stewart both said, "Good night," and Harry and I walked out of the apartment.

"Why don't you whoosh in front of those two?" I asked. "It's not like they don't work for the Chairman too."

"It's not necessary."

"It's way too late to be debating what is or isn't necessary."

Before I finished I found myself standing in Courtney's and my hotel room. Courtney was breathing deeply and evenly in the bed nearest the window.

Moving slowly and quietly, I hung my parka in the closet and undid my shoulder holster, draping it over the parka's hangar. I tiptoed into the bathroom, quickly accomplished my evening ablutions, and dressed in modest, old-fashioned pajamas that Harry had provided. I slid under the sheets of my bed. Looking at the ceiling as if that were the night sky, I whispered, "Thank you," then rolled over and dropped off to sleep.

Room service arrived with breakfast at a horribly early time. At least it was horribly early for a guy who'd been breaking into an art gallery the night before. Courtney was fine with the timing.

I gobbled down my food after rushing through a very brief, very hot shower.

"Rough night?" Courtney asked as I chugged coffee.

"No, surprisingly. Just a late one."

"Are we all set for the next phase of our plan?"

"We are. Want to watch Naomi kick it off?"

"Absolutely."

We caught a taxi on Seventh Avenue and raced downtown with nothing but green lights until we turned right onto 17th Street. The cab pulled to a stop in front of Naomi and Stewart's building about 10 minutes after we had left the hotel. It paid to travel in Manhattan early on a Saturday morning.

A few breathless minutes later, we summited to the fifth floor and knocked on the door. Once again, Stewart let us into the kitchen, handed us coffee and tea, and led us to Naomi, sitting in front of a monitor. Harry stood near by.

"We all set?" I asked.

"Of course," Naomi grinned. "It's 9:28. As soon as

we hit 9:30, the malware activates. Anyone who tries to access the networks at either Sinclair's London office or O'Malley's gallery will be greeted with this—"

She touched a key and displayed a dialog box occupying most of the screen. The message in white on a black background read:

------ **WARNING** -----

Your network is now under our control.
All data has been encrypted.
Your network is frozen.
If our demands are not met, the data
will be destroyed in the next 24 hours.
If our demands are not met, all network
hard drives will be destroyed in the next 24 hours.

Nigel Sinclair must call this number:
203-555-1718

The clock is ticking.

Indeed it was—two small clocks, one showing New York time and the other London time, tick-tocked away in the lower lefthand corner of the screen. A loud ticking sound emanated from the computer's speakers.

"Will you know when someone triggers—"

A ping echoed. And another. And another . . .

Naomi turned down the sound. "Yes, we'll know."

"Assuming they have sophisticated tech, won't they

be able to trace the phone number?"

As we talked, we heard more pings.

"It's a burner phone. And it's in Connecticut, call-forwarding to us. If Sinclair's folks can track to the nearest cell tower, they'll find out that the phone is in Stamford."

"Isn't there a delay with call-forwarding?"

"A few seconds."

"How'd you get the phone set up in Stamford?"

"Harry did it."

"What a guy," I grinned. "I wonder how long before the self-obsessed Mr. Sinclair rings us up."

"I'm just guessing, but 10 to 20 minutes. Users running into our ransomware message will call IT. The IT director will try a few tricks to see if they can access files on the server. Once they realize that they can't get to their stuff, they'll call Mr. Self-Obsessed."

"While we wait," Stewart said, "anyone want more coffee or tea?"

I followed him to the kitchen to top off my coffee. Courtney was fine with her tea.

"Listen," Stewart began as we returned to the office. "I analyzed some of the Sinclair files that Naomi downloaded last night."

"Let me guess," I said. "More LLCs and off-shore accounts?"

"Lots more. I've got no proof, but I think they're O'Malley's handiwork."

"Why O'Malley?"

"Just a feeling."

"That's good enough for me," I said.

Stewart resumed, "The accounts and LLCs are legal and almost impossible to untangle. *But* . . . Naomi found some encrypted files that we hope are the books for Sinclair's criminal operations."

"Do criminals actually maintain accounts for their illegal activities?" Courtney asked.

"They do when you're talking about multiple revenue streams amounting to tens of millions of dollars."

"That's a lot of money," she said, stunned.

"And it's incredibly complex. Tons of cash from illegal sources that needs to be laundered. Lots of expenses like staff and vehicles with the costs probably being paid by your legit businesses. And you're dealing in at least two currencies: the dollar and the pound."

"Even criminals need accountants," I said.

"I'm . . . that makes sense . . . wow," Courtney said. "What are you going to do with those encrypted files?"

"I'll crack 'em open," Naomi said, "and Stewart will analyze them."

"If they are, in fact, the books for Sinclair's illegal operations," Harry added, "we'll turn them over to the authorities and that will be the end of Mr. Sinclair."

"That sounds simple," Courtney sounded hopeful.

"I'm sorry," Harry responded, "but it's rarely as simple as it sounds."

"Not when Jack's around," Naomi said.

"You make it sound like it's my fault."

"Don't whine. And I was just making an observation."

"It sounded like you were assigning blame."

"You are such a Catholic school boy."

"Ouch."

Naomi, Stewart, and I laughed. Harry was blasé. Courtney was hesitant to join in the merriment then realized it was okay and chuckled.

A phone's ring tone sounded through the computer speakers, and a message displayed on Naomi's monitor:

INCOMING CALL FROM 203-555-1718

"That was fast," Naomi said and looked around. "Ready?"

"Yup," I said and took a seat beside her.

Naomi nudged a microphone close to me, handed me a Bluetooth earpiece, and said, "The earpiece will prevent feedback. And don't worry, your voice goes through a filter. You'll sound like a killer robot on Red Bull." She clicked "Return" on her keyboard as I inserted my earpiece. Out of the corner of my eye, I saw that Stewart was handing earpieces to Harry and Courtney.

"Hello," said Nigel Sinclair, sounding every bit the cultured Brit. "To whom am I speaking?"

"First things first: Who are you?" My voice had a gravelly basso profondo growl. I sounded like the Voice of

147

Doom.

"I'm Nigel Sinclair." He didn't sound all that impressed with my doomsday vocalizations. "Who are you?"

"I'm the man who is in control of your computer systems." The word "control" had a wonderfully ominous tone through the basso profondo filter.

"Really?" Sinclair said calmly, with complete indifference to my powerful performance. "What do you want?"

"You will guarantee that no harm comes to Courtney Wilson. No harm of any kind. She will not be subjected to violence or kidnapping or being killed. Most of your files will be unlocked as soon as you make this guarantee. Others will be released slowly over time."

"Which files will be released?"

"Not your most sensitive files. Not your shadow accounts."

"Shadow accounts?" Naomi mouthed at me.

I shrugged.

"I see you know what you are doing," Sinclair said.

"Yes, I do," the electronically enhanced growl made the simple phrase "I do" resonate with threat. "Your shadow accounts will be saved for last."

Next to me, Naomi was grinning and nodding and flashing a thumbs up.

"When will you release my data?"

"When I see fit."

"You think you have me in a box, don't you?"

"I *do* have you in a box."

"Despite what you've done to my computers, I can continue operations. I have money in my London bank accounts. Enough to operate for quite a while. Enough to buy me time to hunt you down."

"That's very unfriendly of you."

"I assume you are the man who saved Courtney Wilson's life."

"I am." What an astoundingly powerful phrase when spoken by the Voice of Doom.

"I will kill you."

"You? You personally? You won't pay somebody else to do it for you?"

Sinclair didn't respond immediately.

Harry leaned over and whispered, "I think you're getting off-topic."

I nodded and spoke again. "I said I have you in a box, and I do. We have your shadow accounts—the encrypted accounting books for your illegal activities. Even when we unlock those files, we'll still have copies. As long as Ms. Wilson is safe, the files will stay hidden away. If anything happens to her, the files will be decrypted and released to the FBI, Scotland Yard, and Interpol."

Silence on Sinclair's end.

"Do you understand me?" I asked.

"Yes."

"Are you going to meet our demands?"

149

"Do I have a choice?"

"I'll assume that was a rhetorical question."

"It was. I will not harm Ms. Wilson."

"Is that a guarantee?"

"If I say so, yes it's a guarantee."

"We'll begin unlocking files on Monday morning."

"I'd like to ask a question, if I may."

"Go ahead."

"Do I have to promise not to harm you?"

Harry put his hand on my shoulder. I could see Naomi turn toward me.

"I wouldn't want to demand too much from you."

Harry withdrew his hand. Naomi frowned and focused on her monitor.

"You're a fool," Sinclair said. "You have no idea what I'm capable of."

"I feel the same about you," I growled and gestured with my hand across my throat to cut the call.

Naomi disconnected. "Really, Jack?"

"Do you think it was wise to provoke him?" Harry asked.

"He's going to feel and think however he's going to feel and think," I replied. "Trading barbs with him wasn't going to change anything."

"I hope you're right," Naomi said.

Courtney added, "He sounded pretty angry to me."

"I wouldn't want him coming after me," Stewart agreed. "Do you think maybe you're writing a check your body can't cash?"

"For crying out loud," I responded. "We got the bad guy to agree to leave our client alone. Why is that a bad thing?"

"It's not, but . . ." Naomi's voice trailed off.

"Do you believe him?" Stewart asked.

"I believe some of what he said," I answered. "He's buying time to find me and deal with me."

"And give his IT guys time to attempt the unlocking of his files," Naomi pointed out.

"Yup."

"He probably thinks he's got some time before we break the encryption and access his books."

"Yeah, I bet he does think that. Sinclair believes that until we open his books, he can do whatever the hell he wants. On the other hand, once the books are open, we've got him by the short hairs." I paused, thought about it for a moment, then asked in a British accent, "Sinclair here. Mr. IT Director, how long will it take these blokes to crack our books?"

"Is that a Monty Python gag?" Stewart asked.

"No."

"Well, you sound like John Cleese."

"Never mind," I spoke to Naomi, "If you were Sinclair's IT people, how long would you estimate for our cracking the encryption?"

"If I'm his IT department, I'd take a long, hard look at the malware hack that was installed and guess that we might crack it in 3 or 4 days."

"Is that how long it will take you?" I asked.

Naomi treated us to a huge, Cheshire cat grin. "With Harry's help, I'll probably have it done by tomorrow."

"Okay. So we probably need to survive Sinclair's antics for the next 3 days."

"I'd like to emphasize the word *probably*," Naomi said. "I'm making an educated guess about someone else's educated guess."

"Your guess is what we have to work with, so that's what we'll go with. As soon as you crack open the files, we'll give Sinclair a bit of data to prove we've opened his criminal books. That should be enough to make him back off."

"If it doesn't?" Courtney asked. "Am I ever going to get my life back?"

"We'll get him to stop," I reassured her.

"How?"

"We'll figure something out."

"I think you may be ignoring something," Harry said.

"And that would be?"

"Sinclair's personality. Or rather, his mental and emotional makeup."

"Yeah . . . he suffers from narcissistic personality disorder. So?"

"You may remember the events following Election

Day."

"Of course, I do. It was only 4 months ago."

"And you drew a parallel between Sinclair and the current occupant of the White House."

"Yes. They're both narcissists. Get to your point, Harry. Please."

"Do you remember how much time transpired before the current occupant declared that he had actually won the popular vote?"

"A few days, maybe a couple of weeks."

"Do you remember his claims regarding the attendance at his inauguration?"

"Yes. What's your point?"

"Why do you think he said those things, without any evidence whatsoever?"

"He has to be acknowledged as the best. As a winner."

"Exactly. He hated the idea of being branded a loser."

Stewart observed, "And since Sinclair is the same kind of narcissist, he won't be able to admit he's lost. He'll attack."

"Regardless of the consequences," Naomi said.

"Yes," Harry agreed. "Sinclair will attack."

10

SATURDAY MORNING – THE MARK

AMANDA RUNDLE strode into Sinclair's suite, shook hands with him, and took a seat without waiting for one to be offered to her.

Sinclair smiled at her confidence and asked, "Can I get you anything to drink? Juice? Tea? Scotch?"

"Tea would be nice, thank you." Like Sinclair, she had a cultured accent. Her hair was a brown bob, her eyes ice-blue. She was dressed in a midnight-blue pant suit and a white blouse. At first glance, a standard police-detective wardrobe. But Sinclair noticed the quality of the cut and the fabric was well above what someone working for Scotland Yard or Interpol could afford.

Sinclair went to the suite's kitchenette and poured hot water into a cup. "English Breakfast all right?"

"Perfect."

"Do you want lemon? Cream? Sweetener?"

"No, thank you," Rundle grinned. "I imagine it's been a long time since you made someone a cuppa."

"Yes." He served her with the cup on a tiny plate.

"Is this a special occasion?"

He sat on the couch opposite her. "I assume you

read the file that was prepared."

"Just before I fell asleep. Your jet is a very comfortable aircraft."

"I'm glad you liked it."

"It's the only way to travel."

"I have a new problem."

"Oh? Something or someone beyond Courtney Wilson and the mystery man who saved her?"

"It appears that someone hacked into my network. My people are locked out of everything."

"Do you have an idea who it could be? Maybe the mystery man?"

"My IT director tells me that it took a very skilled person to hack my system. Elite level. I think it's highly unlikely that the mystery man, as you like to call him, has that kind of ability."

"You think he's a little too good at the rough and tumble of it all?"

"Yes, that's exactly what I think. And that is the reason I think we may be facing a formidable team."

"Have you had a ransom demand?" Rundle asked.

"Yes. Just a few minutes ago. I had to guarantee that Ms. Wilson will come to no harm. Beginning Monday, they will start releasing my files."

"A slow, timed release?"

"Yes."

"There's something else, isn't there?'

Sinclair nodded, "They claim to have unlocked my

books."

"Where your true accounting ledgers are?"

"Precisely."

"And they're threatening to release those books if Ms. Wilson comes to any harm—and they're going to withhold a copy to ensure you cooperate in perpetuity."

"They're blackmailing me."

"And doing a good job of it."

He bristled, "What are you going to do about it? How are you going to help me?"

"Am I correct in assuming that—despite your guarantee—you do not intend to cooperate with their demands?"

"That is correct. My father was far from being a sophisticated man, but I still live by one of his axioms: When threatened, attack. Continue to attack until the threat is resolved."

"You said, 'they *claim* to have unlocked' the books—does that mean you don't believe them?"

"My IT director says it's not possible. We likely have 3, possibly 4, days before they break the encryption."

"Which means we have a 3-day window in which to secure Ms. Wilson, your files, and the mystery man. I am assuming you will want to deal directly with him."

"Yes, I do. But all of my troubles start with the woman."

"She does seem to be the origin. And if we find her, we'll find her protector."

"How do you plan on finding her?"

"Old-fashioned police work. I've reached out to a former colleague at Interpol and asked that Courtney Wilson be detained for questioning. Interpol issued an alert for her to many international law-enforcement agencies, including the NYPD. Interpol checked her credit card activity—there's nothing since Tuesday, a day before your first attempt on her life. NYPD has checked the airports and passenger ships in the New York area—no one with Ms. Wilson's ID has departed the area."

"Maybe she paid cash for a bus ticket to suburban New Jersey," Sinclair suggested. "That wouldn't rise to the attention of Interpol or NYPD, would it?"

"NYPD is showing her photo around the major train stations and bus stops. They're also looking into the rental-car companies in case she and her mysterious protector have rented a car and drove out of town."

"Unless fortune smiles on me, I doubt this plan of yours will find her in the three-day window."

"Maybe you'll find this reassuring: I think Courtney Wilson and her mystery man are still in New York, hiding somewhere. Your team last encountered them in Greenwich Village almost a day after the initial attack by your team. Only hours after the second attack. I think if they were going to depart the area they would have done so before that last encounter."

"I hope so."

"Also, the malware attack and the ransom demand

are not what you'd expect from people on the run. Ms. Wilson and the mystery man are not trying to escape you—they're counter-attacking. That leads me to believe they're still in New York."

"And you have a plan for finding them in the city?"

"I've contacted another former colleague, this one at the NYPD, a detective who is unaware that I no longer work for Interpol. She's aware of the Interpol alert to detain Ms. Wilson. She and I will make the rounds of the large, midtown hotels, show Courtney Wilson's photograph from the file, and ask if anyone has seen her."

"That sounds like a slow approach. Again, I don't think I have the time."

"It is slow. But it's thorough and could produce results. Also, if they're hiding out in a hotel, it's likely to be a large hotel and not one of the posh boutiques like this one. Easier to hide at a large hotel like the Marriott Marquis at Times Square or the Hilton Midtown. Hunting for her at those places will narrow the possibilities."

"I hope you're right."

"Do you have a better idea?"

He simmered in anger for a moment, then grudgingly admitted, "No, I don't."

"That settles it then. I'll try to persuade my NYPD contact to put some more detectives on the hotel-to-hotel search to aid in our hunt."

"I hope this works. I need to find that woman."

Rundle finished her tea, replaced the cup on its

saucer, and left the suite. Sinclair stood and picked up her cup and saucer to carry them to the kitchenette. When he was still a few feet away, he threw the cup and saucer into the sink, shattering them.

*   *   *

Naomi and Harry were hard at work decrypting the books. Stewart was again re-examining the LLCs and off-shore accounts to see if he could find anything we could threaten Sinclair and/or O'Malley with. Courtney was mostly working with Stewart, but occasionally switched over to see what the super-hackers were up to.

Since I could add absolutely nothing to the proceedings, I took a walk. After 20 minutes, I'd made my leisurely way to Buona Tazza, my favorite downtown café, on Minetta Lane. I ordered a cappuccino, found a table near the front where I could stare out the window and watch the passersby out on the sidewalk. Since I was a regular, the barista was nice enough to bring my cappuccino to me. I savored a sip then a second. Took a deep breath.

Called Kim.

"This is Kim Gannon. Please leave a message, and I'll get back to you."

I should have been prepared for the possibility that I would end up dumped into voice mail. Kim could be on the phone. Or worse, she was screening her calls and

159

avoiding me.

Like I said, I should have been prepared. I wasn't. "Hi, Kim, it's me. I'm . . . sorry. Sorry about the way things have gone lately. Sorry that you're . . . wait, let me back up, sorry that *I* have hurt you. I'd really like to talk. Okay. Guess that's all . . . except . . . I love you."

I finished my cappuccino, luxuriating in every drop of its espresso and foamed milk. It was a really good cappuccino. And it did absolutely nothing to help with my confusion and pain regarding Kim.

Checking my phone, I thought I might have time to share a meal or grab a cup of coffee with my friend Mike Bracken. Father Mike was the Jesuit priest who was supposed to take Kim and me through our Pre-Cana preparation and then preside at our wedding at St. Ignatius Loyola Church where he was the associate pastor.

"Hey, Jack, how are you?" he answered cheerfully.

"Uh . . . I've been better. I know it's really short notice, but do you have time for a sandwich? Or a cup of coffee?"

"Actually, I do. I just had a cancellation, which happens to leave me free to deal with your issues."

"The coffee shop on Madison? Half an hour?"

"I'll see you then."

I splurged on a cab to head to uptown. As the taxi headed north, I called Harry.

"Everything okay?" I asked.

"Your presence is not a requirement for our well-

160

being."

"So glad you missed me. I take it you can live without me for a bit longer. A couple of hours?"

"If it means you are going to an AA meeting, yes, of course."

"As a matter of fact," I sighed resignedly.

"Good. See you later."

Within 15 minutes the cab pulled to a stop in front of a coffee shop on Madison Avenue, a couple of blocks away from St. Ignatius Loyola. Mike was already at a table when I entered. He was, like me, an Irish Catholic. He had a thick head of prematurely gray hair and horn-rimmed glasses. He smiled broadly and stood up to give me a hug.

"I had a feeling I would be hearing from you soon," he said, waving me to a chair.

"Really? What made you think that?"

"It wasn't quite 3 weeks ago that you and Kim met with me. You were supposed to get me some paperwork—"

"Baptismal certificates, Kim's annulment decree, and my late wife's death certificate."

"Yes. We were going to set up another meeting. But, until today, I haven't heard a word from either of you."

"Sorry about that."

"It's your wedding."

"Yeah. That's the plan, anyway. . . ."

"What's worrying you, Jack?"

"Well, Kim's not talking to me. That's probably significant."

"Probably. Why isn't she talking to you?"

"It's uh . . . it's the same problem we've had over and over."

"Your work with 'some very dangerous people,' as Kim put it."

"Yup. That's it."

"You told me you can't change the nature of your work even thought it sometimes requires you to deal with dangerous people. Do you still feel that's true?"

"It *is* true."

"And you can't change it?"

"Nope."

"And you won't stop doing it?"

I took a deep breath and exhaled slowly. "I feel like this is the point where I'm supposed to say, 'I love Kim, so I'm going to walk away from this calling of mine.' But I . . . I . . . just can't. Not now, anyway. I know that makes me a crappy husband-to-be since I'm prioritizing something over the woman I love."

"Your situation is probably more complicated than prioritizing one thing over another. Do you think it's possible, that over time, your feelings about your calling might evolve? That you might find it easier to walk away from the more dangerous aspects of your work?"

At that moment, the waiter, a small, dark-haired man with a thick salt-and-pepper mustache appeared at our table and asked if we knew what we wanted for lunch. Mike ordered a turkey sandwich, and I followed suit.

"I don't know," I said in response to Mike's question. "Right now, I am literally keeping a young woman alive while a British villain straight out of a Bond movie tries to kill her."

"That is . . . something I don't think I've ever heard anyone say before."

"Oh? Oh, listen, can we keep this conversation confidential please? Seal of the confessional?"

Mike grinned, "Yes, it's confidential. I have so many questions—"

"I'm sure you do," I interrupted, "but could we please stay on topic regarding Kim and me?"

The waiter arrived with the sandwiches, asked if we wanted anything to drink, and left when we said we were fine with water.

"I think . . . ," I struggled to find the precise way to express myself, "I think that . . . maybe, after my current case is done . . . maybe I could move away from the dangerous work. As Kim pointed out, having a family is a pretty important calling."

"Yes it is."

"But the problem is . . . I think Kim wants an answer right now. This minute. I'm up to my eyeballs in snakes and alligators, metaphorically speaking, and I just can't give her the answer she wants."

"Are you afraid she's going to give you an ultimatum? You must choose her or your work?"

"I guess I am. To be completely honest, I think

she's already given me that ultimatum. She's not talking to me, not returning my calls. I feel like . . . until she hears what she wants to hear, we're . . . nothing."

"I'm sorry to hear that."

"Me too." I took a bite of my sandwich and made the ill-mannered choice to speak while chewing. "There's something else."

"Yes?"

"I . . . I feel like . . . Kim's being unfair to me. She's not really listening when I say that I'm following a calling."

"Do you think she's not hearing what you say, or is she deflecting because she can't argue with your calling?"

"I don't know," I said quickly. Then, "No, no, that's not right. She's deflecting."

"You love her so much you're defending her even in this conflict between the two of you."

"I guess I am."

"It's what you do."

"Excuse me?"

"You protect people."

"I try, anyway."

We ate in silence for a few moments.

Then I asked, "Don't you have some magical words of wisdom for me? Aren't you an expert on people following their callings?"

"Please excuse my brevity, but no and no."

"No and no?"

"Most of my pastoral work is listening. Being

present for people. Giving them my attention."

"I need more than your ears."

"You'll have to turn to God for more."

"Whatever He's saying to me, I'm not hearing it."

"You may need to keep praying."

"Can't I have a white-light experience like St. Paul on the road to Damascus?"

"You *could*, but do you really think that hoping for such an unlikely event is a good way to proceed?"

"No. So all you've got for me is: Keep praying."

"Yes," he smiled. "And use your head but listen to your heart."

I paid the check and gave Mike a hug goodbye as we parted in front of the coffeeshop.

"Hang in there," he said. "Keep praying."

"I will. Early and often."

"That's voting."

"I think it works with praying too."

He grinned, "Certainly worth trying." He walked off toward St. Ignatius Loyola.

I had about a half-hour to kill before going to an AA meeting, so I walked up Madison to 90th Street, turned left and walked to Fifth Avenue, and turned left again, heading downtown. I enjoyed the bare-trees scenery of Central Park and when I passed the Guggenheim Museum, I gazed upon it and tried for the bazillionth time to appreciate Frank Lloyd Wright's innovative design. It was interesting, but it just didn't speak to me. Oh well.

I checked the meeting app on my phone to be sure that the Metropolitan Meeting was still being held in the basement of St. Ignatius Loyola (yes, Father Mike's church) at 3:15 P.M. on Saturdays. It was. I turned left on East 84th Street and walked the couple of blocks to the church's entrance on Park Avenue.

AA meetings are held in every kind of room imaginable, but to my mind, the classic setting is a church basement. With a forty-cup, stainless-steel coffeemaker gurgling in the corner, percolating its way through a meeting's worth of coffee. The basement at St. Ignatius, or undercroft, had been renovated a dozen years ago and had none of the grimy, subterranean feel of some New York City church basements I had been in. But it was still a basement. With the regulation coffeepots (one with coffee, one with hot water for tea and instant decaf). And plates of store-bought cookies. I got myself a cup of coffee and manfully refrained from consuming a dozen cookies. I had to stay in fighting trim.

The meeting started. A middled-aged Black man introduced himself by saying, "I'm Charlie, and I'm an alcoholic."

Everyone responded, "Hi, Charlie."

Charlie read the AA preamble and then introduced the speaker, a slender, thirtyish white woman with long dark hair streaked blonde.

"I'm Leslie, and I'm an alcoholic."

"Hey, Leslie."

Leslie told a gripping story of growing up knowing that she was different, feeling isolated and afraid. In her teens, she was finally able to admit that she was a lesbian but had already begun medicating herself with alcohol and "dry goods" (as alcoholics refer to drugs).

"It's impossible to come to terms with yourself when you drink and drug so much you have no idea who you are or what it means to be who you are," she said. "I didn't feel that I could tell my family or friends that I was a lesbian. And I was terrified that they'd figure it out for themselves and reject me.

"What I didn't think of, what never occurred to me, was that most of the people who wanted to be close to me, couldn't be because of my drinking. I was a nasty, self-loathing bitch, and when I was drunk, which was most of the time, I was nasty to everyone else. My family and friends just wanted me to be happy. But I couldn't see that because of my alcoholic haze.

"Finally, my parents put together an intervention, I was my usual nasty self, shouting and cursing, but they wore me down, and it worked. I went off to rehab, and I've been sober for the last 4 years.

"Turned out that my parents and friends knew I was a lesbian and were fine with it. They didn't disapprove of me, they disapproved of my drinking. Actually, that's not quite right. They were *worried* about my drinking. They were scared for me, afraid I was going to kill myself.

"Now, I'm sober and slowly learning to accept

myself. I actually enjoy who I am a lot of the time. Okay, maybe it's only sometimes—I'm getting *better*, not *perfect*. One day at a time, I'll probably get to a point where I'm happy with who I am *most* of the time. That would be great."

There was a round of very warm applause as she finished, and then other people in the room shared what was going on with them. I confess that I didn't listen. I just kept thinking about what Leslie had said. I wasn't a young woman or a lesbian, but didn't I have the same problem she had? Of course the drinking, but also the struggle to be happy with who I was. And with who I could be.

Protector. Recovering alcoholic. In the employ of the Chairman. Husband? Father? Content with a safe 9-to-5 existence as a corporate-security consultant?

Not for the first time I left an AA meeting thinking self-awareness is a very good thing but also very painful. And confusing. . . .

11

When I returned to Naomi and Stewart's railroad flat, Naomi greeted me with, "I've got bad news, Jack."

Naomi, Stewart, Courtney, and Harry were sitting in the middle room with the computers and monitors. Courtney and Harry were sitting on metal folding chairs. I stood in the doorway since there didn't seem to be any empty chairs available.

"I'll take the good news first."

"I didn't say I had any good news."

"I was using the power of positive thinking."

"You're suffering from a power outage," Naomi said. Usually, she would have grinned at making such a comment, but her expression was glum. "I'm still running the algorithms to crack the encryption."

"So that would be classified as '*no* news.'"

"Yes. But while the algorithms are running, I've been digging through the server logs and found that at 12:02 A.M. Greenwich Mean Time, Sinclair's network automatically established a VPN to an off-site data center where all the files—including the criminal accounting books—that have been modified or updated in the preceding 24 hours were backed up. We hacked in at approximately 2:00 A.M. our time, or 7:00 A.M. in London. In other words, Sinclair had only lost 7 hours of updates to his system when we froze him out. Given that those were overnight hours on a Saturday morning, I doubt he lost much at all."

Stewart said, "He can be back in business pretty soon. But we still have all his files and can use them as evidence."

"If and when we get to the point where we need evidence," I responded. "I'm guessing Sinclair will need clean computers to relaunch his network."

"He will. My malware has him locked out so his IT people can't start over. They'll have to buy and install all new machines then install all their programs and then load their data. Even with a large team of very skilled people, it's going to take a couple of days at least."

"But we still have the evidence," Stewart said. "We still have leverage."

"Only once Naomi cracks the criminal books and you analyze them."

"I think you're forgetting something," Harry said.

"Oh?" I asked, not really wanting to know what I was forgetting.

"You're not taking into account Sinclair's basic nature. He attacks anything that constitutes a threat to him. He wants to eliminate Courtney. Thanks to the successful hacking of his computers and seizing his criminal ledgers, he now wants to eliminate this entire team."

"But he doesn't know who we are," Stewart said. "Does he?"

"No. Although he is aware that Courtney has a protector."

"Thank God for that," Courtney sighed heavily.

"Yes, exactly," Harry said.

"What was your point in bringing up Sinclair's reaction to threats?" I asked.

"You were discussing the data as leverage against Sinclair. Leverage will not work against him. You need a plan of attack."

"Are you advocating violence?"

"In this particular instance. . . ."

* * *

SATURDAY EVENING – THE MARK

NIGEL SINCLAIR MARCHED across the hotel lobby, dug a phone out of his suit jacket pocket, went out the hotel entrance, and climbed into a black limousine.

"I want to hear good news," he said into the phone as the limo pulled away.

"Lucky you," Amanda Rundle replied. "I have some for you."

"You found Courtney Wilson?"

"Of course."

"Where is she?"

"Hilton Midtown. It was only the third hotel we checked. No one saw her at check-in, but when we asked room service, one of the servers recognized her."

"Where are you now? Is she with you?"

"I'm in her room. The hotel was very willing to cooperate with the NYPD and let us in. No, at the moment, she's not here."

"What are your next steps?"

"I explained to my NYPD colleague that this woman is not dangerous, but that I do need to interview her, and that I didn't want to take up anymore of her department's valuable time. They were willing to leave me to my own devices. Which leaves me free to . . . *acquire* Ms. Wilson when she arrives."

"Nicely done. Who's with you?"

"Yes. I have two members of my team in the room. Three in the lobby."

"I'm flying back to London tonight. I want both Ms. Wilson and her protector alive with me on that flight."

"We'll do our best to deliver them both. May I ask why you want her protector?"

"I want to look him in the eye before he dies."

"I will do what I can to make that happen."

*   *   *

"My suggestion is that you," Harry looked

pointedly at me, "make a direct attack on Sinclair's criminal operations in London. Go after his sex-trafficking ring and/or the drugs and/or the weapons dealing."

"You do know that I am only one guy."

"This is no time for modesty."

"You can do it, Jack," grinned Naomi.

Harry said. "I will guide you to Sinclair's illegal operations, and you will take them out."

"Cutting off Sinclair's cash flow," Stewart pointed out.

"Maybe providing more evidence?" Naomi asked. "Something we can use to force Sinclair to back off?"

Stewart shook his head, "There are too many layers. I can't find any direct connection between Sinclair and the sex-trafficking, drugs, or weapons-dealing activities."

"Maybe there would be some proof where those activities are actually happening?"

"Based on the casserole of LLCs and off-shore accounts," Stewart replied, "I don't think you're going to find a thing."

"And by 'you,' you mean me," I said.

Stewart shrugged.

Harry spoke, "I think your friend Joanne at the FBI might help you with a very useful contact at Scotland Yard."

"Oh?" I responded. "That's what you think?"

"Yes."

"How useful?"

"Very. Former SAS."

"What's SAS?" Naomi asked.

"A highly trained Royal Army unit, kind of like our Green Berets," I replied.

"Always nice to be part of a winning team," Naomi said with a wide smile, holding her arms out as if to encircle everyone in the room.

"Yes like this one." I turned to Courtney. "Have you had enough of these folks? Would you like to go back to the hotel and grab another room-service dinner?"

"I'd rather go home and make myself a cup of tea, but since that probably isn't an option. . . ."

"Sorry, no."

"I guess it's going to be room service then."

We grabbed our coats, said our goodbyes, and walked down the building's seemingly interminable steps and out to the sidewalk.

"Okay if we walk to Sixth?" I asked. "We can enjoy a little fresh air and probably catch a cab more easily over there."

"Fine." Courtney began walking east toward Sixth Avenue, and I fell in alongside her.

"I'm usually a subway guy," I said. "I love the speed and convenience of the trains. Always felt like once I had mastered the subway I was a master of the city."

She chuckled. "I know what you mean. Learning the subway system here is very empowering."

"Over hundred years old with almost two hundred fifty miles of track and more than four hundred stations awaiting the swipe of your MetroCard."

"So why are we taking a cab?"

"Since I've had to leave you cooped up in the hotel all the time—"

"Or with Naomi and Stewart—"

"At their less-than-swanky office, I feel I should give you the deluxe treatment and hail a cab for you."

"Thank you."

We reached Sixth, an no sooner had I raised my hand then a cab pulled to a stop to pick us.

"The Hilton Midtown please," I said.

We arrived without incident a few minutes later. I tipped too generously, but what the heck, we were safe and sound.

As we headed across the gigantic lobby toward the elevators, I noticed a tall, thin, red-haired white man to our left fall in surreptitiously behind us. My internal radar began pinging. We hadn't gone another 10 feet before a Black woman began trailing us on our right flank. My radar was pinging more loudly.

We reached the elevator bank as a bellman was trundling a full baggage trolley into the middle elevator. I gently grabbed Courtney's right arm and quick-stepped her behind the bellman. She pressed 17 but as the doors began to slide shut, there was a "bing," and the doors rolled open again.

The red-haired man entered swiftly and muttered, "Sorry to hold you up." Was that a British accent or was my imagination in overdrive?

A split-second later, the Black woman also entered the elevator, sliding in next to Courtney, who was on my right. The baggage trolley was to my left. Red Hair was between me and the elevator door, his back to the trolley. There was barely enough space for one other person in the elevator, but sure enough, a squat white man with a crew-cut and a close-cropped beard stepped aboard. None of the three late arrivals had pressed a floor button. My internal radar was pinging like mad.

The elevator doors closed, and we began ascending. I saw that the button for the ninth floor was lit up. The bellman must be delivering bags to that floor. I slowly reached my left hand out and grabbed the handle of an overnight bag.

The elevator settled gently to a stop on the ninth floor. As the doors rolled open, I tightened my grip on the small suitcase. The bellman said, "Have a good night," and pulled the trolley out of the elevator. I maintained my grip on the overnight bag, and it slid out between the brass bars at the end of the trolley. No one noticed. The doors closed, and we began climbing again.

"It was nice of you to wait," I said.

Courtney said, "What?" at the same time as Red Hair grinned and spun toward me.

I yanked the suitcase up and shoved it into his

chest. He thumped against the elevator doors. I twisted around as Crew Cut swung a blackjack at me. I shielded myself with the suitcase and used it to ram him into the wall. I twisted back and whacked Red Hair again with the luggage. He slumped to the floor.

Crew Cut was back with the blackjack. I was able to block the blow with my right arm, which hurt like hell. I managed to hold onto the suitcase and used it like a battering ram against Crew Cut, smashing him back against the elevator wall. He tried to swing the blackjack, but, holding the suitcase with my right hand, I jabbed him in the face with a hard left. Jabbed him twice to ensure he got my point. He dropped to the floor.

Behind me, I heard Courtney struggling with the woman, who had a gun in her right hand. Courtney was gripping the woman's right wrist, forcing the gun down so it was aimed at the floor. The woman's left hand was cupped under Courtney's chin, and Courtney was gripping the woman's left wrist, trying to free herself. Courtney's height gave her a serious advantage over the other woman, and she seemed to be holding her own.

I should have paid attention to my own dance partners. Red Hair shoved a gun into my chest and said, "Hold still, you wanker."

"Wanker? Me?" I asked, dropped the suitcase and in the same instant spun to my right so that my left arm knocked the pistol away. I reversed and threw a right hook, catching Red Hair on the jaw. The force of my punch

177

rocked him back on his feet and sent him crashing into the elevator doors. He slumped to the floor, and I grabbed the pistol out of his hand.

The elevator stopped on the seventeenth floor. The doors rolled open. Crew Cut jumped me from behind, grabbing me in a bear hug. A white woman with short dark hair, wearing a black duster coat, was waiting in the hallway and aiming a weapon at us.

Courtney and the other African American woman were still wrestling for control of the woman's gun. They toppled out of the elevator onto the hallway floor.

The woman with the short dark hair aimed her weapon at us. It was a Taser. I spun around and heard the click as she pulled the trigger. The electrodes hit Crew Cut in the back, and he released me immediately and fell to the floor, his body jerking around like an electrocuted cartoon character. Since the electric charge of a Taser is localized between the probes, I wasn't affected, but it didn't matter. The elevator doors rolled shut, trapping me inside and Courtney outside in the hallway.

The car began to descend. The Taser cords pulled tight, snapped off of Crew Cut's back and were yanked back to the elevator doors. A second later, the doors began to roll open then stopped as the elevator abruptly jerked to a halt. The emergency stop alarm sounded.

"God dammit!" I paced in the tiny bit of free floor space in the elevator. "Do something useful, Tyrrell."

I checked both men for wallets, phones, and guns.

They both had British drivers licenses. And compact little Samsung flip phones. And Glock G17 pistols.

Was it just me, or had the emergency alarm been sounding for an eternity?

"Harry?"

"Yes," he replied, whooshing in with his usual smooth suddenness.

"Could you please get me out of here?"

"Where do you want to go?"

"Wherever Courtney is."

Harry peered skyward, then at me. "I'm sorry . . ."

With no sensation of time passing or my moving, I was standing with Harry on the corner of West 54th Street and Sixth Avenue.

". . . I can't take you to her," Harry finished.

"This is no damn time to be arguing about my needs and free will and all that crap. She could be killed. Take me to her *now*."

"I can't. But I can assure you that she is alive and is being taken to London."

"Shit!"

"That is a remarkably brief yet accurate summation of the current situation."

I took a deep breath and exhaled slowly. "Thank you for getting me out of there."

"You're welcome."

"I don't suppose you covered our tracks?"

"Of course. There's no video to identify you, no

DNA or fingerprints in your hotel room. I had checked you in under a false name, and you've already been checked out. Courtney's and your luggage is back at your apartment."

"Wow. Thanks. Again."

"You're welcome. And . . . I am truly sorry about Courtney."

"Me, too. So. London?"

"London."

"First, my apartment?"

"Yes."

"Will you be whooshing me to London?"

"Yes, I will *transport* you there."

"Can I bring guns?"

"Yes."

"*Lots* of guns?"

"Yes."

12

SATURDAY NIGHT – PRIVATE JET

COURTNEY WILSON, in plasticuffs, boarded Sinclair's jet. Amanda Rundle was immediately behind her. The co-pilot ignored the cuffs and shut the cabin's hatch as soon as the women were clear. He returned to the cockpit.

Rundle pointed Courtney to a seat facing Nigel Sinclair. She cut off the plasticuffs and sat down in the plush leather chair next to Courtney.

Sinclair smiled at them, picked up a phone, and said, "We're ready for departure."

The pilot replied, "We're beginning to taxi now are are first in line for takeoff. We will land in London around noon, local time."

"Good," Sinclair said and hung up. To Rundle he said, "I'm not happy with the fact that we only have a single passenger. I told you to invite both of them."

"The gentleman was highly resistant."

"That's your problem not mine."

"I had to make a decision in the moment. Take her, our first-priority target, or possibly experience complete mission failure." Rundle shrugged, "I took her."

Sinclair put his hand on the phone. "Maybe I

should leave you here to find and collect the mystery man."

"That is, of course, up to you. But I think he will follow us to London."

Sinclair pulled his hand away from the phone. "What makes you say that?"

"Everything we've seen of the mystery man is that he is determined and resourceful. He's taken out every team you've sent. He and his team have launched a successful malware attack on your network. He now has your files, and he's threatened you. Let me repeat that for emphasis: He's made direct threats against you. What makes you think he won't follow you to London?"

"I agree with you. This could actually be a fortunate turn for me. Up till now, I've been playing against him on his turf. Now, we're going to my home pitch."

"Precisely."

Sinclair stared out the window into the dark. He turned back to Rundle.

"What about her?" he pointed at Courtney.

"Money and taking precautions when we departed and then again at our entry point in London should allow us to smuggle her into England without her passport information being recorded."

"Ahh, good." To Courtney, he said, "Can I get you anything?" He raised his hand, and a flight attendant, a short, slender white woman in a burgundy suit, appeared.

"May I get you a drink?" The flight attendant asked. "Or a blanket?"

"No thank you." Courtney replied.

Sinclair requested Scotch, neat. Rundle declined any drink.

Looking back and forth from Rundle to Sinclair, she said, "You two have made a big mistake."

"Oh?" Sinclair grinned. "Would you care to enlighten me as to the error of my ways?"

"I don't know anything. I didn't see anything the day we sort of met in the hallway at Bargen-Meijer. There was no point to anything you've done."

"I'll be the judge of that." He took the Scotch, in a Baccarat double old-fashioned tumbler, from the attendant and sipped it. "Aren't you going to tell me that your hero is going to save you and make me regret this?"

Courtney smiled mirthlessly. "You already know that."

* * *

A double shoulder holster with two Ruger SR9s lay on my bed next to two medium-size, dark-gray duffles. One duffle was packed with clothing and toiletries; the other, assorted guns, ammo to match the assorted guns, grenades of the bang and smoke varieties, and dozens of plasticuffs.

"Is it possible you have overdone your packing?" Harry asked.

"Yeah, I probably don't need that many clothes."

"I was referring to your weapons collection."

"I'm going light on the weapons. You never really know what you're going to *need*—" I growled the word "need" since its definition was a bone of contention "—when you're launching an assault on a well-organized criminal operation in somebody else's town."

"Yes. Well, launching assaults is your area of expertise, not mine."

"You can say that again."

"Launching assaults—"

"That's enough out of you." I glanced through the contents of each duffle one more time, couldn't think of anything else to add, and zipped them up. "Would you please make hotel arrangements for me?"

"Already done. You're registered at the Sheraton Grand London Park Lane."

"On Piccadilly, facing Green Park?"

"That's correct."

"Good choice, thanks."

"I thought it best to avoid anything that . . . might remind you of Laurie."

"Very considerate of you. I don't need memories of spending the night at the Grange Clarendon with Laurie Mandelbaum before she was murdered."

"London is full of . . . harsh memories for you."

"That's for sure."

"Will you be able to handle your current case?"

"Don't have much choice, do I? That's where the bad guy is. Where the damsel in distress is. A man's gotta do what a man's gotta do."

"That would be an excellent slogan for a T-shirt."

I sighed and admitted, "I wish it didn't have to be London. Laurie was . . . my first love . . . and I couldn't save her." For crying out loud, Tyrrell, snap out of it. "But I have to do whatever I can to save Courtney. So it's off to London I go." I slipped into the shoulder holsters. "Thanks for booking me into the Park Lane. It'll . . . make things easier."

"Nothing ever makes your operations *easier*."

"True." I rechecked the Rugers, making sure they were secure in their holsters. "I guess I should call Joanne for the name of her SAS friend who works at Scotland Yard."

"Jack," she answered. "What the hell have you been up to? There are English thugs packed into NYPD holding cells. Or handcuffed to hospital beds."

"Gee, isn't that bizarre."

"Do they work for Sinclair?"

"I wish I could prove that. My guess is that they work for one of his many LLCs. Or they may work off the books for cash. Either way, there won't be a direct connection to him."

"Were you responsible for their being locked up?"

"No, their own misbehavior led to their arrests."

"Are you saying you had nothing to do with it?"

"Well . . . not . . . nothing."

"Probably better if I don't know."

"Probably."

"Okay, so what can I do for you?"

"Do you, by chance, have a contact at Scotland Yard?"

"Someone to help you with Nigel Sinclair?"

"Yeah, someone like that."

"With a great skill set and a willingness to keep his or her mouth shut?"

"That sounds perfect."

Joanne chuckled. "As a matter of fact . . . Kamal Tiwari. He was in SAS in Afghanistan. He and I were part of the same team on a couple of ops. I don't remember if you were part of those ops."

"His name sounds familiar, but I don't think I worked with him."

"Not sure if he's investigating Sinclair. But he meets all your other criteria. And, if he's willing to join your little crusade, you can trust him with your life."

"I probably will have to."

"Is there anyway I can talk you out of this whole thing?"

"I wish you could, but my client's life is on the line."

"In that case, I'll call Kamal and get back to you. Is it okay if I call him in a couple of hours? It's only 5:30 in the morning there."

"No problem."

"When will you get there? Or are you there already?

"Almost there." I wasn't going to explain the workings of Air Harry to FBI Special Agent Joanne Agar. "Thanks for your help."

"You're welcome. And, Jack?"

"Yes?"

"Godspeed."

We disconnected.

"Are you ready to go?" Harry asked.

"Almost. I need to make another call."

"I'll wait for you in the living room."

"Thanks," I said and watched him walk out of the bedroom and turn down the hallway. I guessed the distance between the bedroom and living room wasn't worth whooshing through.

I sat on the bed next to the two duffles and called Kim. She didn't answer. Was she screening her calls and avoiding me? Or just too deeply asleep to hear her phone?

"Hey, Kim, it's me," I spoke into her voicemail. "I'm, uh . . . I'm sorry to call so late. I have to go to London on this case. . . . Just wanted to tell you I love you. Maybe we can talk when I get back."

I hung up and muttered, "Oh, shit." I stood up and walked to the living room. "Okay, ready to go."

Harry gave me the Mona Lisa-smile treatment, "Not quite."

"No, I'm—"

My phone rang. It was Kim.

"You're going to London?" she asked.

"Yes." I walked back down to the bedroom. As if that would prevent Harry from knowing exactly what we were discussing. "My client was kidnapped and taken there."

"And you gotta do what you gotta do."

"You know me so well."

"I do know you so well. And I don't know what to do with you. You're off to London to do God knows what with I'm assuming some extremely dangerous people. Once again I'm supposed to be the dutiful girlfriend and wait for you."

"You could pray for me while you wait."

"That's not funny."

"It wasn't supposed to be."

"We can't make a life like this. At least, I can't."

"I get it, I do. And I understand. Can we please talk about this when I get back?"

"Yes. And you'd better come back."

"I will."

"You'd better. I mean it."

"I will. I promise."

"Come back to me."

"I will. I love you."

"I love you too." She hung up.

Looking up as if the Chairman lived someplace in

the air above, I said, "Thank you." I tugged on my parka, which had been on the bed next to my duffles, grabbed the strap-handles of each duffle, and took a step toward the bedroom door. Stopped. And looked up again. "If you could help me figure out the rest of my life, I'd really appreciate it. And keeping me alive long enough to live the rest of my life would be nice, too."

Harry was waiting patiently in the living room. "Coat on, luggage in hand, it looks like you are ready to depart."

"I am."

"Good."

We materialized in a Park Lane hotel room with a king-size bed and windows that—I assumed—had a view over Green Park. The colors of the walls, drapes, and carpet were beiges and browns, and the furniture was luxuriously upholstered. Not exactly my taste, but it was much more elegant than the rent-by-the-hour motel off of Route 495 in Weehawken, New Jersey that I had driven past on my way into and out of the Lincoln Tunnel.

I walked to the window and gazed down into the park. In the pre-dawn dusk of a pre-spring March day, it was peaceful. No early dog walkers. In the glow of Piccadilly's street lights, I spotted a few buds on the trees at the edge of the park, hinting at the glories of the season to come. Buckingham Palace was to my right, almost due south of the Park Lane, invisible at that moment. I wondered if I should stop by to say, "Hello," in case the

Queen was in residence. Believe me, stranger things had happened to me than being allowed to meet Elizabeth II. I sighed, knowing that I wouldn't have the time for a social call at the palace. South over the park and on the South Bank of the Thames was the London Eye, Europe's tallest observation wheel at almost four hundred feet. The Shard, the tallest building in England, rose to the east of the London Eye. The place where Laurie had been murdered.

"This is very nice," I said to Harry. "Thanks."

"You might as well be in a good hotel, even if your stay is likely to be very brief and very busy."

"Don't remind me. I think I'll take a quick nap before calling Kamal Tiwari."

"You have 3 hours."

"Can I ask a question?"

"Of course. As long as you're prepared for an answer you may not like."

"I'm always ready for that with you. Anyway, why did you suggest I bust up Sinclair's sex-trafficking and drug operations? Isn't my mission to save Courtney? Couldn't you just whoosh me to wherever she's being held, let me rescue her, and then vamoose?"

"Remember what Jacob Marley's ghost said to Scrooge?"

"Mankind was my business. That's my slogan, too: *Mankind is my business.*"

"With that slogan in mind, you might want to consider whether your mission is to help more people than just Courtney. You might have been called here to save other victims of Sinclair's crimes. Maybe Courtney's mission was to lead you here."

I collapsed on the bed. "Is everyone always called to something?"

"What do you think?"

"Yes."

Harry walked to the window and stood for several minutes enjoying the view from *my* hotel room. "Are you comfortable with your way of proceeding now?"

"Comfortable? No. But I am *committed*, God help me." I sat up, shrugged out of my parka, and slipped out of my shoulder holsters, tossing both the parka and the holsters to the side of the bed. I lay back down and closed my eyes.

"Could you please wake me in 3 hours?"

"Yes." Harry turned off the lights.

I was asleep in seconds.

*   *   *

From Kim Gannon's Diary:

London. LONDON!

Jack and—I hope—Harry are in London. Trying to save Jack's latest client. Knowing Jack, I'm positive this means lots of violence, or as he likes to call it, "mayhem."

I'm so angry. Part of me just wants him to get back safely so I can tell him that we're finished and not feel guilty about it.

Part of me is plain terrified.

I love him. I don't want to lose him. But I don't know how we can have a life together if he's constantly off saving someone.

I love him. But I think I have to say goodbye.

13

I'm not sure if you can describe a three-hour snooze as a power nap, but afterwards I took a hot shower and dressed in a black turtleneck and black cargo pants. Yes, breakfast was a little early to be sporting my cat-burglar look, but there wasn't a lot of room in my luggage for anything besides weapons.

Due to the time difference between New York and London, and the instantaneousness of travel via Air Harry, I had arrived in the wee hours of Sunday morning. And so, to breakfast in the Palm Court, an elegant Art Deco restaurant. But not just any breakfast. A veritable breakfast feast: Multiple egg options, bangers (sausages to you Americans), kippers (small, smoked herring), assorted fruits and berries, tea (never touched the stuff), and, of course, coffee. Finally, to top it all off, the bread pudding was . . . sublime. It took every ounce of willpower not to go back to the buffet table for more. Lots more. I would have happily drunk coffee and eaten bread pudding all day. Instead, I had to go off and commit acts of mayhem on Sinclair's criminal enterprises.

In the middle of my third cup of coffee, I looked up and saw Kamal Tiwari walk across the Palm Court toward me. At least I thought it was Kamal. He matched the self-description he had given me over the phone: slender, just under six feet tall, with a thick shock of black hair, and sharp, handsome features. (He hadn't used the word "handsome." But he was.) He smiled as he neared my table. I stood, and we shook hands.

"It's a pleasure to meet you, Mr. Tyrrell."

"Please, call me Jack. And the pleasure is mine."

"Joanne Agar tells me that we are like-minded individuals."

"Oh? We both want to see Nigel Sinclair at the bottom of the Thames?"

"Something like that."

I gestured toward the buffet table, "Would you like something to eat? Maybe coffee or tea?"

"I'll have coffee."

Kamal went to the buffet to get his coffee, and I sat back down but decided to wait on the last few bites of my bread pudding. Something to be savored after we had planned the destruction of Nigel Sinclair.

I said as Kamal returned to the table, "Joanne said that we may have been in Afghanistan at the same time, but I'm sorry, I don't recognize you."

"I don't recognize you either." His accent—I recognized the irony of my thinking he had a British accent in London—was cultured. Oxbridge, I assumed. "But that shouldn't stop us from participating in a joint operation or two now."

"I agree," I grinned. "I may have jumped to conclusions, but I'm guessing that Scotland Yard is pretty darn sure that Sinclair is as crooked as a barrel of fish hooks, but that you haven't got any evidence."

"As you say," he returned my grin. "We are convinced but powerless. Joanne mentioned that you operate privately with amazing resources."

"That's one way to describe it."

"And you're not averse to stepping outside the law to bring justice."

"That is completely accurate."

"Then—if you will allow me to use an old-fashioned turn of phrase—we are well met."

"I like that. May I explain what I have in mind?"

"Please do."

"My current client was kidnapped by Nigel Sinclair in New York and flown to London last night. I know this to be true but can't prove it."

"As usual with that bastard."

"Yup. Joanne Agar gave me some information on Sinclair from FBI profilers. They think he has narcissistic personality disorder. When threatened, he attacks."

"It doesn't matter if the threat is real or not," Kamal agreed, "it doesn't matter if the threat is large or small, Sinclair attacks. Our profilers have that exact assessment."

"The key point here is that Sinclair doesn't negotiate, so there's no peaceful way to get back my client."

"And since our lack of evidence precludes us from attacking him through the legal system, you intend to attack him directly. Outside the system."

"Yup."

"As a first point of attack, may I suggest a townhouse on Upper Grosvenor Street here in Mayfair? It's the home of Sinclair's upscale brothel," Kamal said. "On any given day, there are twelve to fifteen young women forced into working as prostitutes in the building. Very genteel. Extremely pricey. Feels like a men's club. A long way from street prostitution."

"Isn't prostitution legal in London?"

"It is. But owning and managing a brothel is not. And it's against the law to buy sex from someone younger than eighteen. We're pretty sure that some of the women are younger than that."

"How has this place escaped the police so far?"

"As I said, it is in an upscale neighborhood and operates like a men's club. Several very well-connected people are members. Apparently, as long as they are sexually satisfied, they don't care if the girls are sex-trafficked and under-aged."

"And there's no direct connection between the brothel and Sinclair."

"The ownership of the house is clouded by many layers of paperwork," Kamal continued. "So, does this sound like a good place to start our attacks on Sinclair?"

"Oh, yeah," I replied. "I don't suppose Sinclair

takes advantage of his own disgusting sex services? Maybe we could put him and the brothel out of business on a night when he visits."

Kamal grinned, "That would be a marvelous bit of synchronicity. But it would require you to surveil the house or follow him around town until he shows up there."

"Much as I'd like to catch him in the act, I think we should concentrate on saving the girls as soon as we can. Tonight?"

"Certainly. I hope you don't mind an impertinent question?"

"Impertinence is kind of a specialty of mine. Fire away."

"Are you bringing weapons tonight? And do you have some you can spare?"

"For you? You bet."

*   *   *

Kamal knocked on my hotel room door promptly at 6:00 P.M. He was wearing a charcoal-gray wool coat over a medium-gray suit and a blue shirt with white collar and cuffs. His tie was midnight blue with thin, diagonal stripes of red and gold. He was every inch the prospective member of Sinclair's exclusive brothel. If I said so myself, I was his equal in a Navy-blue suit, a white shirt and a burgundy-and-gold repp tie.

I introduced Kamal to Harry, who was very fashionable in a mono-colored outfit of black suit, shirt, and tie.

"Will you be joining us on tonight's operation?" Kamal asked.

"No," Harry smiled. It was a full smile, not the quick-flash Mona Lisa expression he usually treated me to. "I'm strictly intel, not ops."

"Harry's understating his role," I said and pointed toward the arsenal spread across my bed. "He's also the armorer."

"My, my," Kamal said, scanning the assortment of deadly objects. "As a member of law enforcement, I have to frown on your possessing such a lethal array of tools."

"But as a member of this operation?" I asked.

"I heartily approve." He glanced at Harry, "How did you get all of this into the country?"

"I promise you these weapons were smuggled in solely for the sake of this mission against Sinclair," Harry said in a firm, persuasive tone.

Kamal nodded, reassured. When Harry gave you his word, it was impossible to doubt him. It was an angel thing. Or a Jedi mind trick.

"I hope you don't mind," I said, "but I asked our team in New York to see if they could find anything about the brothel in the files we took from Sinclair."

"The files you *took*?" Kamal's eyebrows arched impressively. "Was this an extralegal taking?"

I shrugged. "Yes. But it happened in New York. Well, to be accurate, we hacked into Sinclair's computers from New York. So you probably don't have any jurisdictional worries."

"Hmm," he chuckled. "I doubt my bosses or the Crown Prosecution Service would see it that way."

Harry spoke in his firm, angel-thing-Jedi-mind-trick voice again, "I can assure you that no one can trace back the hack and that you will never be attached to this."

"I don't know why," Kamal nodded, "but I believe you. What did your New York team come up with?"

"We're about to find out," I said and dialed Stewart's number, putting my phone on speaker.

"Hey there!" Stewart answered. "How's London? What's the weather prediction for tonight?"

"Looking a little stormy." I turned to Kamal and whispered, "He's not really referring to the weather."

"So I gathered," Kamal responded. "Do we have to speak in code?"

Harry shook his head, "No, the phone's secure."

"Just a little stormy?" Stewart continued, feigning disappointment. "Aren't you going to give the Brits a sample of Tyrrell Style?"

"Tyrrell Style is not a thing. And," I said, "you should know you are on the line with Detective Chief Inspector Kamal Tiwari of Scotland Yard."

"Oh. . . . Sorry."

"That's all right," Kamal said. "I'm here in a strictly

unofficial capacity. And looking forward to seeing what Tyrrell Style is."

"I'm sorry Chief Inspector, I meant no disrespect."

"Please, not to worry. May I ask to whom I'm speaking?"

"My bad," I said. "Kamal, this is Stewart Budman, the world's greatest forensic accountant."

"My honor," Kamal responded.

"Well, I wouldn't say I'm *the greatest*—"

Harry cut him off, saying firmly, "He is certainly *one of* the top forensic accountants in the entire world."

"Thanks, Harry. I appreciate that."

A female voice broke in, "Hey, this is Naomi, I'm the hacker, and isn't it time we got down to business?"

"Kamal, this is Naomi Fukushima."

"Nice to meet you, Chief Inspector."

"Please, Kamal."

"Nice to meet you, Kamal. And before someone else says it, I'll tell you that I am one of the world's greatest hackers. With Harry's help, there's almost nothing I can't do with a computer. Now that we've exchanged credentials and talked about Tyrrell Style—and, Jack, there *definitely* is such a thing as Tyrrell Style—can we please talk business?"

I asked, "Have you cracked Sinclair's account ledger?"

"Some of them. The account ledgers are multiple files, all separately encrypted. Once I finally broke the first encryption, I had their encryption convention. Now I'm cracking open the files much faster. But I think Stewart has enough info from the first couple of files to point you in the right direction."

"For sure," Stewart said. "Based on a couple of months worth of cash flow, it looks like the brothel generates around £8 million a year. That's a conservative estimate. And, of course, the townhouse itself is worth about £50 million."

"Any other sex-trafficking operations?" I asked. "I'd love to hurt Sinclair and help his victims at the same time."

"I don't see anything like that in London. Do you want me to keep looking?"

"Yes. But do you see anything else we can, uh, *adjust* that will hurt Sinclair while helping others?"

"Could I interest you in illegal weapons sales?"

"Oh yeah."

Kamal interjected, "Are these small-arms? Dealt from a farm in East Sussex?"

"Yes, that's what it looks like. Can't tell for sure, but the sales transactions number in the dozens and the matching cash deposits are too small for it to be anything like Stinger missiles."

"Probably hand guns and assault rifles," Kamal said. "We've thought Sinclair was operating out of a farm in East Sussex, but we've never had enough evidence for a search warrant."

I grinned. "To paraphrase *The Treasure of Sierra Madre*: We don't need no stinkin' warrants. Stewart, what's your estimate of the cash flow?"

"About the same as the brothel. But the farm isn't worth anywhere near what the Mayfair townhouse is."

"Still, if we cut off £16 million in revenue that's gotta sting." To Harry I said, "Will you be able to brief us on security at the Mayfair townhouse and the farm in East Sussex?"

"Of course."

"Great. Stewart, good work, thanks. Naomi, please keep cracking open those files."

She replied with a question, "You don't think going Tyrrell Style on Sinclair's £16 million is going to make him negotiate with you?"

I looked at Kamal before answering. He shrugged. "I don't know. He seems to be an attack-attack-attack kind of guy."

"But he's never been attacked himself. At least not on this level."

"I hope we can . . . persuade him. Okay, thanks guys. We've gotta go."

"Have fun," Stewart said.

"Yeah," Naomi chimed in. "And be safe."

"Always," I said.

"Yeah, right." She disconnected before I gave her even the briefest reply.

"Well," I said, "should we order dinner and plan

our operations?"

"Are you thinking we'll do both in one night?" Kamal asked, surprised. "Isn't that awfully ambitious?"

"Yes, but that's why we'll get away with it. Sinclair won't expect two attacks. Especially when they're not near each other. Speaking of which, how far is it to East Sussex?"

"About 2 hours by car."

"Even with—what's the nickname for your police lights and siren?"

"Blues and twos," he grinned. "If we take a police car, we can get there faster. A bit more than an hour."

"Yes, please, blues and twos."

"I can arrange that."

"So . . . what do we want for dinner?"

I'd love to tell you that we had some amazing meal from room service. But I was so preoccupied with the coming operations, I was barely conscious of what I consumed or the dinner conversation. I was aware that Harry was dancing past a number of getting-to-know-you questions from Kamal.

"Where are you from originally?"

"Here and there. Mostly New York."

"How do you and Jack come by all of your intelligence?"

"I'm sorry, but I'm not really at liberty to explain. Still classified. And so complicated that I'm not sure I could adequately explain it even if I were able to."

"Sounds very impressive. Or sinister."

"Not sinister," I jumped in for just a moment. "I can guarantee you that there is nothing sinister about Mr. Mitchum."

"Have you two been working together for a long time?"

"Seems like forever," I said.

"Yes, eternity," Harry added.

Kamal chuckled, and I tuned out. I was too busy thinking deep thoughts. It would have been a very good thing if these were penetrating insights into the upcoming operations. But I was thinking about the women in my life. I stood up from the table and walked to the window, staring out over Green Park, its scattered white lights shining in the night.

It had been 7 years since my beautiful, loving wife, Maggie, died because of my drunken selfishness. It was only 5 months since I had failed to save Laurie—the first woman I had ever loved. The woman who suddenly reentered my life, desperately needing my help. The woman who had been murdered right here in London. Only 5 months since I had failed to save her. And now Courtney's life was hanging by a thread in the same city where Laurie had been killed. Based on my track record, Courtney's prospects weren't good.

And Kim. Her life wasn't in danger. But our relationship was. Our hopes of marriage and a family were very . . . very what, Tyrrell? Maybe this fight with Sinclair needs to be the end of your career as a do-gooder. Maybe. . . .

I wondered if the Chairman would accept my hanging up my guns. I wondered if I could accept it.

Grabbing my parka off the bed, I said, "I'm just going downstairs. Get a bit of fresh air. When I get back, we can weapon-up and get going. Sound like a plan?"

"Of course," Kamal said agreeably.

Harry just nodded, giving me a look that made me think he knew what was going through my head.

Once outside, walking along the sidewalk on Piccadilly, I called Kim. It was early afternoon in New York. She was probably at her desk, working. The chances of her being able to take a quick call from her fiancé were good. Assuming she was willing to talk with me.

My call went straight to voicemail. I had the sinking feeling that came from knowing she was screening calls and that there was no way in hell she was going to take mine.

Her voicemail greeting played, and then I was on: "Hi, Kim, I . . . uh." I exhaled trying to gather my thoughts. "There's so much to say . . . and voicemail is not really the best way to say it. . . . I love you. I'm sorry I've been such a disappointment."

Harry appeared at my side, falling into step with me as I paced in front of the hotel.

"Did you leave Kamal by himself?" I asked.

"He's taking a power nap."

"Good idea. I should try that."

"You should."

"How did your call with Kim go?"

"It didn't. Voicemail. And didn't you already know that?"

"No, I didn't. I do not know everything."

"How I loved hearing you admit that. Could you please repeat it?"

"No. I'm sorry you weren't able to talk with her."

"Not sure it would have made a difference." I watched London's black beetle-like cabs and red double-decker buses go by on Piccadilly. Wonderfully British. But they provided no answers for my worries. "We should probably go upstairs, wake Sleeping Beauty, review the tactical situation at the brothel, and strap on our guns."

*   *   *

From Kim Gannon's Diary:

Jack just called for the gazillionth time. I know he's doing the best he can, but really? Does he think if he keeps apologizing eventually the apologies will make everything better? And what's he apologizing for? That he's hurt my feelings? That he's choosing his calling with Harry over marriage and family with me? Or just saying "I'm sorry" because he doesn't know what else to say?

I love him but . . . he's driving me crazy. We're on a break. Let's take a break. Leave each other alone for a while. Maybe a very long while.

I'll probably have to talk to him at some point. Unless his activities in London end up getting him killed.

Oh my God, I can't believe I wrote that.

It was just flippant, stream-of-consciousness writing, but what is wrong with me? How could I say something that horrible? That unfeeling? He's the man I love. Is there really any situation in which his death would be a good solution to our problems? I'm ashamed of myself, even if this is my diary. Thank God it is my diary. I may have to burn it after that piece of heartlessness.

I do love him.

And the end of his message—he apologized for disappointing me. He could never disappoint me.

He makes me absolutely crazy. But he could never disappoint me.

14

We ordered coffee upon our return to the hotel room. Kamal seemed remarkably refreshed by his quick nap.

"Care to brief us on security at the brothel?" I asked Harry.

"There are multiple security cameras with no exploitable blind spots."

"Since we're going to approach the brothel as customers, masks are probably not an option," Kamal said.

"No need. I can handle the cameras for you. I'll arrange a continuous loop of video, so the activity inside and out will appear perfectly normal."

"May I ask how you will accomplish that?"

"With a method that cannot be replicated."

"Oh."

"While you're at it," I said, "would you mind jamming all the phones? I don't have the necessary equipment."

Harry glanced at the ceiling then at me. "Yes, I can do that."

"Pardon the interruption," Kamal said, "but if you could jam the security cameras on Grosvenor House—the large hotel directly across the street—and also any CCTV at Park Lane to the west and Park Street to the east, that will help us remain undetected in the aftermath of this operation."

"Good thinking," I responded.

"Yes, I will handle that," Harry nodded.

"Perfect. What's the set-up in the house itself? Number of guards and their locations?" I asked.

"Four floors," Harry replied. "Kitchen, dining room, and sitting room on the ground floor. The first floor—what Americans call the second floor—"

"I'm well aware of the differences in British and American floor nomenclature," I said.

"One can never be too careful when dealing with you. As I was saying, the first floor consists of a large living room with a bar at one end, and a couple of smaller rooms, which are used as offices. One contains all the monitors fed by the security cameras. There are twelve bedrooms on the third and fourth floors. A small elevator is at the rear of the house."

"Sinclair wouldn't want any of his aging guests to be too fatigued by climbing the stairs."

"Some of his guests are younger than you."

Kamal chuckled at Harry's remark.

"Okay, human security?"

"There's a doorman outside the front door. Unarmed of course—"

"Of course," interjected Kamal. "This is a civilized

country."

"Of course," I echoed. "What else?"

"A man at a desk just inside the front door, and three others who spend most of their time in one of the offices on the first floor."

"On ready status?" Kamal asked.

"Exactly. Occasionally they have to help an inebriated guest out to a cab. Other than that, they never leave the premises."

"Are they armed?" I inquired.

"Not the man at the desk, but the other three carry Walther PPKs. And blackjacks. All of them are very handy with blackjacks."

"What's the background of this security team? What kind of training have they had?" Kamal wondered.

"All former military. Two are veterans of the Metropolitan Police as well. Not at your and Jack's level of expertise, but you should take them very seriously."

"Are we liable to run into any *well-connected* guests tonight?" I asked. "Politicians? Law enforcement?"

"Possibly even Sinclair himself?" Harry answered my question with a tone that said, no such luck.

"So, that's a no?"

"No, it's not a no. I have no idea who will be there tonight."

"Kamal, any other questions?"

"I think we've covered all the essentials."

"Let's pick our weapons and go."

Kamal put the soft-sided, leather briefcase he had been carrying whole time on the bed. He flipped the shoulder strap out of the way and snapped the briefcase/bag open. He quickly filled it with items from my traveling armory: two Tasers, smoke grenades, flash-bang grenades, and dozens of plasticuffs.

"Is this sufficient?" he asked.

"Looks good to me."

He snapped shut the briefcase and reached for a single shoulder holster and placed a Sig Sauer P226 in it. "May I?"

"Be my guest," I replied, as I took off my jacket and slipped into my double shoulder holsters. I slipped back into the suit jacket and placed Ruger SR9s in each holster under the jacket. Two extra seventeen-shot magazines went in my inside jacket pockets. I handed Kamal a pair of extra fifteen-shot magazines for his Sig. I fervently hoped we would not have to use the extra magazines. To be completely honest, I was hoping not to use the guns at all.

"Ready?" I asked.

"Ready."

We said goodbye to Harry and left. Out on Piccadilly in front of the hotel, Kamal suggested we walk. "It's only a few blocks from here."

"How convenient."

Upper Grosvenor Street was as posh as it gets. It stretched from Hyde Park on its western end to Grosvenor

Park (once upon a time the home of the American Embassy). Kamal and I stood on the south side of the street, with our backs to the Marriott Grosvenor House hotel. We were looking at the Georgian-style terraced housing that ran along the north side of the street. One house in particular.

"Stewart said that place would cost about 50 million pounds," I said.

"Ah, if you have to ask . . ."

"Humor me. How much?"

"Since it's not within my reach, I'm not sure. But I agree with Stewart."

"50 million pounds?"

"For a little place in a posh neighborhood like this? Yes."

"How little a place?"

Kamal pointed, "As Harry told us, it has twelve bedrooms. My understanding is that the rooms on the ground and first floors feel very much like a men's club with leather chairs, cigars, food and drink—"

"And beautiful young women forced into making disgusting old men feel . . . *happy*." I growled the last word.

"Yes," Kamal agreed. "I feel the way you do about what's going on inside this house. But we need to harness our anger until we are, in fact, inside."

"I'm harnessed."

"Oh, yes, I can see that."

I gave him a bitter grin, "As harnessed as I'm gonna get."

"Well then, shall we proceed?"

We crossed the street. I adjusted my tie, shot my cuffs, and brushed imaginary lint off the lapels of my suit jacket. Kamal observed this procedure and smiled. "I presume you've done this sort of thing before."

"What? Break up the operations of a brothel by whatever means necessary?"

"Yes."

"Actually, my last operation of this type was at a Manhattan establishment like this only 4 months ago."

"Are you forming a pattern?"

"Maybe. Any time there's a chance to put a place like this out of business that's good by me. It's disgusting that grown men abuse young women."

"I couldn't agree with you more wholeheartedly."

"In that case, shall we?" I held my hand out, palm up, gesturing toward the front door of the building across Upper Grosvenor Street.

Like many of the townhouses, Sinclair's brothel had a minuscule front yard, bounded on three sides by a short wrought-iron fence. Double wooden doors with an arched transom window were recessed inside an almost-white sandstone arch. Not recessed in any way was the very large, very white, uniformed doorman. The uniform wasn't military. Big epaulettes, shiny brass buttons, royal blue with bright red trim. To my mind it screamed of a

213

banana-republic dictator with a teeny weeny ego.

There was nothing teeny weeny about the man who filled the ludicrous costume. He had me by 2 or 3 inches and 40 pounds. He also had me by a good 10 years and many, many pints. He was intimidating but not terrifying.

"Evening, gent-ul-men," he said in a baritone reminiscent of a Monty Python sketch. "This is a private club."

"Yes, we're aware of that," Kamal replied smoothly. "We are interested in joining."

"Very good, sir. See Mr. Barton at the desk. He'll get you awl signed up. First, I have to do a litt-ul security check and pat you gent-ul-men down. You don't mind, do you?"

He began patting me down without any further ado, stopping when he came to my twin holsters.

"Well now, what do we 'ave 'ere?"

I answered by bringing my knee up into his balls at the highest speed I was capable of. He groaned and staggered for a second then reached out and gripped my wrists. I was about to give him another knee to the groin, when Kamal pistol-whipped the back of his head.

His eyes rolled back, and he collapsed. Kamal and I both grabbed an arm to hold him up.

"Shall we deposit him at the front desk?" Kamal asked.

"I like the way you think." I reached for the door knob with my left hand while continuing to hold up my part of the doorman's bulk with my right. "Ready?" I grunted.

"Ready."

I twisted the knob, pushed the door, and we stepped in with our load. There was a second set of beveled-glass doors across a small foyer. We could see a man sitting at a desk through the glass. We were moving fast, hoping to catch Barton, the desk man, before he could react. We shoved our way through the glass doors. Barton stood up, brought up a gun and aimed it at us.

Kamal and I threw the doorman over the large, carved wood desk that had a top large enough to park an MG. And, as I may have mentioned before, the doorman was far from tiny. But we gave the throw a terrific effort, and the doorman's body made it most of the way over the desk then toppled over the desk's edge onto the floor.

Barton was forced to step back, his gun hand reflexively dropping. I was moving even as the doorman was falling to the floor. I planted both hands on the desk's top and vaulted over it, my feet swinging around and slamming into Barton's chest.

He flew backwards and crashed to the floor. His gun went clattering away. I landed on my feet at the same time.

Kamal, Sig Sauer in hand, had already stepped into the large sitting room to the left and was covering the four waiting guests with his pistol. The four were relaxing with a drink, book, or newspaper before they took advantage of

215

some poor, underage girl. So sorry to disrupt your plans.

As I grabbed Barton's pistol, I heard a groan behind me and saw that he was struggling to his feet. I hammered the back of his head with his own pistol. He thumped face first onto the floor. A quick glance back into the living room showed that Kamal was busy plasticuffing the guests' hands behind their backs.

He peered up at me, "Do you need some help?"

"A smoke grenade would be nice."

He grinned, reached into his briefcase, and tossed me one. I hustled to the bottom of the stairs, looked up and saw two men at the top of the stairs, each with their pistols aimed at me. I ducked behind the ornately carved-wood rail post—no point in ducking once they fire—and heard the bullets whine past and thud into the floor.

Kamal appeared at my side. "I think maybe a flash-bang is more in order."

"Be my guest."

He pulled the flash-bang's pin and tossed it at the top of the stairs. The grenade exploded with a bright flash of light and a loud, sharp bang. Kamal handed me a Taser as we went up the stairs. We needn't have bothered. The two men lay on the floor of a long hallway, disoriented and incapable of aggressive action. Off the hallway to the left a large archway opened into the house's living room. The hall ran to the rear of the building where the security office was. A man crouched at the side of the office door, pistol in hand, and fired. Lucky for us, he missed as his bullets dug into the hallway wall to our right.

We both dove inside the living room. Kamal rolled to his feet, his Sig covering several more brothel guests. They ignored their drinks, cigars, and reading materials and stared at his gun.

Pigs, I thought. No, that wasn't fair to pigs. Come on, Tyrrell. Time to deal with the last guard. I tossed the smoke grenade halfway down the hallway. Let it spew for a minute.

"Would you like another flash-bang?" Kamal inquired.

"Yes, please."

He lobbed another grenade to me. I yanked the pin and hurled it to the end of the corridor. It was satisfyingly loud. I was pretty sure I heard a thump, which I hoped was the last guard hitting the floor.

With a Ruger in my left hand and a Taser in my right, I charged through the smoke ready for anything. As it turned out, I could have strolled down the corridor with my hands shoved deep in my pockets. The last guard was on the floor, semi-conscious. I debated pistol-whipping or Taser. I hit him with the gun butt instead. These guys did not deserve the tender mercies of a Taser.

"All right to proceed?" Kamal called through the smoke.

"Absolutely."

He emerged from the smoke in a second then knelt and cuffed the last guard. "The guests in the living room are secure."

"Which leaves the rutting pigs in the bedrooms upstairs."

Kamal noticed my white-knuckled grip on the Ruger in my left hand. "Would you like me to round them up and bring them down here?"

"Yes," I exhaled in relief. "Thank you. I shouldn't get so worked up."

"It's impossible not to get worked up over this kind of criminal behavior."

"You seem fine."

"You didn't see me when I was cuffing the guests," he grinned. "I'll go get the others."

"What do we do with the young women?"

"I have a friend in social services. As soon as the customers are secured, I'll call her. She'll take good care of them."

"As if there's enough care in the world to make up for what's happened to them."

Kamal patted me on the shoulder, "We're doing what we can. Let's keep moving."

"You're right. Thanks."

He went up the stairs with the Sig in his right hand and a Taser in his left. Based on the looks of the middle-aged, over-weight johns we'd found in the sitting and living rooms, I thought the worst Kamal would confront was spluttering indignation.

I bent over the guard, grabbed him by his shirt

front, and hauled him to his feet. He groaned, a semi-conscious vocalization not a genuine attempt to communicate. I gently slapped his cheeks—okay, it wasn't all that gentle—until he came around. I stopped when he blinked several times and focused on my face.

"Are you out of your mind?" he moaned. "Do you know what you've done? You're out of your bleedin' mind. You've messed with the wrong damn people."

"Yeah, I'm sure you're right about that. But my mental health is not your concern. What you need to worry about is I'm the guy who just shut down this operation. And that I've got a gun."

"Fuck you."

Did all low-level thugs read the same job manual complete with a glossary of obscenities? The F-word always seemed to be thrown at me by goons like this guard.

"Okay. I was going to play nice," I said, "but I think I'll get a better response from you by playing rough."

I grabbed the back of his collar and half-dragged, half-led him down the corridor to the arched opening of the living room. When I had been in this room a few minutes earlier, I hadn't registered what it looked like. Too busy with bad guys, I guess. It was a large, elegant room with overstuffed furniture and a huge Persian carpet. A fire roared in the hearth at the far end of the room.

The johns were lying on the floor, plasticuffed to each other and to the brass foot rail of the bar. They were a sorry bunch, like a high school football team that had just been drubbed by their cross-town rivals. Their drinks had been left on end tables next to chairs and couches, and three cigars were still burning in ashtrays.

I led the guard to one of the chairs and forced him down into it. I pulled out plasticuffs and said, "If you try to kick me, I will hit you so hard *your mother's nose* will bleed."

"Fuck you," he repeated.

"Charming." I knelt down beside his legs, so that if he did try for the kick, he'd have a very hard time delivering a kick with any power. I slid the cuffs over his left leg to the ankle and then did the same for his right.

As I cuffed him, I said, "Listen. You still have a little bit of time before I use some ultra-persuasive methods to force your cooperation. So . . . are you going to cooperate?"

"Fu—"

"I get the point," I said, cutting him off. I stood up, reached for one of the still burning cigars, and held it an inch from his face.

"See here!" one of the johns called out in an overly plummy British accent. "This is too damn much. Who the hell are you?"

"I'm the guy with a gun. And a burning cigar. And no compunction at all about using either one of them to keep you quiet. And to make this . . . *gentleman* talk."

"This is outrageous. Torture is a war crime."

"I agree. It is a crime. Then again, every man in

this house is guilty of a crime. So shut up. As for torture, it's not very useful. Sooner or later, people being tortured will say anything to get it to stop. Their answers become meaningless. Organizations like the CIA have to do painstaking research to see if the information has any value. But . . . I'll be able to confirm the veracity of the answers very quickly. And if necessary . . ." I leaned in close to the guard, "continue the interrogation. So . . . ! Torture it is."

I brought the cigar to within millimeters of the guard's right cheekbone. He pulled his head back as far as he could. I jammed my Ruger under his chin and growled, "Hold still."

His eyes were wide; his mouth gaped open.

"I gotta tell you I don't know much about cigars," I said conversationally. "But I would imagine that the heat at the tip of a cigar is probably around 400 degrees. Celsius. Ouch."

"Hey!" Kamal's voice was low but firm. "I think that's enough."

I faced him, winked, and asked, "Everybody comfy upstairs?"

"All taken care of. I called the Met and told them I had confirmed an informant's tip that a brothel was operating at this address."

Waving my hand around the living room, I asked, "You call a bunch of unconscious guards and handcuffed johns *confirming* a tip?"

"I was compelled to take action to make sure no further harm came to the young women."

"Are you going to take all the credit for this?" I laughed.

"I rather thought I would. You don't mind, do you?"

"No, anonymity suits me just fine."

"Social services is on the way. The police will be here as well to arrest the . . . customers. Hopefully, we can charge some of them with buying sex from an under-age woman."

"Do you need to wait for your fellow officers?"

"No," Kamal grinned. "I am in hot pursuit. I said I'd call as soon as I have something definite for them."

"I like your style." I returned my attention to the guard. "So, okay, I'm getting real curious what would happen if I applied the super-hot tip of this burning cigar to your skin. Are you curious?"

"No . . . no," he grunted.

"Really? You're not?"

"No . . . please . . . ?"

"Please. I like that. Would you please tell me where the other girls are?"

"Other girls?"

"The girls who work here but aren't here tonight?"

The guard was terrified. "I can't . . . I can't . . ."

"Your choice. Burning tip it is." I moved the cigar microscopically closer to him.

222

"Noooo!" he wailed. The johns joined him, shouting in horror. But the guard continued "No. 101 River Road in Barking, please, please, 101 River Road."

I turned to Kamal, who nodded. "I know where that is," he said.

The guard was sobbing now, a typical reaction when someone breaks. I felt sick to my stomach, but I wasn't done yet.

"Thank you," I whispered. "You've been very cooperative. But I need to know something else: Can you contact your boss?"

"We don't 'ave any direct contact with him. We were hired in the blind and paid in the blind."

"Don't you have contact information in case of an emergency? Like this?"

His courage and defiance were seeping back into him. He glared at me, ready to F-bomb me again.

I moved the cigar even closer to his face. Feeling the heat, he whimpered.

"I want your boss's contact information," I said, ignoring the self-loathing rumblings in my stomach.

"There's . . . there's a burner in the desk drawer in the security office," he was beginning to sob again.

"Passcode?"

"No passcode."

"You sure?"

"Yes . . . yes . . ."

Kamal disappeared down the hallway and returned

223

a moment later with a cell phone. He tossed it to me.

"It only has a single number programmed into the contacts," Kamal said.

I was glad to have the phone because if I'd had to threaten the guard with anymore torture, I was going to throw up.

"How many women at the River Road establishment?" Kamal asked the guard.

"I dunno. A dozen. Maybe more."

"What's the layout? And what's the security like?"

"Well, like alarms and such?"

"Yes, of course. How many guards? How many doors? Alarm system?" Kamal struck me as deadly serious.

The guard hesitated, and Kamal said, "Give me the cigar."

"No, no, no . . . I'll tell you what I know. I promise, I will." He babbled about multiple doors all locked from the inside, each with all at least one armed guard directly inside, total of three guards, the girls sleeping on tiny beds separated by temporary partitions. Silent alarm system but he had no idea where the alarm actually went. "You can be damn sure it h'ain't going to the Met."

Kamal turned to me. "Unless you crave even more action tonight, I think breaching the River Road location is a job for SCO19. What you Americans colloquially refer to as SWAT."

"Sounds good to me."

"I'll call it in."

"Yes, please. And once you have confirmation that those young women are freed, off we go to Sinclair's farm."

"I'd like to suggest that we leave here right away," Kamal said, "since the police and social services will be arriving any minute."

"Thank you for keeping me on schedule. Give me just a minute." I leaned over the guard. "Where's the loo?"

"Down the hall near the kitchen."

I barely made it to the bathroom and flipped up the toilet seat before tossing my cookies. I hated torture. If the guard had held out any longer, I probably would have let him get away with it. I rinsed my mouth out and splashed water in my face.

Kamal was waiting for me at the front door. "Are you all right?"

"More or less. Let's go."

We crossed Upper Grosvenor street to the Marriott Grosvenor House London hotel and found a bar and restaurant that had a view of the street.

A middle-aged white woman with her dyed-blonde hair pulled back in a bun showed us to our table and said, "Sorry, luvs, but the kitchen is already closed for the night. We're only serving drinks now."

"Do you have coffee?" I asked.

"Yes, fresh made as a matter of fact."

"Perfect."

"Make that two, please," Kamal added.

As we waited for the coffee, four police cars

braked to a stop in front of the brothel. They were followed by two ambulances as well as two unmarked cars and two passenger vans.

"You really know how to order up an emergency response," I remarked.

Kamal nodded, smiling. "Speaking of which. . . ." He pulled out a phone and placed a call. He identified himself as DCI Tiwari and said that he'd discovered that a location on River Road was being used as a holding cell for a dozen or more young females. Yes, sex-trafficking. Better send SCO19. He gave them the rundown on the layout, the guards, and the silent alarm.

"Yes, thank you," he said, disconnecting. "They'll call me back after the breach."

"How long do you think it will take?"

"SCO19 will take its time consulting building plans and blueprints. They'll form an incursion plan, surround the building, and execute. Depending on how formidable the response from the guards . . . it could be quick or take hours."

"I don't think our hosts will let us sit here for hours."

"We'll move to the lobby."

Our waitress returned and set down two coffees along with a small pitcher of cream and various sweeteners. "Do you want anything else? I might be able to rustle up a couple of scones."

"That's very nice, but we're fine," Kamal said.

"Thanks," I agreed.

"Right then," she said and peered through the window at the show underway across the street. "You've got a proper bit of entertainment."

"Lucky timing on our part," I replied.

"If you go for sirens and emergency lights."

"Sometimes I do."

She shook her head, smiled, and walked away.

Across the street, the young women, with blankets over their skimpy dresses, were being led to one of the passenger vans while the men were being led to another van with no windows, the modern equivalent of a Black Maria.

We watched the proceedings in silence. The vans, ambulances, and two of the marked police cars drove away, leaving only two marked and two unmarked police cars out front. Our waitress appeared as if by magic to refill our coffees and leave a scone in front of each of us. "Last ones left. Wouldn't want them to go to waste."

"Thank you," we both said.

We drank the coffee and happily consumed the scones that we hadn't ordered.

Kamal's phone buzzed. "Tiwari speaking." He nodded a few times, grinned, and said, "Very glad to hear that. Well done." He disconnected.

"Everything went well at River Road?"

"The guards gave up the minute SCO19 announced themselves on a bullhorn. They put up no fight. Thirteen young women were recovered."

"That's really good news."

"Yes, isn't it?"

"I think we should go perform an encore at Nigel Sinclair's farm, don't you?"

"Why not?"

15

"No point in hailing a cab for the short walk back to your hotel."

"I agree." I left way more cash than our coffee and scones had cost. We waved to the waitress as we walked out.

She called out, "Good night, luvs."

Out on the sidewalk, we stopped and watched the police going in and out of the brothel turned crime scene. "What do you think will happen to the johns?" I asked.

"Any we can connect to having sex with under-aged females will go to jail. Anyone who was with an older girl will get a stiff talking to and get sent home."

"At least they'll have an arrest on their records."

"Depends on how politically well-connected they are. I recognized two MPs and at least one senior-ranking police officer being arrested. It's unlikely they'll spend more than a few hours in holding."

"We did all that hard work for nothing?" I sighed.

"We shut down the brothel and liberated the young women. I'd say that's something."

"A very worthwhile something. Thanks for reminding me."

We turned away from the brothel and began our walk back to the hotel, heading down Park Lane with Hyde Park on our right. Park Lane curved to our right, making it a less-than-direct route, but we could take in the Wellington Arch at the roundabout of Park Lane and Piccadilly. And the hotel wasn't very far from the arch. A minor, and scenic, detour.

"Do you do this sort of thing often?" Kamal asked.

"This sort of thing?"

"Breaking up the villains' operations. Going where the police can't."

"I guess you could say 'pretty often.'"

"How did you start this kind of work?"

"Well, my late wife introduced me to Harry, and he introduced me to . . . this way of helping people out." I didn't think I should tell Kamal that my late wife was already dead at the time she introduced me to Harry. Or that Harry worked for the Chairman.

"Does Harry always provide you with intel and weapons?"

"Pretty much."

"Where does he get such resources?"

"You wouldn't believe me if I told you." An understatement if I had ever made one. "And, meaning no offense whatsoever, but I'm like Harry, I'm not really at liberty to explain his special status. Sorry."

"I understand. Joanne Agar said I could trust you, and that's good enough for me."

"Thanks. And really, I'm sorry I can't explain more fully, but—"

"No need. Really."

"Thank you."

We paused for a moment to admire the Wellington Arch. It was vaguely reminiscent of the triumphal arches built in ancient Rome.

"Boy," I said, "You smash a French emperor and the term 'Waterloo' becomes a part of the everyday language, *and* you get a victory arch. Nice."

Kamal smiled. "It *was* a *major* victory against a brilliant and powerful foe. And it turned the tide of history."

I grinned in response. "I guess."

We turned left on Piccadilly, toward my hotel.

"Other than driving all the way to East Sussex with blues and twos," Kamal said, "do you have a plan for our expedition to the farm?"

"My immediate plan is to return to my room and order room service, which we will enjoy while discussing the East Sussex operation with Harry."

"I wholeheartedly endorse that plan. Especially if it includes Scotch."

"It will."

"What's your favorite tipple?"

"Cappuccino. Accompanied by something chocolate."

"Ahh," he said with appreciation. "Have you been

231

to England before?"

"Yup. Seen a lot of the usual tourist sights: Buckingham Palace, Westminster Abby, St. Paul's, the British Museum, Tower of London, and the Churchill War Rooms. Loved the War Rooms."

"I do, too. Have you ever been here on one of your, eh, operations?"

"Yes. I was here last October."

We stopped in front of the hotel, neither of us moving toward the front door. I had the uncomfortable feeling that Kamal wasn't done asking questions.

"How did that go?"

"My client was killed."

"Oh, so sorry."

"Thanks. But I got the bad guy."

"If you don't mind my inquiring, what do you mean when you say *got*?"

"I killed him immediately after he murdered my client," I admitted huskily.

"Oh." After a moment of silence, "Was your client special to you?"

"She was. Laurie. The first woman I ever loved. I met her in college, years before meeting my wife."

"Had you fallen in love again?"

"No, uh . . . I was just helping an old friend."

"And your only option was to kill the murderer."

"No. I probably could have taken him in alive, but I had done that once before, and it got Laurie killed. So, I shot him in the head."

"And that's your idea of justice?"

"It was. In this case. I don't run around killing every bad guy I encounter, although a fair number of them do end up dead. But this . . . this was different.

"Listen," I continued, "if you don't want to work with me anymore, I completely understand. But even if you don't, come up to the room and let me buy you a drink."

"I appreciate your honesty."

"Thanks."

"And I will take that drink."

"Of course."

"And I will keep working with you."

"Why?"

"Sometimes . . . the only way to achieve a just result is to kill the bad guy."

I gestured toward the entrance of the hotel, "Let's drink to just results."

Harry was ushering a room service waiter out as we walked down the hall to my room. "I thought you might like a drink and something to eat."

He had anticipated us very well. There was a bottle of Ballantine's Scotch for Kamal, a hot cappuccino for me, a plate of savory crackers and cheese, and biscotti.

"Thank you," I said. "This is great."

"Some libations and snacks to revive and relax you after your labors," Harry replied.

"And sustain us as we plan our next moves."

"I was afraid there would be next moves. How did this operation go?"

"A complete success," Kamal responded as he poured two fingers of Scotch. "The brothel has been shut down, arrests have been made, and most important, twenty-five young women have been freed."

"Congratulations," Harry said.

Kamal bowed in acknowledgment, and I said, "Let's get to planning our little assault on the farm."

Harry spread out a map on the table.

"You prepared this in the time we were at Upper Grosvenor Street?" Kamal asked. "That's remarkable."

"Harry does the remarkable as if it were routine."

Harry nodded and treated me to one of his Mona Lisa smiles. "Now, Sinclair's farm is a little more than thirty acres. The main building, the family house, is set back approximately a hundred feet from the road and is reached by a paved driveway from the road. Other structures on the farm include a pool house, a tiny cottage near the tennis court, and, most important for your mission, a small barn and stable with capacity for eight horses."

"Does Sinclair keep horses?" I asked.

"He does, but only two."

"Does he ride? Or are the horses a cover for his weapons dealing?"

"Sinclair does ride, but only occasionally. The horses are primarily for cover. Many vans going in and out with food and supplies for horse care."

"When in fact the vans are carrying weapons back and forth."

"Exactly."

I pointed to the map, "Is this a secondary driveway? Leading to the barn and stable?"

"Yes. A gravel driveway, lined by trees most of the way. The drive is invisible except where it actually joins the main road."

"And the distance from the paved driveway to this, secondary drive? About a quarter-mile?"

"Yes."

"You have a good eye," Kamal observed.

"My misspent youth in the Army." I asked Harry, "What about guards? Alarms? Cameras?"

"Six guards, all former military. They take four-hour shifts, always armed when they're on duty."

"What kind of armament?"

"Pistols, all 9mm. Do you want the brands and models?"

"No, thank you. Back to alarms and cameras."

"No alarms, but there are multiple cameras along the gravel drive to the barn and stable. Wide-angle, infra-red, and constantly monitored."

"By a guard at the barn?"

"Exactly."

"Is this secondary drive the only route to the barn?"

"Yes."

"Could you handle the cameras for us? Provide a

continuous loop of video that shows an empty driveway?"

"Of course. But I would suggest you shut down the blues and twos long before you turn down the driveway."

"Sounds like a plan. I don't suppose Sinclair is in residence tonight."

"He is at his Eaton Square townhouse."

Kamal gently coughed, "May I suggest that I call and arrange for SCO19 to handle the farm? Save ourselves a bit of bother?"

I shook my head, "I think we need to apply direct pressure to Sinclair's operations. Convince him that we're serious about shutting him down. When we're done there, I'll call him from a captured phone taken from one of his guards. Tell him that we're responsible and we're going to keep it up until he gives us Courtney."

"You're assuming that we will be able to call Sinclair after our visit to his farm. It's possible that we won't live that long."

"Are you worried about a bunch of trained, armed men guarding a cache of illegal weapons?"

"Just a little bit."

"You may have a point," I admitted. "But I think it's almost impossible to penetrate Sinclair's narcissistic shell. He's got to know his opponent can defeat him. He can't just dismiss it as bad luck that the police discovered his arms business."

"Sinclair's narcissism does seem to shield him from reality."

"It certainly does. What do you think? You and me and the weapons in East Sussex?"

He grinned. "I have an uneasy feeling about this, but I agree with you about Sinclair. Let's go."

Harry said, "I thought you might like to change for this late-night excursion." His hand pointed toward the open sliding doors of the closet. Two sets of black army fatigues hung from the rack. On the floor were black boots. "I'm sure you'll find the clothing is a near-perfect fit," Harry said.

"*Near*-perfect?" I asked impishly.

Kamal smiled, "You are a true wonderworker."

"That's kind of his job description," I said.

We dressed and booted up. The clothes were perfect. The right size for each of us; new but broken-in so there would be no chafing in all the wrong places.

"These might come in handy," Harry said, holding out two black Kevlar vests.

"I'm grateful," Kamal said. "But your thoroughness is giving me some concern."

"Not to worry. Harry just wants us to be properly dressed for the party."

I grabbed a black backpack out of the weapons duffle, dropped in six grenades, equally divided between flash-bangs and smokers. Since we hadn't fired our weapons earlier, we didn't need more ammunition, but I did grab four more Tasers.

"Are you going to bring your briefcase this time?"

I asked.

"I think not." He popped the case on my bed, opened it, scooped out the remaining grenades and plasticuffs, and placed them all in my backpack. "I'm ready when you are."

"Let's go."

We collected his police car, parked on Down Street a couple hundred feet west of the hotel. I wasn't sure if it was a legal parking spot, but with the police markings on the car that was not an issue. The police car was a Ford Mondeo Estate, about the same size as a Subaru Outback sold in the States. Not a huge sedan or SUV as so many American police departments used. We didn't speak as Kamal fired up the blues and twos and maneuvered the Mondeo through London to the A13 highway, headed east past Greenwich and Barking. Once on the A13, Kamal cut off the sirens. Somewhere around Aveley, we turned south on the A282 and drove over the Thames at Dartford on the Queen Elizabeth II Bridge, a long suspension bridge. Several miles south of the bridge, the A282 magically transformed into the M25. I had a sneaking suspicion it was the M25 the entire time, but far be it from me to argue with the British road-designation system.

"We'll be on this road for a bit then take the A21 south almost to the front door."

"Thank God for the A21."

He smiled. "I find your American highway system as stimulating as you find ours."

"Have you been to America often?"

"A half-dozen times. My brother and his family live in Los Angeles."

"Oooh, Los Angeles. Now that's a highway system. Right up there with northeastern New Jersey."

"Oh? Is the traffic very dense in that part of New Jersey?"

"Rivals L.A."

We talked about his brother and sister-in-law who had met in Los Angeles, been married for 13 years, and had three children.

"What about you?" I asked. "Married? Kids?"

"Didn't Joanne give you the rundown on me?"

"Not a personal rundown. She did give me a brief version of your professional resume. The main thing was that she said I could trust you. The only thing that really matters."

"Thank you," Kamal said. "I was married. Now divorced. No kids. The usual story: It's difficult to build a life with your spouse when you have an all-consuming police job. What about you?"

"Well, I'm sort of engaged."

"Is that a Facebook status? 'Sort of Engaged?'"

"It should be."

"Why are you 'sort of?'"

"Basically we have the same problem you had. My fiancée and I are having a tough time balancing our life together with my work."

"You mean she has issues with your behavior on nights like tonight?"

"I think she has issues with my getting punched and stabbed and shot on nights like tonight."

"When was the last time you were shot?"

"Four days ago."

"Oh my. Really? Were you badly injured? Four days and you're already running around fighting villains?"

"Flesh wound. In my love handle. Exactly where I was shot before—just enhanced an existing scar."

"Is your love handle the only place you've been shot?"

"I wish."

"No wonder your fiancée is worried about you."

"Whose side are you on?"

"Your fiancée's. My ex-wife's. No sane man would disagree with their positions."

"Are you saying you're insane?"

"I must be."

We both laughed softly.

"Joanne said you saved her life in Afghanistan."

"She exaggerates."

"Joanne Agar is a woman of many fine qualities; however, being prone to exaggeration is not one of them. She also told me that you were awarded a Silver Star and a Purple Heart. Was that an exaggeration?"

"Well . . . no. Would you mind if we don't discuss Afghanistan? I'm sorry, but I find it depressing. Not exactly the frame of mind I want for going on a covert operation."

"Right you are," he said as he took the exit to the A21.

"On the home stretch," I observed.

"Yes."

"From what I can see through the dark, this area is heavily wooded area."

"We're near the High Weald national park, so yes, it's heavily wooded."

"Weald?" I asked.

"The word comes from German through Middle English. It means wooded area or forest. You've heard of the Cotswolds?"

"Of course."

"The suffix 'wold' is a variant of 'weald.'"

"Wow, I didn't realize you were a Detective Chief Etymologist."

"I have many talents."

In addition to woods, the area was hilly. Harry's map of the Sinclair estate was not topographical, so we had no idea what kind of geographic challenges we might be facing.

As we exited the A21, Kamal turned off the car's blue emergency lights and dropped the cruising speed to the local speed limit.

"I take it we're almost there," I said.

"Almost. Care to take a scenic detour to Wadhurst Castle? It's almost on our way."

"Maybe the next time we're shutting down an illegal arms business."

We made a left then a right, passing through what I assumed was the town of Wadhurst. We were on the B2100, which I saw from a road sign was also known as Wadhurst Road, the road Sinclair's farm was on.

"Where did all this fog come from?"

"It settles in the hollows in the hilly countryside," Kamal replied. "Might come in handy."

We passed a wide, paved driveway that led to a house that was barely visible through the fog. A quarter-mile later, we pulled over near a gravel drive that opened to our left.

I put in AirPods and called Harry.

"Yes, Naomi successfully hacked into the farm's security system. The communications and alarm from the barn and stable to the house have been deactivated. The cameras are showing an all-normal video loop," he said calmly.

"Hello to you too. Our drive was fine. Are you enjoying my hotel room?"

"Yes. Did you need anything else?"

"No. Thanks."

"You're welcome." He clicked off before I did.

"It's safe to proceed," I said to Kamal.

"Safe from the alarms and cameras anyway."

"Yeah," I sighed for dramatic effect. "Harry won't help us with the guards."

Kamal turned left into the driveway and drove slowly down a long gentle slope.

"On the map this driveway appears to be about a half-mile long," Kamal said. "I thought we'd go to its mid-point and leave the car there."

"Sounds good to me."

We reached a part of the drive where it bulged outward on both sides. Kamal stopped the car and checked the odometer.

"Halfway. This part of the driveway was probably widened to allow vehicles going in opposite directions to pass each other."

"How handy for us."

Kamal executed a three-point turn and parked the car facing back toward the road.

"Just in case we need a quick exit," Kamal said.

"Very thoughtful."

We got out, walked around to the now-open rear hatch, and pulled on our Kevlar vests. I shrugged into my backpack full of weapons.

"Let's review the set-up one more time," I said.

"Yes, let's," Kamal agreed. "The barn and stable are approximately a quarter-mile down the road from where we are now. This road curves to the left into the barnyard, which is packed dirt."

"The stable will be on our right, stretching longitudinally out from the barn, which will be directly in front of us," I said.

"The stable originally had stalls for eight horses, along with hay storage, a tack room, a feed room, and a wash stall, all lining up on either side of the central aisle."

I nodded. "The aisle runs the length of the stable, with large sliding doors at either end. The four horse-stalls nearest this driveway have been converted into weapons storage. A wall across the width of the stable cuts off these stalls from the rest."

Kamal completed the description: "On the other side of the wall are the remaining stalls with their two equine residents, the tack room, feed room, wash stall, and hay storage. The only access to the weapons storage is through an exterior sliding door at the stable's end. There are no windows."

"The important thing for us to remember," I said, "is the guards don't go into the horse stalls. Three of them stay in the weapons-storage area. And, of course, one man roams the grounds."

"The last two guards will be sitting in a small room in the barn next door, watching the security monitors." Kamal pursed his lips. "Which leads me to make a suggestion? Do you mind?"

"Of course not."

"If we run into the roaming guard first, we deal with him. After that, we take care of the guards in the security office. The camera feeds will look normal; the guards will think all is well."

"And they might be a bit too relaxed for their own

good?"

"Possibly."

"I like the way you think. And if we don't spot the roamer first, we'll find him after we take out the security office."

Kamal reached for an assault rifle.

"Is that standard police issue?" I asked, surprised.

"I asked for it when I arranged for the car. I'm an authorized firearms officer."

I said, "I really don't want to use those things."

"They give us a huge boost in firepower."

"That's why I don't want to use them. Way too easy to kill someone."

"It might be way too easy for you to be killed without one."

"Maybe," I said, shaking my head. "You should use whatever weapon you're comfortable with."

"Well, in the interest of you as comfortable as I can—" Kamal put the rifle back in the Mondeo. "I do hope we won't regret this. You realize getting into the weapons storage is going to be quite the challenge. Three guards in a relatively small space with a single entry point."

"And I was feeling so optimistic until just now."

He grabbed a small flashlight from a kit near the spare-tire well. I pushed the button to close the hatch. We walked downhill, with Kamal pointing the flashlight directly in front of our feet so we didn't trip over anything while simultaneously containing the light to a short, tight beam. With the fog, we probably weren't visible from 50 or 60 feet away. After several minutes of walking, the ground leveled off, and we saw lights through the fog. Kamal turned off the flashlight, and we approached, moving so slowly that a tortoise would have been impatient with us.

The drive bent to our left, and the trees stopped at the bend. We could see the barn and stables. Floodlights on the corners of both buildings illuminated the scene. The fog wrapped around the structures like a special effect in a horror movie. The stable was on our right, stretching toward us. The tall barn was behind it, slightly offset to the left. Both structures had stone bases, roughly 3-feet high, with everything above the base made of wood. Very rustic and pretty. Very much in keeping with the horses. Not so much the cache of deadly weapons.

We stopped where the driveway bent into the barnyard, taking cover behind the trees on the edge of the open space. We waited. And watched.

Out of the fog, from behind the stable, walked a tall, heavy-set man in camouflage fatigues with irregular splotches of dark gray, blue, and green. At least that's what the colors looked like in the flood-lit fog. He was carrying an assault rifle.

He stopped when he reached the point where the drive opened out into the barnyard, about 20 feet away from our hiding spot. He slowly scanned the foggy night. His eyes passed right over us.

16

Kamal leaned in close to me and whispered, "Care to rethink the assault rifle?"

I shook my head.

He shrugged.

The guard walked to our left, farther away from the stable, stopped, and scanned the grounds again. Now, he was at least 30 feet away from us, his body eerily backlit by the floodlights, a dark figure only partially visible in the fog. It might have been a trick of the mind, but I had no problem at all seeing his damn assault rifle.

I whispered into Kamal's ear, "Can you move to his right? Stay inside the tree line. Make some noise to pull his attention in that direction?"

Kamal nodded and slunk off. His SAS training was on full display; I couldn't hear him, and I was only a few feet away. I dug into my backpack and pulled out a Taser with my left hand. My right hand went across my body and drew a Ruger from the left-side holster. I crept forward until I was at the very edge of the barnyard.

The guard had moved farther away from me and stopped again. He was scanning the trees when a thudding noise came from his right. He immediately crouched in a combat-ready position, his assault rifle at the ready. Creeping slowly, he walked toward the noise.

I slipped out from behind a tree and began to walk on the packed-dirt barnyard as fast as I could toward the guard. His attention was focused on the noise; something he imagined was in front of him. He had no idea that danger was approaching from behind. But then he did. He whirled around. I ran toward him, closing to within about 10 feet as his gun came level with my chest.

His finger tightened on the trigger as I fired my Taser. The prongs hit him in the chest. His body spasmed. The assault rifle fell from his hands, and he collapsed on the ground. It wasn't a silent swan dive, but it was a lot less noisy than his firing the rifle would have been.

Kamal appeared by the guard's prone body. He picked up the assault rifle and whispered, "I hope you don't mind if I appropriate this."

"Do what you gotta do," I replied, checking around for the sight of more guards. None were appearing.

"You took a bloody crazy chance going up to him that way," Kamal said as he grabbed two extra magazines from the guard's camouflaged fatigue jacket. "It's a miracle he didn't kill you."

"You'd be amazed how often miracles occur. Let's get him out of sight."

We pulled the guard to his feet, threw his arms over our shoulders, and carried him a few feet past the treeline to a large oak. We plasticuffed his wrists behind him, dumped him on the ground behind the tree, and duct-taped his mouth.

"I think duct tape might be America's greatest invention," Kamal observed.

"A woman named Vesta Stoudt invented it during World War II to help seal ammunition boxes. The military called it 'hundred-mile-per-hour' tape because you could use it to fix anything from a jeep fender to your boots."

"I had no idea."

"Miraculous, wouldn't you say?"

"Yes, I would."

We walked back to the edge of the barnyard and surveyed the tactical situation.

"Assuming we are still going for the guards in the barn's security office, I would suggest we go around the stable," Kamal said.

I nodded in agreement. To our left, the barnyard opened to a meadow that ran uphill away from us back to the farm's main house and Wadhurst Road. The hill was dotted with trees and bushes, providing very little cover. On the other hand, Kamal's proposed route allowed us to stay under the trees as they curved around the stable almost to the barn. We crept back toward the gravel drive, crossed it, and circled the stable.

"Your training was excellent," Kamal whispered. "You move like a wraith."

"You, too."

We had made our way to a point opposite the

northern end of the stable, which was the entry for the horses. There were no flood lights on this side of the stable, so the structure was in a foggy silhouette. The nearest light was affixed to a corner of the barn, about 30 feet away from the stable. The gap between us and the stable was about the same. The trees we were hiding under continued to our right, heading north, but the treeline was receding like a middle-aged man's forehead—to the east, away from the barn. We were as close as we could get and still be hidden by trees.

"Cover me," I whispered and scuttled from under the trees to a dark shadow at the corner of the stable. I scanned in every direction, saw nothing, and waved at Kamal to join me.

We peered at the barn from around the corner of the stable. The barn footprint was rectangular; it's long side stretched away from us. It's short side was the nearest part, but had no access point except for a window in the corner overlooking the stable. The barn's main entry, a large sliding door, was centered in the long side.

"I think with this fog we can crawl to the barn and not be seen," I said.

"Especially if we take the scenic route. Circle to the right to stay away from the floodlight."

"Yup."

With my Ruger in my right hand, I lay down on my belly and began crawling in a long right arc toward the barn. I was aiming for the far corner, where there was no floodlight. I glanced over my shoulder and saw that Kamal had slung the assault rifle onto his back and was following me with his Sig Sauer in hand. I felt as if I crawled for as long as it takes to have your wisdom teeth removed. But after what was probably only 15 minutes, I reached the far corner of the barn. Kamal joined me within seconds.

It was such a relief to get off my belly and take the pressure of my weight off of my elbows and knees.

Kamal whispered, "Now I remember why I don't miss being in the SAS."

I grinned. "I was thinking I'd go around the far side of the barn and enter through the small door at the opposite end of this barn." I pointed to the window nearest us, the security office window, and said, "You can cover me from there."

"Cover you through the window? Possibly shooting out the glass?"

"If you need to start shooting, breaking the glass will be the least of our worries."

"Yes, I can see that. All right, off with you."

"Yes, sir."

I made my way around the barn very quickly since I was able to walk upright. I found the door, which was a normal-size door, but like all the other doors on the barn and stables it was a sliding door. It did not appear to be locked. I gripped the handle and pulled very carefully. The door budged open a half-inch but made no noise. I continued to pull it open. Very, very slowly and quietly. I slid inside when the door was open less than a foot. The interior was dark except for the light spilling through a glass wall that formed one side of the security office at the other end of the barn. I was grateful for the light. Without it, I probably would have bumped into one of the two tractors parked or one of the many harrows, cutters, and tillers that were parked on the barn floor near the tractors. All of this farm equipment was probably positioned for easy access for anyone doing farm work. It was a nightmare obstacle course for me.

As I snuck across the barn floor I saw a man and woman in the office watching the security monitors. Little did they know that the interesting show wasn't going to be on the monitors. Not tonight, anyway.

I managed to navigate silently almost to the office door. I hadn't knocked over anything or bumped into the business end of a pitchfork. The two guards were still zeroed-in on their monitors as if they were watching the end-of-season recap of *Doctor Who*.

The wooden door to the office was to the right of where the guards were sitting; they could probably see it out of the corners of their eyes. The door was the only part of the office not made of glass. Once I reached the door, I would be completely out of sight. But getting there without being discovered would be tricky. I hid behind the giant rear tire of one of the tractors—a couple of quick steps would get me to the door. But those quick steps would be in the full wash of light spilling through the glass wall. And quick movement was the kind of thing that a human being's peripheral vision picked up quite well.

I was debating whether I should make a dash for the door or do an extremely slow crawl to it when the male guard stood up. He said something I couldn't understand, walked across the office, out the door, and crossed the barn to a couple of porta-potties in the corner opposite the office. He leaned past one of the potties and flicked on a soft overhead light. I stayed frozen behind my tractor tire.

The guard was quick about his business. As he stepped out of the porta-potty, he stopped at a small sink and washed his hands. It made my heart warm to think this man was upholding the high sanitary standards of British barns. He switched off the overhead light and made his way back to the office.

Behind the tractor tire, I gripped a Taser in my right hand. As the guard walked to the office door, I fell in behind him, taking two soft-as-a-feather steps. As he put his hand on the doorknob and pushed the door open, the woman turned and saw me over his shoulder. I slammed the back of his head with the butt of my Taser. He staggered forward, crashing onto the desk and knocking over two of the computer monitors.

I fired the Taser at the woman, but she was already on her feet, moving very fast to my left. The Taser probes missed. She had a gun in her hand and aimed it at me. I dove for the floor as she fired three times. Bullets whined past me and shattered the glass-wall panels. Another shot dug into the floor inches from me. I rolled toward the desk and pulled on the male guard's legs. His body tumbled down, landing on me the instant that the woman fired again. She hit him twice and cursed loudly.

I yanked out my Ruger—not easy with a body on top of me, but the situation gave me an adrenaline rush that helped me—and pointed my gun and fired. I aimed center mass, pulling the trigger three times. All three bullets hit her, and she collapsed backward.

Shoving the dead man off me, I stood up and swore under my breath. Both guards dead. Not the hoped-for result. Dammit.

I could see Kamal through the window, jerking his thumb over his shoulder toward the stable. Even through the window glass, I could hear him say, "We need to move." I picked up one of the monitors and threw it through the window. I jumped up on the desk nearest the window, used my gun to rake out the remaining nasty little shards of glass in the frame, and leapt out of the barn.

"I gather that we've decided against the silent approach," Kamal observed.

"It would seem so." I paused, looking back into the wrecked office. "I didn't want to shoot them."

"I know."

I closed my eyes, took a deep breath, then exhaled. I felt terrible, but our mission wasn't finished. "Okay, the guards in the stable are isolated inside. Harry's already deactivated the alarms and phones, so they can't get help."

"But we are faced with the almost impossible task of forcing our way through a single entry point that the guards' attention will be focused on."

"Not to mention a wide array of weapons to use on anyone who tries to get them. 'Anyone' meaning us."

"I do understand that," Kamal acknowledged. "Have you, by chance, formulated a plan?"

"Actually . . . yes. How do you feel about destruction of property?"

"As long as it's Sinclair's, I don't have a problem with it."

"Good. I noticed a sprinkler system in the barn. Let's go to the horses' side of the stable and see if there's one there."

Guns drawn, we advanced to the near end of the stable. While Kamal stayed ready with his seized assault rifle, I pulled the unlocked door open slowly and quietly.

A soft glow from low-wattage light bulbs permeated the stable. I smelled the hay immediately that was stacked to our left in the storage area. Lined up on the same side of the structure were three horse stalls. To our right were open doors to the feed and tack rooms, and a larger opening to the wash stall. Finally on the right was one last horse stall. Harry's intel said that the unpainted plywood wall that cut across the stable was backed with 6 inches of sound-proof insulation and additional plywood on the weapons side.

I looked up and saw the pipes and heads for the

sprinkler system. The pipes ran parallel to the center aisle and disappeared into the plywood. I pointed at the pipes and smiled.

Kamal nodded. He was standing next to one of the stalls, looking into it.

"Are the horses asleep?" I whispered, not able to see their faces clearly in the soft light.

"Yes, they are dozing. Let's wait a few minutes and see if they wake up. Horses sleep in multiple power naps a day."

"Hopefully they wake up soon, and we can lead them to the barn to keep them safe," I stepped to the front of the stall next to where Kamal was standing. "What if they don't wake up soon?"

"We'll talk a little louder. See if we can't wake them gently," he said, his voice rising subtly in volume. "Horses sleep on their feet so they can run from danger. You could say they are on alert. With that in mind, we need to be gentle so as not to frighten them."

"Frightened and probably noisy horses are not what we need," I agreed.

The horse in the stall next to me shifted on its feet. Then shifted again. I saw it blink its eyes. It shifted one more time and gently snorted. The horse took a step closer to me and stopped.

Kamal opened the gate to the stall and stepped inside, murmuring quietly and reassuringly. He gently rubbed the horse's neck. It occurred to me that I should do likewise. I walked into "my" stall, softly telling the horse what a good boy he was. I stroked its neck. I assumed it liked the stroking. Otherwise it would have moved away, right? A 1,000-pound animal doesn't have to put up with neck-stroking if it doesn't want to.

After a few minutes of our talking and rubbing the horses, Kamal told me to pull a bridle off its peg on the front post of the horse stall. The horse accepted my slipping it on. Thank God, I thought. The last thing I wanted was a pissed off horse.

"Grab that horse blanket," Kamal said, "and throw it over his middle. Then we'll lead them to the barn. Pretend you know what you're doing. Your horse will respond better to confidence."

My horse accepted the blanket and allowed me to lead him out of the stall, down the stable aisle, and out through the sliding door about 10 feet behind Kamal and his equine charge. Inside the barn, we tied the reins to a wood beam that ran from the floor to the roof. There was a lot of open space around this beam, so it was perfect as a place to park the horses. "Park" was probably the wrong terminology, but what the heck.

"What do you think our three guards in the weapons storage in the stable are thinking right now?" Kamal asked as we returned to the stable. "It's been quite a while since the gunfire."

"Assuming they heard it, which I'm pretty sure they did, I hope this period of nothing happening has gotten on their nerves."

"Anxiety undermines performance."

"Yup. Now, do you want to set off the sprinklers or play with grenades?"

"Grenades."

"Grenades are so unrefined for a gentleman like you."

"That's true," Kamal grinned. "But whoever sets off the sprinklers is likely to get wet, and since you asked for my preference, grenades."

"Rock, paper, scissors?" I asked.

"I think grenades trump all three."

"You've got a point," I said. I opened my backpack and pulled out two smoke grenades and two flash-bangs, handing each one to Kamal.

He asked, "Do you think that two smoke and two flash-bangs will be enough?"

"Plenty. I'll shout as loud as I can when the sprinklers go off, just in case you can't hear inside. I'll try to run around the stable in time to help you greet the three coming from inside."

"It will be good to have you join the fray whenever you arrive."

Kamal jogged off toward the door to the weapons end of the stable. I went inside the horses' side of the stable and checked for a smoke detector. As I had expected, there was one above the hay storage. I stepped into the feed room, found an empty feed bucket, and carried it into the hay storage. I positioned the bucket on a bale of hay, about 5 feet directly below the smoke detector. I pulled the pin on a smoke grenade, dumped it in the bucket, and ran out.

Smoke billowed from the bucket, and within seconds the smoke detector activated and the sprinklers went off.

I didn't quite burst my vocal cords when I shouted, "It's a go!" but it was faintly possible the people of Wadhurst might have heard me. I ran for the other end of the stable.

Kamal had pulled the pins on the smoke grenades, and they lay on the ground, gushing smoke. He held a flash-bang in one hand and tossed me the other as soon as I rounded the corner. We heard loud thuds as sliding bolts were drawn on the inside, at the top and bottom of the door. Then the door slid open.

The first two men stepped cautiously through the door, out into the smoke, guns drawn. We dropped our flash-bangs like a one-two punch, and both guards sprawled on the ground, groaning and barely conscious.

The third guard barreled out of the stable through the smoke and tackled Kamal, slamming him onto the ground. They landed so hard I felt Kamal's pain—the guard had to be almost three hundred pounds. But, despite a pronounced beer gut, the guy had plenty of muscle and could move fast. He shoved himself up so that he was sitting on Kamal's chest. The guard threw two quick punches into Kamal's face and was about to hit him again when I intervened.

I pistol-whipped the side of his head, knocking him clear off Kamal. He rolled away. I leaned over to check Kamal. A mistake. Make sure the enemy is down and out before you look after your team. The huge guard was on his feet and rushing toward me. I couldn't get my gun up in time to shoot—the guy crashed into me and slammed me to the ground in an almost identical move to what he had done to Kamal. I didn't black out, but I wanted to.

The guard shifted his body to pin my arms against my body, his extremely generous butt grinding me into the ground.

But I still had my pistol in my right hand. Trapped under his leg, but with the gun pointed at his foot. The guard slammed me in the face with a fist the size of Montana. Okay, maybe not that big. Maybe only Delaware. But it was a hell of a big fist. I literally saw stars and knew that one more punch and I was goners.

"Help me, God," I whispered as I pulled the trigger and shot the guard in the foot. He screamed in pain and jerked back away from me.

"I can't believe I didn't shoot myself," I muttered and looked to the sky. "Thanks."

The guard was cursing. More important, the bastard was getting to his feet. Holy moly. I stepped closer to him and pistol-whipped him again. He sank to one knee, clearly struggling to maintain consciousness.

"I'm sorry about this," I said and pistol-whipped

him one more time. He collapsed in a heap. I dug into my backpack, pulled four sets of plasticuffs and double-cuffed his wrists and his ankles. Then I cuffed the wrists and ankles of the other two guards who were still moaning and groaning from the effects of the flash-bangs.

By the time I turned my attention back to Kamal, he was sitting up, holding his jaw. He said, "Thank you, I think you just saved my life."

"My pleasure."

"Pleasure? Really? Did you shoot him in the foot, or was that a semi-conscious hallucination on my part?"

"Uh, no. I shot him in the foot."

"It's a miracle you didn't shoot yourself."

"Like I told you, you'd be surprised how often miracles happen."

17

"I think it's a miracle I survived," he pointed at the big guard, "that man's attack."

"Can you stand up?" I offered him a hand, which he grasped so I could pull him to his feet. His left eye was swollen, and his lip was bleeding.

"Shall we go look at the weapons?" he asked.

"Let's."

We walked through the wisps of smoke from the grenades that hadn't drifted away yet. Inside the stable the sprinklers had stopped, but there was water dripping everywhere. The center aisle was as wide in this part of the stable as it was where the horse stalls were. There was a card table with chairs around it, and against the plywood wall that blocked off the stable's center aisle stood a small table with a microwave, plug-in tea kettle, and coffee pot. On one end of the table was a five-foot high wooden cabinet, on the other end, a refrigerator. There were no stalls, only a few wooden beams from floor to ceiling. Unlike the dirt of the active stable, the floor was cement. Stacked on that cement were a dozen or so wooden crates marked with stenciled lettering: Glock 9mm, Sig Sauer 9mm, Heckler & Koch HK416, Tavor TAR-21. Pistols and assault rifles. A veritable Fanny Farmer assortment of sweet lethality.

"This is nasty," Kamal observed.

"Oh yeah. I wonder what the turnover is on these items."

"Whatever it is, it's too bloody much."

"Gotta agree with you there."

"I have to contact the local police. Get some officers here to impound the lot of this."

Harry stepped through the sliding door and said, "That is an excellent idea."

"Where did you come from?" Kamal asked. Since I was accustomed to Harry's sudden comings and goings, I never bothered with a question like that.

"I followed you in a car. It's parked next to yours."

"What brings you 'round these parts?" I asked.

"You. I thought you might need a lift back to London." He raised a red-and-white plastic case to shoulder level. "And administer first aid where needed."

"Why would first aid be needed?"

"When you're involved, first aid is always necessary.

"Oh? And my ride back to London?"

"It occurred to me that Detective Chief Inspector Tiwari will need to wait with the suspects and the weapons."

"You make a good point," Kamal said. "After all, one can only get away with so much by claiming 'hot pursuit.' I do need to wait for my East Sussex colleagues."

Harry opened his first-aid kit and handed Kamal an instant ice pack. "For your face."

"Thank you." Kamal gave the pack a hard twist to break the inner seal and activate the chemical cooling agent. He placed the ice pack on his cheek just below his left eye.

Harry knelt next to the big guard. He slipped off the man's left shoe and sock, poured a bit of disinfectant on the top and bottom of the wound. "Through and through," Harry said. "Is this the position he was in when he was shot?"

"Not exactly," I replied. "A couple of feet to your left. And he was on top of me."

Harry twisted around and studied the stable wall. "You should dig the bullet out of the wall. About 2 feet to the right of the sliding door, a foot above the ground."

"How the—never mind." I walked over to the stable and found the hole exactly where he said it would be. I pulled a knife from my pack and dug out the bullet.

While I was recovering the evidence, Harry was doing his usual thorough job of bandaging the guard's wound and applying a tourniquet on the man's calf. "Can't have him bleed out before the locals make their appearance." He spoke to Kamal, "Unless you have further need of Tyrrell, I suggest he and I should make our exit. Less explaining to do when your colleagues arrive."

"Yes," Kamal said and shrugged out of his holster,

handing it and the Sig to me. "UK police have to sign out weapons, and there is no way for me to explain my possessing this pistol."

"But there are ways for you to explain everything else?" I asked with a smile.

"I'll think of something."

"Perhaps you'll be divinely inspired," Harry offered.

"Miracles do occur," Kamal grinned. We shook hands, and he said, "Thanks again. And good luck."

"Good luck? Why do I need luck?"

"Something tells me you're not done with Nigel Sinclair."

"Ah," I said, as if the light was dawning. "Hopefully this is the end of things."

"Hope is not a strategy," Harry said.

"Stop that," I said.

Kamal walked outside with us, and pulled his phone from a pocket. As I walked past the big guard, I stopped and patted down a couple of his coat pockets until I felt a bulge. I dug down, and found his phone.

"Oh, Grandma," I said, "what a nice smart phone you have."

"The better to make harassing phone calls to the bad guys, my dear," Kamal replied with a grin.

Harry and I began to walk up the driveway. Once we were out of sight of the stable, I asked, "Are we going to whoosh out of here?"

In the tiniest fraction of time, I found myself standing in my hotel room at the Park Lane.

"Thank you," I said.

"You're welcome. Do you want some ice for your face?"

"Do I need it?"

"Of course." He walked toward the door, but before he got there, someone knocked very politely on the other side and said very quietly, "Room service."

Harry let in the room-service attendant, who wheeled in a small cart with an ice bucket and two cups of cappuccino. The items were placed on the table where we did all of our in-room entertaining. Harry tipped the young man 10 pounds.

"Thank you, sir," he said enthusiastically and smoothly wheeled the cart from the room.

"You're showing off," I said.

Harry shrugged and handed me a cappuccino. He then dumped a handful of ice cubes into a napkin, folded the fabric over, and gave it to me. I took a long sip of cappuccino and placed the improvised ice pack on my left cheek. Harry went into the bathroom and returned with bottles of ibuprofen and acetaminophen. I popped two of each, washing them down with more cappuccino. I leaned back in my chair and closed my eyes. I was torn between wanting to nod off for 20 minutes and taking another life-saving sip of cappuccino. The cappuccino won. I sat up straight and drank more of the wondrous beverage.

My phone buzzed with a text alert. It was from Naomi:

> We've cracked most of the files.
> Stewart is sure this stuff will
> cause Sinclair a lot of pain.
> Almost certainly jail time.
> Should I e-mail you a damaging
> sample?

I dictated a text response into my phone:

> That's fantastic. You two are the
> absolute best. Yes, please send
> the sample.

I reread it to make sure the voice-recognition software hadn't created some bizarre message. It hadn't. I hit send. And received Naomi's next message within seconds:

> Check your e-mail. Be safe.

I drank more cappuccino, opened my laptop, checked my e-mail, and found Naomi's sample.

There was no point in my reading what Naomi had e-mailed. I didn't have Stewart's forensic skills. But if he said the sample was bad news for my buddy Nigel, then it was bad news.

* * *

PRE-DAWN SUNDAY –
EATON SQUARE HOUSE

NIGEL SINCLAIR lounged in an overstuffed leather couch in his townhouse living room, holding a glass of Scotch and staring down at the large Persian carpet. Amanda Rundle stood patiently a few feet away, unsure if he had heard what she had just said. Was he lost in thought? Or just lost in the intricate design of the carpet that he seemed unable to take his eyes off of.

"I'm sorry, sir, but the news is accurate. Our sources have confirmed that in the overnight hours the house on Upper Grosvenor Street in Mayfair, the dormitory on River Road in Barking, and the farm in Wadhurst have all been seized by the Metropolitan and East Sussex police."

Sinclair lifted his gaze and focused on Rundle's face. "How bad is it?"

"Guards are under arrest. All of the female employees have been taken away by social services. The guests are all under arrest, although some of them may be released. The weapons at the farm were seized. The operations have been totally destroyed."

"How much?" Sinclair asked, shifting on the couch to consider a thin-haired, stout man in an ill-fitting suit.

"As Ms. Rundle said, the operations have been completely wiped out."

"I don't need a situation report from you. I need an accounting. What are my financial losses?"

"Approximately £16 million in annual revenues. The properties themselves were worth approximately £70 million."

"I've lost £86 million in one night?"

"Yes, sir, I'm sorry."

Sinclair took a long pull of the Scotch, finishing it. He extended his hand, and Rundle took the glass from him and poured two fingers of Scotch in it.

Handing the glass back to him, she said, "I want to remind you that you don't face any legal exposure here. All three properties were owned and operated by a number of shell companies. Impossible to trace back to you."

"And," the stout man said, "all revenues and expenses go through offshore accounts that do not lead back to you. I'm sorry for your losses, sir, but I want to assure you that you are safe."

Sinclair stared at him for a minute then growled, "Get out."

The man hurriedly scuttled away.

Sinclair drank more Scotch, resumed his analysis of the patterns in the Persian rug, and muttered, "£86 million." His head snapped up. "How? How did this happen?"

"The operations against the Upper Grosvenor

house and the farm were high quality. The security systems were deactivated, and the cameras played a stream of innocuous video to the monitors. A two-man team took out all the guards at the house on Upper Grosvenor and at the farm. As for the River Road dormitory, it was seized by SCO19."

"Who did this? Do you think it was the same two men at the townhouse and the farm?"

"I do. This seems like the work of the same team from New York that we've been dealing with since you first tried to capture Courtney Wilson. High levels of physical and technical competence. You've never been challenged at this level until she entered the picture."

"Are you saying I made a mistake?"

"No, sir, I am not saying that. But Ms. Wilson does seem to be the catalyst."

"What are we going to do about her?"

"There are two options. We negotiate Ms. Wilson's return. Or we fight—" She was interrupted by the ringing of her phone. She checked the phone's display, puzzled. "Sorry, I should take this. It's the burner phone from the Upper Grosvenor house."

Sinclair waved dismissively at her and got up to refresh his drink.

"Hello," Rundle said. "Oh. . . . Yes. . . . Yes." She muted the phone and said to Sinclair, "This man claims to be Courtney Wilson's defender. He wants to speak to you."

"Put it on speaker."

She did as she was instructed and set the phone on the carved-wood coffee table in front of the couch.

"Hello, Nigel Sinclair? Are you there?"

"Yes. With whom am I speaking?"

*   *   *

"I'm Courtney Wilson's protector," I said. "And as bad as last night was for you, I'm only getting started closing your illegal businesses down. I haven't touched your drug operations—yet. And you deal weapons from another location. I'm going to make sure you have nothing left."

"Do you have the faintest idea who I am?" Sinclair managed to sound urbane even as he growled at me. I wondered if that was something he picked up at Cambridge. "Do you realize how much trouble you are in?"

"Actually, I know more about you than anyone this side of your proctologist. My teammates have hacked your computers, stolen your files, analyzed those files, hacked your security system, and helped me reduce your revenues and assets by £86 million. In one night."

"That's a very precise estimate of my losses."

"It's on the money, if you'll pardon the expression. The forensic accountant I work with is world-class. Thanks to him I know—down to the penny—how much money you are making. Making illegally. And socking away in

271

offshore accounts."

"Are you telling me that you are personally responsible for last night's attacks on my operations?"

"You could say that."

"The same man my people tangled with in New York."

"Yup. Same guy." I picked up the second burner phone I had captured at the farm and called the one number programmed into it. I said, "Oh, you're about to get another call." I heard the ringtone on my end.

I heard a woman say, "It's a call from the one of the burner phones at the farm."

"You don't need to answer that." I disconnected the second burner. "I just wanted to prove to you that I actually was at that pricey townhouse in Mayfair and the bucolic farm in East Sussex."

"You've made your point," Sinclair sounded less urbane.

"Relax, Nigel. I'm pretty sure that we can settle this. All you have to do is give me Courtney."

"You think you hold all the cards."

"I know that you will have a very hard time accepting this, but I *do* hold all the cards."

He snorted derisively, "And you think you can make me negotiate."

"It would be less painful for both of us."

"I don't give a shit about your pain. Or Courtney Wilson's. I don't negotiate with anyone."

"Even if negotiating would save you from further financial loss? Even if it can save you from legal exposure?"

Speaking very slowly for emphasis, Sinclair repeated, "I . . . don't . . . negotiate."

"Please remember, I'm offering you a way out of this mess."

"Fuck you!" he shouted.

The line went dead.

"That could have gone better," I said.

Harry shook his head. "You were never going to have a productive conversation with Sinclair."

"He doesn't negotiate," I conceded.

"So I've heard."

"All right, we know he's now in attack mode his normal way of doing things. I'm going to have to go directly at him," I said quietly.

"Won't that put Courtney in greater jeopardy?"

"Yes. But I'm all out of ideas. Can you think of other options?"

"No, I can't."

We sat quietly for a few minutes. Harry and I finished our cappuccinos. I can't begin to explain to you why my brain went in the direction it did, but I started wondering about something other than the Nigel Sinclair problem.

"We're missing something," I said, breaking out of my reverie.

"Excuse me?" Harry asked.

"There's something we're not seeing."

"What makes you say that?"

"I don't know. I have this uneasy feeling that there is more to the whole picture than what I'm seeing. Can you please help me out here?"

Harry glanced upward then back to me. "Sorry, I don't know of anything that you are not seeing. And we still need to deal with the problem at hand."

"When you're right, you're right. Where is Sinclair holding Courtney?"

"At his townhouse on Eaton Square."

"Talk about real estate where if you have to ask, you can't afford it," I commented. "So, we attack there."

"Are you hoping he'll surrender Courtney under the pressure of a direct attack?"

"I doubt he could ever be realistic enough to admit defeat. I just want to save Courtney. And we seem to be completely out of ideas."

"What will you do if he threatens Courtney? Holds a gun to her head?"

"I'll burn that bridge when I get to it."

Harry responded, "You excel at burning bridges. But please let me clarify: Are you planning to kill Sinclair?"

"I wouldn't say I'm planning it, but I'm not averse to that outcome. It would be a just result that I could live with."

Harry considered that for a long moment and stared at me without speaking.

"You have something to say?" I asked.

"This is one of your free-will moments. You're making a choice that may lead to your killing Sinclair."

"A man can dream," I replied.

"It's also in the realm of possibility that he and his team will manage to kill Courtney. And you."

"I hope it doesn't come to that."

"Hope is not a strategy."

I went to the duffle on my bed, my *unused* bed, and replenished my backpack with more smoke and flash-bang grenades and plasticuffs. There were two unused Tasers leftover from the earlier excursions. I zipped the duffle closed.

"Are you planning on going right now?" Harry asked, watching me.

"Yup. I want to hit Sinclair while he's still feeling the sting of our earlier operations."

I checked the magazines in both Rugers, and added four bullets to one of them. I returned the guns to the holsters and said, "I'm ready to go get Nigel Sinclair. Would you mind escorting me there?"

"This is a bad idea."

"This is a *terrible* idea," I corrected him. "But it's better than no idea at all."

"On occasion, doing nothing is the best idea," Harry said.

"Not this occasion," I replied.

18

Eaton Square was quiet in the hour just before dawn. The square itself was formed by six rectangular private gardens covering almost fifteen acres and bordered by Greek Revival townhouses with white-stucco exteriors, pillars, and black, wrought-iron railings. The square and the houses have remained in pristine condition through all the years—with the kind of money the residents of Eaton Square had, it could have been nothing else. Buckingham Palace was less than a mile to the northeast; Harrod's less than a mile to the northwest. Belgrave and Sloan Squares were much closer than that. Many celebrities and important people had lived in Eaton Square over the years, including a number of lords, ladies, dukes, at least two prime ministers, the Oscar-winning actress Vivien Leigh, and *two* James Bonds: Sean Connery and Roger Moore.

Our focus, however, was solely on one angry narcissistic billionaire. Harry and I arrived in the garden opposite No. 13 Eaton Square. Given the early hour and the lack of any signs of life, we made no effort to hide ourselves, which was good since the early March foliage provided no cover.

"Why are we in the park opposite Sinclair's front

door?" I asked.

"As opposed to being on an adjacent rooftop? Or Sinclair's rooftop?"

"Exactly."

"I think you'll find the easiest way into the residence is through the front door."

"Really?"

"The kitchen, pantry, servants' dining room, and security office are on the ground floor. A living room, dining room, drawing room, and Sinclair's personal office occupy the first floor. Four large bedrooms, including Sinclair's, take up the second floor. Sinclair's room, on the back of the house, is far and away the largest of the bedrooms. The walls, doorframe, and door have been reinforced to make a forced entry all but impossible."

"Are we talking panic room?"

"Not quite that secure. But it would be very difficult to breach."

"Okay, and the other bedrooms are large and feature en-suite bathrooms."

"Let's just say that any of the other bedrooms make your place in the Village look. . . ," he trailed off.

"Cozy? Tiny? Minuscule?"

"Any of those words would suit. To finish: The third floor, the top floor, has—"

"The servants' quarters. Right?"

"Yes," Harry acknowledged my interruption with a small sigh of impatience. "The butler and housekeeper are a married couple who share a small apartment on that floor. The other six rooms are singles. There are two bathrooms off the hall."

"How many servants besides the butler and housekeeper?"

"Two: a cook and a driver, who doubles as a bodyguard."

"You said there was a security office—does that mean the bodyguard isn't alone in providing protection for Nigel?"

"He is not. Six guards form an around-the-clock security team. Two on duty in the security office—"

"Watching video feeds, blah, blah, blah."

"Yes. Exactly. The other four are off duty and stay in the mews house."

"The mews house?"

"It's a small house at the back of the property, facing out onto Eaton Mews. There's also a garage that houses Sinclair's—

"Bentley Flying Spur."

"Yes."

"Returning to the important issues, why shouldn't I access the house from the roof? Drop down the rear of the building and go through a window?"

"Sinclair's windows are bulletproof. Getting through one of them would take too much time and cause too much noise."

"Rooftop door?"

"Solid steel, sliding bolts on three sides, all on the inside."

"Does the house have an elevator? Maybe added in modern times?"

"It does. On the rear of the building. The elevator shaft was added in the 1950s. The solid-steel service door has to be accessed from the outside and has a sophisticated alarm system that would take you a very long time to bypass."

"Couldn't Naomi hack into it?"

Harry shook his head. "The entire property has a completely self-contained, closed-circuit alarm system. If the alarm goes off, it only sounds in the security office and the mews house."

"So. . . ," I said thoughtfully, "my best approach is to walk right up to the front door and knock."

"Yes."

"Given how late, or rather, how early it is, I'm guessing that one of the security guards will answer the door."

"Yes."

"With a gun in hand?"

"Yes."

"Will he have a panic-button remote to set off the alarm in his other hand?"

"He will."

"Are you sure this is the easy way inside?"

I stared at the front door and considered the

280

challenges of a guard with a gun and a remote. "I don't suppose you could help me out with the guard who answers the door. You know, magically disable the remote?"

"I cannot."

"What about talking your way inside? You're smooth as satin sheets."

"Satin sheets? You are procrastinating."

"Anybody in the house besides our gracious host and his staff?"

"Courtney, of course."

"In one of the guest rooms on the second floor?"

"Yes, with a guard sitting in the hallway in front of her bedroom door."

"Is that guard one of the two who are regularly on duty in the house – or is he an extra?"

"He's one of the two regulars."

"Okay. Anyone else?

"Amanda Rundle, Sinclair's security chief, is ensconced in another guest room."

"Rundle's the woman who took Courtney at the Hilton?"

"Yes."

"Anything going on between Sinclair and Rundle?"

"I don't think so."

"Why not?"

"His mistress, a Ms. Linda Huntington, is sleeping next to him at this very moment."

"Do I have to worry about Ms. Huntington?"

"Excuse me?"

"Assuming I somehow get by the guard at the front door, do I have to worry that Ms. Huntington is going to show up with a gun or knife and do damage to me?"

"Ah, I see. No, you don't have to be concerned about her."

"If I don't manage to stop the front-door guy from pushing the panic button, what's the response time from the guys in the mews house?"

Harry looked up as if seeking divine guidance then at me. "A minute or two."

"Assuming—and this is an absolutely gigantic assumption—assuming I can get past the guy at the front door, subdue the guard upstairs, deal with Amanda Rundle and Nigel Sinclair, and then secure Courtney all inside of a minute or two—will you whoosh us out of there?"

"Yes."

"You answered awfully fast. You already know that I'm not going to make it, don't you?"

"I agreed to transport you if you can accomplish your mission inside of the time limit."

"I don't trust you."

He was not perturbed by my insulting response. "Placing your trust in anyone is a personal choice."

"Thanks for the Hallmark-card wisdom."

I turned away from Harry to try to impress upon him how frustrating he was. I was pretty sure that he could not have cared less about my frustration. I resumed staring at the front door, hoping that inspiration would strike. But no. All I got was Harry, commenting about my time usage.

"You're still procrastinating."

"I'm thinking."

"So you say."

"Look, I'm trying to get Courtney out of there in one piece. How do I know that the guard outside her bedroom door isn't instructed to kill her if attacked?"

"Because Sinclair wants his files back."

"Are we sure that his understanding of the situation is the same as ours?"

"Interesting question," Harry nodded. Once again, he glanced skyward for the answer then at me. "Sinclair has instructed his security team to keep Courtney safe."

"Thank you. That's good to know." I continued to focus on the front door.

"Jack?"

"Okay, I'm procrastinating."

"Why?"

"It's been a hell of a long night. I'm exhausted. And to be honest . . ."

"Yes?"

"I'm scared. I feel like I'm running out of gas." I felt his eyes on me, so I turned to face him. "I'm . . . not sure I can do this."

"I didn't expect self-doubt from you."

"I'm a man of many surprises. Like I said, it's been one very long night. I've been incredibly lucky so far. I just feel like . . . I'm out of luck."

"Luck. Really?"

"You're saying that the Chairman is smiling down on me?"

"What do you think?"

"I think if I don't say that the Chairman gives me what I need, you're going to keep asking me questions to lead me to that conclusion."

"I would, except that we are running out of time. Sinclair's staff will be up soon and become an unnecessary complication."

"So, I should get my ass in gear and trust in the Chairman."

Harry shrugged.

"Okay," I sighed. "Like U.S. currency says, 'In God We Trust.'"

Harry's Mona Lisa smile came and went.

I took a deep breath, pulled a Ruger from its holster, and said, "Direct frontal assault." I walked across the street to No. 13 and spotted the camera to the right above the door. I climbed up the four steps. A doorbell sat under a brushed nickel speaker. Above the speaker was another camera lens. Oh joy. My right side was my "good side." I knocked on the door.

"Yes?" A low rumble of a voice said.

"Basil Fawlty," I said. "I apologize for the early hour, but I need to speak with Mr. Sinclair."

"Go away," the rumble replied.

"It's an emergency regarding his American guest."

I heard a click and the speaker went dead. Then I heard a door opening—probably the inner door to the house's foyer. And then the tumbling of the front door locks. The door opened about 4-inches wide, and a coffin-shaped face belonging to a tall, thin man peered out at me. Based on the Glock I could see in his hand, I figured he was planning to control me not with his height but with 9mm bullets.

"What do you want?" he asked. His voice was only a tiny bit less rumbly in person.

"I need to see Mr. Sin—" I tucked my knee up to my chest and kicked straight out, hitting the door with the force of a pile driver.

The door smacked into Coffin Face, blasting him backward into the foyer, where he crashed onto his back. I jumped inside, leaned over him, and slammed him across the head with my pistol. He dropped the Glock and the small panic-button fob. They clattered onto the marble floor.

He was groping for his gun and had just gotten his fingers around the butt when I pistol-whipped him again. He was unconscious. I twisted around to find the fob. A small red light on the fob was blinking. Damn. The guy had set off the alarm. Tyrrell, you need to move fast.

Footsteps from the back of the townhouse pounded toward me. I reached up and smashed the light overhead with my gun, plunging the foyer into dusky darkness. The footsteps slowed. They were creeping forward now. I stepped behind the open foyer door and tugged a Taser out of my pack.

My incursion into hostile territory was taking way too long. I needed to deal with guard No. 2 and be on my merry way. I looked up and whispered, "Please help me." I dove onto Coffin Face's unconscious form, twisting in the air and firing the Taser through the foyer doorway.

I landed on Coffin Face as the Taser caught guard No. 2. As cushions went, Coffin Face's body was a tiny bit softer than the marble floor. Guard No. 2 was doing the high-voltage shimmy. She collapsed to the floor. I scooped up the guns of both guards and dropped them in my pack. No time to waste on plasticuffs.

Through the door, I spotted the staircase to my right. I climbed the stairs quickly and quietly, with a Ruger in my right hand and my last Taser in my left. People were moving around upstairs. Speed is of the essence, Tyrrell. I hurried past the first floor, not bothering to check it. I didn't slow down as I reached the second floor and went along the broad hallway.

Quick as I'd been in gaining entry and dealing with the guards below, I hadn't been fast enough. Not near fast enough. To my left in the hall, Amanda Rundle stood in the hallway behind Courtney with a knife to her throat. In the soft light, the blade gleamed as if it were polished silver. To my right, Nigel Sinclair stood with a Sig Sauer pointed at me. All three of them were wearing pajamas.

"Wow," I said softly. "Sorry to interrupt your pajama party. Was this invitation only?"

Rundle said to Sinclair, "He's the mystery man from the Hilton in New York. He did follow us."

"I can hear you, you know," I said. To Courtney, "You all right?"

"Sort of."

I smiled. "Hang in there."

Sinclair said. "Drop your weapon or my security director will kill Ms. Wilson."

"Kill Courtney, and I'll kill both of you."

"In case you are unaware, I know how to use this gun," he grinned mirthlessly.

"I don't want to get into a dick-measuring contest with you, but please believe me, I can shoot a thousand times better than you." It occurred to me that Sinclair might be stalling for time. When the other guards arrived the odds would shift heavily in his favor. "Listen, Nigel, why don't we make ourselves comfortable in your room? I hear it's quite nice."

He glanced at Rundle, and she shrugged. At least, I think she shrugged—it was hard to tell with her standing behind Courtney.

Rundle spoke to me, "Take a step back into the stairwell. Ms. Wilson and I will walk past you. Mr. Sinclair will have a clear line of sight to you from his position in the hallway. If you shoot me in the back, he'll kill you."

"I'd never shoot you in the back," I said

indignantly. "I also would never hide behind someone with a knife to their throat."

"Step back," she said.

I did as I was told, and Rundle and Courtney walked down the right side of the hall. Sinclair was to the left, or far side, of the hall, and indeed had a clear line of sight to me in the stairwell door. Of course, I also had a clear line of sight to him. If it hadn't been for the knife at Courtney's throat, I would have dropped him where he stood. Oh well, as Mick Jagger once sang, you can't always get what you want.

As soon as Rundle passed Sinclair, I stepped back into the hallway and hurried toward Sinclair and the bedroom door. I didn't want them to shut me out, pinning me between the almost-impregnable hall door and the guards who were now clomping up the stairs at great speed.

Rundle and Courtney went into the bedroom; Sinclair backed through the door a split-second later and tried to shut it in my face. I kicked it open. The door whacked him in the face and sent him spinning backward. I stepped inside, my gun on Sinclair, and shut the door behind me. I shot home the two sliding bolts.

"That's enough," Rundle commanded.

"Absolutely," I agreed and stayed where I was with my back to the door, Ruger aimed at Sinclair, looking around the room. It was one hell of a room. For starters, it was pretty damn big. Like park three or four Rolls Royces big. The walls were covered in a dark-red, damask wallpaper throughout. The walls were hung with what looked like landscapes painted by Thomas Gainsborough. The floor had three large Persian carpets. An overstuffed couch and armchairs were placed around an elaborately carved mantel and large fireplace. Away from the sitting area was a four-poster bed that probably could have doubled as a helipad.

A voluptuous, dark-haired young woman in a pink lace teddy cowered in the four-poster bed, playing the dismayed damsel, "Nigel, are you all right? Nigel? What's happening?"

"Be quiet," He growled at her. Clearly a man of no bedside manner.

"But, Nigel—"

"Shut up!"

Sinclair had climbed to his feet and dabbed at his bleeding cheek with the sleeve of his pajamas. "I should kill you," he muttered angrily to me.

"Later," I said.

As if on cue, the guards began pounding on the outside of the bedroom door. The pounding was muffled, like the sound of distant thunder. Harry had said the room was secure, and I believed him.

"I know you don't negotiate," I said in a firm, patient tone. "I understand you don't have to. But I was hoping that I might persuade you to treat the current situation a little bit differently than you have other . . . uh, challenges . . . in your past."

289

"Get to the point," Sinclair said contemptuously.

"You give me Courtney. I give you your files and stop destroying your businesses. Life goes on for all of us."

"What kind of guarantee can you give that you'll do as you say?" asked Rundle.

"I can't. But you don't have any other options."

"I could kill you both," Sinclair said.

"You could," I mused. "But then you'd have to get rid of the bodies and that is so messy. Oh! And the digital copies of your books would go to law enforcement. All those nosey people at Scotland Yard and Interpol and the FBI and who knows who else. Very, very messy. You could end up spending the rest of your life in prison."

"You're bluffing."

"Bluffing? You think I'd come in here without a Plan B?"

"I'm sorry, sir," Rundle said, "but it doesn't make sense that he would come here without a backup plan." She pulled on Courtney's arm with her left hand and led her to one of the chairs near the fireplace. "Sit down."

Courtney did as she was told. Rundle maintained her position behind Courtney with the knife at her throat. Rundle used her left hand to dig into her pajama pants pocket and pulled out a phone. She made a call and said, "Stop pounding on the door. We're all right."

The muffled thunder stopped as she disconnected.

"How 'bout it, Sinclair?" I asked. "Care to swap Courtney's safety for yours?"

He seemed to consider my proposed deal. He scrutinized his gun, my gun, and then Courtney. Finally, he looked into my eyes and said quietly, "I . . . don't . . . negotiate."

Sinclair turned to Rundle and nodded.

19

I could have shot Sinclair in that moment, but Courtney's only hope was that I was fast enough to stop Rundle. I spun around, aimed my gun at Rundle, and fired.

Rundle was already slicing her blade across Courtney's throat. Courtney's eyes were wide with terror, her mouth open, gasping for air. The blood flowed from her neck wound.

My bullet caught Rundle in the left upper chest, went straight through her heart, and exited through her shoulder blade. She fell, already dead.

I took a step toward Courtney, as Sinclair fired. A bullet tore through my right tricep. The force of the shot staggered me. Sinclair fired twice more but missed me as I hit the floor. I rolled over to face him, shifted the Ruger from my right hand to my left, and fired.

It was a miracle I hit him, but I did; my bullet caught him in the left leg. He collapsed, dropping his gun and clutching his leg in pain. I struggled to my feet, took a few steps toward him, and kicked the gun out of his reach.

The guards had resumed their muffled pounding on the door.

"Oh, go fuck yourselves," I muttered.

I turned to Courtney. She was slumped in the chair, covered in the blood from her horrific neck wound. Her sightless eyes were open, staring at nothing.

"Oh, Courtney," I whispered, tears rolling down my face. "I'm so sorry."

Someone was screaming. I realized that Sinclair's mistress had witnessed everything. She was kneeling in the middle of the bed, sobbing and screaming, clutching the comforter to her like a gigantic security blanket. I walked over to her, yanked the comforter away, and told her to shut up. She tumbled back into the covers and was hiding under a pillow, continuing to sob into it.

I spread the comforter over Courtney. "I'm so sorry," I repeated.

Time to deal with Sinclair. I walked over to him. He'd managed to pull off his pajama top and was trying to knot it around his leg in some kind of half-assed bandage. Maybe a half-assed tourniquet. I didn't give a shit. I stepped close to him, with my feet next to his wounded leg. He looked up at me.

"I told you I don't negotiate."

"Yup, you told me."

"You lose."

"I don't think so," I said. And shot him three times. Center mass. He flopped onto the floor. I leaned over him and checked for a pulse. Dead as a door nail.

My arm was throbbing, and I felt dizzy. Probably loss of blood. I stumbled over to the other chair in front of the fireplace, dropped into it, and closed my eyes.

"Harry?"

"I'm here, Jack."

"Oh, thank God."

"Yes."

I waved my hand around, trying to indicate the lethal mess in Sinclair's bedroom. "Sorry about all this. Could you . . . ?"

I think Harry told me not to worry. I don't remember. I might have imagined it as I blacked out.

* * *

I woke up in bed in my apartment on Grove Street in Greenwich Village. Based on the angle of the sunlight coming through the windows, I guessed it was midday. But what day?

Next to the bed was an IV dripping clear liquid into my left arm. My right arm was sore as hell. I gently stretched it, trying to relax the muscles.

Harry walked in with a cup of cappuccino and a couple of ibuprofen pills. "How are you feeling?"

"Oh, fantastic. What day it is?"

"Monday."

"It's only been 24 hours since I went into Sinclair's townhouse?"

"More like 36 hours. Your enfeebled state is

causing you to forget the time difference."

He put the cup and the pills on my bedside table, helped me sit up, and handed me the cup and the pills. I downed the ibuprofen and gulped down cappuccino.

"Better?" Harry asked.

"I will be. Have you been attending to my medical needs?"

"Yes. It seemed so much easier than sneaking you back into the country and trying to explain why you needed treatment for a bullet wound."

I sighed in exaggerated annoyance. "Those pesky requirements that bullet wounds be reported to the police."

"Exactly."

"What happened to Courtney?"

"I'm sorry, but I needed to leave her at the crime scene. Otherwise the police on either side of the Atlantic wouldn't have known how she died and by whose hand. Her body is being flown home today. I'll handle the funeral arrangements for her parents."

"Thank you. Who do the police think killed Sinclair and Rundle?"

"Assailant unknown. Kamal Tiwari is going to suggest a rival had Sinclair assassinated."

"Okay, let me guess," I pointed to the IV drip, "you probably topped me off with a pint of fresh blood—"

"I did—"

"And now it's saline to hydrate and antibiotics to fight off infection."

"Yes."

"What about the wound itself? Through and through?"

"Yes. No muscle or nerve damage. I closed the wounds with eight sutures on each side of your arm."

"How soon before I can throw a curveball?"

"I don't know. Were you able to throw the curve before you got shot?"

"No. More's the pity." I had more cappuccino. The combination of espresso and foamed milk was good for whatever ailed me. "How soon will I be back to normal?"

"When were you ever normal?"

"I set you up for that one."

"Yes."

"How soon will I be fighting bad guys?"

"Why? Are you in a rush to return to the fray?"

"Actually, I am. I'm afraid we have some unfinished business."

"Pardon me for pointing out the obvious—and, in Courtney's case—the tragic realities, but your client is dead. The villain and his right-hand woman are dead. His criminal enterprises will be dismantled by international law enforcement. What could possibly be unfinished?"

"We've been missing something all along. I think we focused on the wrong bad guy when we locked onto Sinclair."

"But he kidnapped and killed Courtney."

"Yes, he did. But why did he go after Courtney?"

"Jack, we've been through all this before. In addition to his having narcissistic personality disorder, Sinclair had a hair-trigger when he thought he was threatened. It didn't have to be rational."

"You're absolutely right," I said. "Absolutely. But what was it about Courtney that made him think she was a threat. Why out of all the people he walked by at the Bargen-Meijer Gallery did he fixate on her?"

"He was convinced she saw something."

"Exactly. He was *convinced*. But who or what convinced him?" I asked rhetorically.

"O'Malley."

"Yup. O'Malley carried a piece of paper around, flashed it at Courtney, and expressed concern about what she might have seen. Nothing too obvious, just enough to get Sinclair's paranoid juices flowing. Once Sinclair felt threatened, there would be no stopping him."

"So, a set up," Harry said.

"Yup. This entire thing happened so that O'Malley could take down Sinclair."

"What was his motive?"

"At any given moment," I replied, "O'Malley is laundering millions of dollars for Sinclair—"

"*Tens* of millions of dollars," Harry clarified.

"*Tens* of millions. If Sinclair went down for killing Courtney, O'Malley could keep all the money he had washed for Sinclair."

"People have certainly killed for much less," Harry

said. "But your intervention couldn't have been part of O'Malley's plan."

"No, no way. But my appearance in this little double-cross drama was a lucky break for him since it led to Sinclair's demise. I'm guessing that if I hadn't stumbled onto the scene, O'Malley would have found another way to rat out Sinclair for whatever happened to Courtney. A guy like O'Malley must have contacts at NYPD or the FBI. He could have slipped someone a tip."

"And when law-enforcement fully investigated Sinclair—" Harry mused.

"They would wrap him up like fish and chips in old newspaper."

"But wouldn't law enforcement discover Sinclair's connection to O'Malley?"

"The only thing they'd find is that O'Malley handled what he thought were legitimate purchases and sales of art," I responded. "Lots of anonymous buying and selling going on in the art world. No way to prove culpability on O'Malley's part."

Harry was quiet for a long time. "You're going to settle the score with O'Malley."

"Oh, yeah." I finished my cappuccino. "Could I please have another?"

"Certainly."

"When can I deal with O'Malley?"

"Not for a few days, at least."

"I *am not waiting* a few days. If I have to totter

over to his gallery with my IV drip in tow, I will."

"Your stubbornness has survived intact."

"Yup."

"I will see if I can influence your healing."

"Speed me along the recovery curve?"

"I'll try."

"Thank you," I said. And meant it.

"You're welcome," he replied and walked off to make me another cappuccino.

I picked up my phone off the nightstand and called Naomi.

"Are you all right?" she asked breathlessly. "Harry said you got shot again!"

"I'm afraid so."

"How many times is that?"

"More than I care to remember."

"Right, sure. Are you all right?"

"Didn't Harry tell you I was fine."

"He did. But I wanted to hear it from you."

"Now you have. I'm fine. Listen, I need some help from you and Stewart."

"Shoot. Oh, sorry, poor choice of words."

"Freudian slip, no doubt."

Harry returned with a fresh cup of cappuccino. I took a quick sip and said, "While we were pulling off our little caper at the Bargen-Meijer Gallery, I don't suppose that when you were hooked up to the gallery's network you . . . ?"

"Of course I did."

"You didn't let me finish my question."

"You were about to ask if I took O'Malley's records while I was getting Sinclair's."

"Ah . . . yes, I was."

"And, yes, I did. And Stewart's already analyzed the hell out of them."

"Anything interesting?"

"Stewart's right here—I'm putting you on speaker."

"Hey, Jack," Stewart said. "Glad you're okay. We were really sorry to hear about Courtney."

"Yeah, thanks." It wasn't a graceful response, but my feelings about Courtney were too raw for any kind of conversation. "What did you find about O'Malley's financials?"

"Exactly what you'd expect. LLCs and off-shore accounts up the wazoo. No obvious signs of any criminal activities. Boy, being an art dealer is one hell of a set-up for laundering money. Dozens and dozens of transactions, mostly cash, mostly anonymous. It's like someone designed a hoity-toity laundry system."

"Hoity toity?"

"You know, artsy fartsy."

"So, you found lots of cash but no evidence of any crime."

"That's right. Sorry."

"No worries. That's exactly what I expected. Naomi?"

"Yes, Jack."

"Is it possible for you to hack into the off-shore accounts?"

"With Harry's help, I can hack into anything."

"Good."

"What are you up to?"

"I'll let you know."

*　　*　　*

Kim appeared at dinner time with tears in her eyes, a fragile smile, and a takeout dinner from Le Coucou, a fabulous French restaurant that had opened last year. (Not everything about 2016 was horrible.)

Harry had supervised my move to the living room couch in anticipation of her visit. He had hovered nearby as I slowly climbed out of bed and pulled on gray sweatpants and a maroon Fordham hoodie. He had continued hovering as I walked down the hall to the living room.

"Excuse me," I said, "but by your own diagnosis, I am not dying. There's no need for you to play helicopter parent."

"I don't want you to fall and ruin my handiwork. The stitches are perfect. There will be almost no scar."

"I'm so proud of you. Now get away from me."

I'd eased onto the couch when I heard a soft knock on my front door.

Harry let Kim in. She kissed him hello on the cheek and came straight to me.

"Don't get up," she said, leaning over to kiss me on the cheek.

Hmm. Not on the lips. Not a great start.

She raised the bag, presenting it to me, the admiring audience. "Dinner from Le Coucou." She reeled off a bunch of French words that I assumed were our menu. My command of French was way too poor to follow her.

"It all sounds delicious," I said. "Thank you."

"I wanted to do something special for your return."

Harry said, "Let me take your coat, and then I'll leave you alone." He hung her coat in the tiny front closet then disappeared. Poof.

I took a deep breath and smiled. I hoped the smile didn't look as forced as it felt. Kim smiled back and brushed a tear from her cheek.

"I'd better deal with dinner," she said and walked into the kitchen.

The kitchen was separated by a long counter from the dining area, which was just one end of my living room. We could have continued to talk, but it wouldn't have been easy, so neither of us made the attempt. It felt like the ultimate awkward pause.

Was the fancy-schmancy dinner with names I couldn't pronounce a warm welcome home? Or a fond farewell? My stomach was in knots: bowlines and double dragon loops. I knew we had to have whatever conversation was coming, but I was afraid of the possible outcome.

Kim came out of the kitchen with a dinner plate in each hand. "Can you sit at the dining room table? Or would you rather eat off of the coffee table in front of the couch?"

"For *cuisine française*, we dine formally." I inched slowly over to the table as she put the plates down.

"Oh?" she scanned the sweatpants, the hoodie, and 3-days of beard stubble. "This is your idea of formal?"

"It's my idea of perfectly acceptable dinner wear when you've been shot twice in less than a week."

She grinned, but her eyes were sad. Too soon, Tyrrell. Way too soon. She went back into the kitchen and returned with silverware and napkins.

"How do you feel?" she asked as we sat down.

"I'm okay. A little sore here and there. Tired as all get out. Not too bad all things considered."

"And how are you *feeling* here?" she asked, tapping her fingers over her heart.

"I've been better."

"Harry told me you lost your client."

"Yes." I really didn't want to talk about Courtney's death, so I cut myself a bite of the fish entrée. It was *magnifique*.

Kim followed my lead, and we ate most of the meal in silence, which I took as a very bad sign. It was completely unlike us not to chat and laugh our way through a meal, no matter how *merveilleux* the food was.

When we'd finished our entrées, Kim cleared the plates, saying over her shoulder as she went to the kitchen, "Cappuccino with dessert?"

"Yes, please."

She returned with two small plates, each with a chocolate tart on it. "Be right back."

I could hear the espresso machine gurgling and hissing as it did its miraculous work. Kim came back to the table with two cups of cappuccino.

We both had bites of our tarts. I couldn't speak for Kim, but I was transported to a higher plane of existence. Chocolate like this, accompanied by cappuccino, elevated me spiritually. Wow. If only my spiritual elevation would last through the conversation I was sure was about to transpire.

"I was so . . . worried about you," Kim whispered. "I couldn't imagine how I could go on if you didn't come back from London."

"Ah, yes, but I did come back."

"But you're not done, are you?"

"Done with the case? No . . . I'm not. There's one last bit of business I have to attend to."

"Even though your client is dead?"

"*Because* my client is dead. There is the urgent matter of getting justice for her."

"Are you going to have to kill someone else?"

"I'd prefer not to."

"Don't joke about it."

"Sorry. But I honestly don't want to kill anyone ever again."

"But these things happen," she said bitterly.

"Not to sound like a defensive six-year old, but it's not my fault that a couple of very greedy men forced a situation where people, including my client, died. And, yes, some of them died at my hand. I hate it. But I didn't have much choice. And I didn't cause it."

Kim's eyes were locked on mine, then she looked down at her dessert.

"I'm . . . I'm seriously thinking . . ." Oh for crying out loud, Tyrrell, just say it. "I think that after I finish this last piece of business, I'm going to retire."

She raised her face and contemplated me for a moment. "Are you doing this for me?"

"Yes. For you. For us. I think it's time."

Her eyes watered. After a few seconds she shook her head. "I can't be the reason you give up your calling."

"I love you—why can't you be the reason?"

"You'll resent me forever. If you give it up, you have to do it for you. Not me."

"I want this, too."

"You want it because I want it, and you're trying to make me happy."

"How is making you happy a bad thing?"

"Because it won't work. Because you'll be angry and resentful. Because you'll worry about all the people you could have helped if I hadn't gotten in the way."

"You're not in the way . . . Oh God, I really haven't got a clue what to say or do next. I'm at a complete loss."

"Me, too." She stood up, the tears flowing freely down her face. "I'm so sorry."

She hurried toward the front door—

"Kim, wait, please—"

She grabbed her coat and was gone. The front door closed with a gentle thud. I wished my heart had dropped as gently.

20

Kim sent me a text a few hours later: "I'm sorry I walked out that way."

I answered, "It's okay, we have a lot to work through."

She didn't reply.

I heard nothing from her for the next couple of days. So I rested up. When I woke on Monday, I had felt like the loser in a twelve-round heavyweight fight. By Wednesday, I could take a shower all by myself, something most nine-year olds can accomplish. Oh well, progress not perfection.

Give me a couple of loaded Rugers, and I can take on the world. Or at least take on Raymond O'Malley.

For the last couple of days, my emotional energy had been spent on Kim. But my mental energy had been spent on O'Malley.

Naomi and Stewart visited Tuesday at lunch time, bringing deli sandwiches and a box of cupcakes from Magnolia Bakery. I was surprised at how my appetite had recovered and devoured my roast beef sandwich. Harry appeared in between the sandwich and dessert courses, and made cappuccinos for everyone. As we savored the cupcakes, we discussed what to do with O'Malley's ill-gotten gains.

"Is that doable?" I asked after we'd gone through what I hoped we could do.

"We can do anything," Naomi smiled.

"With Harry's help," Steward added.

"Can you update me on security at the gallery? I'm guessing he's improved it since our little visit."

Naomi nodded, "Oh yeah, he's doubled the team of guards on site and some of them carry guns, not Tasers."

"What his personal security?" I asked.

"He's driven to and from work every day in a Lincoln Navigator Black Label L."

"That's the extra-long version of the Navigator," Harry explained.

"I know what the 'L' means."

"I just wanted to be sure you weren't wallowing in ignorance."

"So kind of you," I said and turned back to Naomi, "How many security people in the car with him?"

"Only two. His driver and a guy who rides in the back with him and holds the door open for him."

"Both well-trained? Both carrying?"

"Yes and yes."

"Still, two is a hell of a lot less than his crew at the gallery."

"What about going after him at home?" Stewart asked. "He probably doesn't have anywhere near the number of guards around him there."

"He doesn't," Naomi confirmed.

"I'm not going after him in his family's home. His wife doesn't need the hell scared out of her. She didn't do anything wrong." I glanced at Harry, "Did she?"

He shook his head. "She is not involved in any way with O'Malley's criminal activities."

"Okay then," I said. "The extra-long car it is."

"I'll send you the vehicle's license plate number and O'Malley's address and schedule," Naomi said.

"Perfect. I think that takes care of everything. Unless anyone has anything else on his or her mind."

"I was wondering if anyone was going to have the last cupcake," Stewart said.

"We saved it for you," I replied.

"Thanks!" he said and pounced on it with leopard-like swiftness.

"Thanks to you for the food. Just what I needed."

"Harry told us what to get," Naomi said.

"Thank you," I nodded to Harry. "And now, off with you, my mischievous sprites! Do your work!"

They laughed. Stewart shook my hand, and Naomi gave me a peck on the cheek. "Feel better," she whispered.

Why did I think she wasn't just talking about my physical woes? After they left, Harry cleaned up. My phone rang. It was my FBI buddy, Joanne Agar.

"Kamal Tiwari said you were very helpful."

"I was *extremely* helpful."

"Pardon me. I'm sure I mis-paraphrased that. How are you? Where are you? Kamal said you kind of disappeared. Right around the time Nigel Sinclair was killed."

"I'm at home in New York. Things got . . . complicated in London. I needed to make a quick departure."

"Did you get hurt?"

"Well . . . I can neither confirm nor deny that I was shot again."

"Oh my God. How bad?"

"A mere bagatelle."

"Oh sure. That's twice in what—5 days?"

"Something like that."

"Has it occurred to you that you should rethink your life? I'm sure Kim would like you to consider a new career."

"Yes, she finds my life to be . . . I don't know what word adequately captures her feeling. Kim is very . . . very unhappy with our situation right now. How does your wife handle it?"

"It gives my wife the shivers every morning when she sees me take my gun out of its lockbox," Joanne said. "She can't help but worry even though she knows that I spend a hell of a lot more time using a phone and a computer than pulling my weapon. Look, you've never volunteered—and I'm not asking—but I've always had the sense that what you do is extraordinarily violent and dangerous. Much worse than what I do. I'm not sure any significant other could handle being your partner."

"You may be right."

"Sorry."

"You're just giving it to me straight," I sighed. "So maybe it's time for me to hang it up?"

"Maybe. And if you ever want a partner for your cozy little, 9-to-5 security firm, let me know."

"You will be my first call. Well, second—"

"Right after Kim."

"You got it."

"I'm serious."

"Me, too," I replied. "Thanks."

"You're welcome."

We disconnected.

Harry walked into the living room from the kitchen. "Another cappuccino?"

"No, thanks."

"Wait," he said, holding his arms out from his sides as if to balance himself. "Did I just feel the earth tremble? Did you just decline a cup of cappuccino?"

"Yes, I did. Even I have my limits. Especially when 93 percent of my waking time is spent on the couch."

He sat in one of my armchairs. "I am astonished that you were able to recognize your limits."

"Spoken like my guardian angel."

He treated me to his Mona Lisa smile. It might have been my imagination, but I thought his smile lingered a tiny bit longer than usual.

"Do I have to choose?" I asked. "Do I have to choose between following my calling or finding happiness with Kim? Is the Chairman really asking me to make that choice? That's what it seems like to me."

Harry took a long time answering. "Yes, it seems like that to me, too. May I ask you a question?"

"Fire away."

"Did you go into our work together to find happiness for yourself?"

"Mankind was my business," the ghost of Jacob Marley had shouted to Scrooge. The phrase echoed in my brain.

I replied, "No. You made it very clear—right from the beginning—that this was a selfless business. This isn't about cash and prizes for me. It's about helping others."

"And haven't you found that to be satisfying?"

"Sort of. Mostly. I guess. It's hard to finish a case, say goodbye to someone I've come to care for, and know that they'll never remember me. I can't call them and see how they're doing."

"I think you mean that you can't call them to see if they still like you."

"*Like* me? They don't even *remember* me. And right now, in this moment, we're not talking about my clients not having any idea who I am. We're talking about my future with Kim."

"You make a good point that your clients are not

comparable to your relationship with Kim."

"Maybe . . . maybe the Chairman could help me out?"

"How? Are you hoping that He will make Kim feel the way you want her to?"

"Oh . . . no, no," I realized that that was exactly what I was asking for and was horrified. "No, of course not. She has to be able to exercise her free will."

"As do you."

"Yeah . . . yeah, I do. I guess I have to make a choice about the entire rest of my life."

"It sounds easy when you express it in that way."

"You're no damn help at all."

*　　*　　*

Wednesday morning at 9:00 A.M., I was snug in my parka, standing at the corner of Riverside Drive and West 87th Street, ostensibly watching three dogs playing in a Riverside Park dog run. In reality, I was keeping an eye on the entrance of 140 Riverside Drive, The Normandy. An Art Deco building of luxury co-ops that stretched the entire block from West 86th to 87th. Home of Mr. Raymond O'Malley. He owned a pair of apartments that had been merged into one, which meant he'd spent somewhere around seven or eight million dollars to purchase the apartments and another couple of million to blend them

313

into a single glorious residence. To paraphrase F. Scott Fitzgerald: the rich are different from you and me.

But I wasn't here to admire O'Malley's real estate holdings. I was here to intercept him before he went to the gallery. A Lincoln Navigator Black Label L, traveling uptown, pulled to a stop in front of The Normandy. I made a show of checking my watch just in case anyone was watching me then dumped my coffee cup into a nearby trash can. And sauntered across Riverside Drive to the southeast corner at West 87th, heading downtown once I reached the sidewalk in front of the building.

A burly white guy with rosy cheeks and a crew cut got out of the front passenger side of the Lincoln and went to stand next to the rear passenger door. If he wasn't ex-NYPD, I was a prima ballerina. The driver stayed behind the wheel and checked his mirrors continuously. I had just reached the front bumper when the Normandy's doorman held open the front door. At the same moment, the ex-cop opened the rear door of the Lincoln.

Raymond O'Malley strode out of The Normandy to the Lincoln. Expensive wool overcoat, charcoal-gray suit underneath, white shirt, maroon repp tie with blue and silver stripes, and black shoes.

I cut across O'Malley's path and kept going, glancing over my shoulder. The ex-cop greeted his boss, and O'Malley climbed into the Lincoln. I wheeled around, pulled a Ruger from my shoulder holster, and quickly stepped back toward the ex-cop and the still-open door of

314

the Lincoln.

I jammed the barrel of the gun against the back of his neck and hissed in his ear, "Get in!"

He did as he was told, shoving himself in next to O'Malley. I shifted the gun from his neck to his side and pushed it hard into his ribs, just to be sure he didn't suffer any confusion about who was in charge.

"I've got a 9mm Ruger in your ribs—what's your name?"

He croaked, "Lonergan."

"Okay, just so nobody does anything stupid, let's all remember that I have a gun in Lonergan's side." To the ex-cop I said, "And don't try any fast moves. You'll never be quick enough to knock the gun away."

"I won't."

"Please, no one do anything stupid, and I won't have to shoot Lonergan. Got it?"

They all nodded and mumbled something affirmative.

"Good," I said. "Drive up to 89th then pull over."

Twenty seconds later, as we neared 89th, he asked me where he should pull over.

"On the park side. No parking, no standing, I don't care. Pull over."

He continued to follow instructions, stopping the Lincoln in a white-striped no-parking space.

"Turn off the car. No blinkers. Hand me the key."

The driver was obviously hoping to get a gold star,

315

because he was one incredibly well-behaved boy.

"Okay, things are going to get tricky from here. You can do what I tell you and no one gets hurt. Or you can give me a hard time, in which case I will leave you in a whole lot of pain. Makes no difference to me."

All three men mumbled words to the effect of "Sure . . . right . . . got it . . . no worries . . . ."

I switched my Ruger to my left hand. "At this distance, I'm ambidextrous."

"I'm not going to try anything," the ex-cop said.

I dug into a parka pocket for plasticuffs, the all-purpose bondage tool. "Twist around and put your hands behind you."

The ex-cop was cuffed within seconds. "Now things increase in difficulty," I said. "Do I cuff the driver or the art dealer? I think I'll go with age before beastly." I switched the gun back to my right hand, leaned over the front seat and shoved the Ruger into the driver's neck. His eyes were roughly the size of salad plates.

To O'Malley I said, "Twist and stick your hands out behind you."

I proved I was ambidextrous with plasticuffs as well as with a gun.

"For my last trick," I spoke to the driver, "I'd like you to face the window on your left—"

"And shove my freakin' hands behind me!"

"You're such an apt pupil."

And, like the others before him, he was cuffed.

316

I wish I could tell you that I'm the trusting sort, but I'm not. I had the driver and O'Malley get out of the Lincoln then had the driver join his buddy in the back seat. I cuffed their ankles and then cuffed the driver's right ankle to the ex-cop's left ankle. For good measure, I cuffed the driver's right wrist to the ex-cop's left wrist. And to top it off, I yanked off their neckties, none too gently, and used them as gags. I patted them down, collected a pair of phones and a pair of Glocks, all of which I tossed into the way back of the vehicle. I climbed out and closed the left rear door. With the dark-tinted windows, a passerby wouldn't be able to see the trussed-up men inside.

While busy with his security team, I had glanced at O'Malley several times, always sure to make eye contact. Always sure to point my pistol in his general direction. He gave me no cause to shoot him. Which suited my plan. I grabbed him by one arm and led him away from the illegally parked Lincoln to the plaza south of the Soldiers and Sailors Monument. A graceful, 100-foot tall structure, the monument had been designed to look like something out of Greek antiquity. Despite being designated a historic landmark by both New York City and State, it had been allowed to fall into disrepair, and now it's beauty was imprisoned behind a chain-link fence that was—no doubt—supposed to keep vandals from doing any more damage.

We stopped in the plaza near one of the Civil War canons, looking downhill through the bare trees of

Riverside Park to the Hudson River.

"You're the one who broke into my gallery."

"That would be me."

"Did you kill Nigel Sinclair?"

"Yup."

"Are you going to kill me, too?"

"Only if you don't cooperate."

"You realize that my security team has the GPS for the car. A backup team will be here within a few minutes."

"The more the merrier," I said. "Now stop stalling and listen to me."

"Who are you?"

"Listen to you—asking questions as if you're the one who's in charge."

"Who are you?" He repeated insistently.

"Like you said: I'm the man who killed Nigel Sinclair."

"And now you're threatening me."

I wanted to punch him in the face. No threat. No warning. Just smash his face. Instead, I asked, "Why did you set up Courtney Wilson?"

"What?"

"You convinced Sinclair that Courtney was a threat to him. He eliminated the threat by killing her. You used her to set him up. So you could keep his money."

"You killed him, not me."

"My getting sucked into this was a lucky break for you since I ended up eliminating Sinclair for you. But it doesn't change the fact that you threw Courtney's life away just so you could take Sinclair's money."

"You can't prove I did that."

"I don't need to prove it," I growled. "You're going to admit it."

He laughed. "Even if it were true, why would I admit to it?"

"You son of a bitch," let's dial it down, Tyrrell. "Courtney was about the same age as your daughters."

"What? What have my daughters got to do with it?"

"I hoped that you would understand the horrible thing you did by throwing Courtney into Sinclair's path if you thought of her as being like your daughters. Thought of her as the same age, with some of the same hopes and dreams. Thought that maybe she loved her parents the same way your daughters love you."

"Shut up!"

"I'll shut up when you agree to confess."

He spun away from me, looking out over the Hudson. "I didn't do anything. I'm not confessing."

"That's not a workable plan for you."

"Oh? What happens now?"

"I'm glad you asked," I said, stepping in front of him and blocking his view of the river. "I'm going to take all your money. Every last penny that you stole from the recently deceased Nigel Sinclair. Every last dollar you have earned by money laundering. All of your completely legal investments from your prosperous years in financial services. Even from your gallery's bank accounts. And your personal checking account with your wife. You will be flat broke, busted like a blown tire on the Long Island Expressway."

"You're full of shit. There's no way you can get my money."

"Oh, if only that were true." I dug into a pocket and pulled out a sheet of paper. I unfolded it in front of O'Malley so that he could read it. "Now, this is only a partial list of your super secure, super secret off-shore accounts. As of 48 hours ago, the total of these five accounts was $37 million. As of this morning, the total was zero dollars. All five accounts were emptied and closed. That's gotta hurt."

He was flushed with anger. "You can't do this."

"It's already done. And *all* the money from *all* your accounts will disappear if you don't turn yourself in by the end of today. You'll have nothing. Nada. Zero. Zip. Zilch."

"I don't believe you."

"If I were in your shoes, I wouldn't believe me either." I folded the paper and tucked it into the breast pocket of his suit overcoat. "You'll need that. So you can check with your banks."

"Why would I waste my time doing that?"

"Just in case I'm not completely full of cornbread stuffing, you should check to see if the $37 million has, in fact, disappeared."

O'Malley's face went from flushed to pale. "What are you going to do with the money?"

"It's all been given to charity. Your ill-gotten gains have been converted into blessings for those in need."

"Don't lie to me. If you're going to take my money you can at least tell me the truth about it."

"I am telling you the truth. Your anonymous gifts are working wonders with food pantries and diaper banks and homeless shelters throughout the New York metro area."

"What are you going to do with the rest of it?"

"Nothing."

"Nothing. See, when you confess, the NYPD and the FBI are going to want to seize your funds. And law enforcement tends to get persnickety about outsiders seizing money generated by criminal enterprises."

"What do you want me to do?"

"You're going to double check with your banks to see that your $37 million has actually disappeared. Once you've proven to yourself that your money has gone bye bye, you will turn yourself in to Detective Charles Winfield at the 6th Precinct. He's in charge of the case regarding the attack on Courtney that took place a week ago today on West Street."

"What am I supposed to tell Detective Winfield?"

"Everything."

"What the hell is everything"

"You confess to setting up the aggravated assault on Courtney Wilson. And, oh yeah, to laundering money for Sinclair."

"But there's no proof."

"Hence, the confession."

He paced a few steps away from me then turned and walked back. "If I do this . . . I need to provide for my wife and daughters."

"One of my colleagues has done a definitive analysis of your assets, separating your ill-gotten gains from the legal ones. I'll make sure Detective Winfield has it. Your lawyer arranges for you to confess as part of a plea deal, and part of the deal will be that your wife and daughters hold onto the money you made during your career in financial services. A tidy sum of approximately $110 million."

He glared at me.

"That's the right amount, isn't it?" I asked.

O'Malley nodded, cursed, and asked, "What about the gallery?"

"Since that was the vehicle for the money laundering, it's going to be seized. The art will probably be auctioned off by the government."

"What? What?"

"Yeah, sorry about that. Now you know that actions have consequences."

"What kind of consequences?" he looked genuinely scared. The thought of prison time did that to some people.

"You're going to prison. Hopefully for longer than the span of Courtney Wilson's life. That would be justice."

I heard screeching tires and looked over at a black Ford Transit Connect jerking to a stop beside the Lincoln. Four men jumped out of the Transit. One ran to the Navigator. The other three, with guns drawn, scrambled around, scanning in every direction.

"The arrival of your guards changes nothing," I said. "Do you understand?"

"What if they kill you?"

"My colleagues will still take all your money if you don't turn yourself in."

One of the guards spotted us on the monument's plaza and shouted, "Over there!"

I raised my Ruger, aiming it at O'Malley's head. The four men ran toward us and took up positions completely surrounding us.

I said, "It's in everybody's best interests if we all stay calm."

21

"First things first, I want to make sure nobody gets hurt," I said, focusing my attention on each man in turn. "And by 'nobody' I mean me. And Mr. O'Malley here."

"Put your gun down," said one of the guards, a tall pinched-face white man with blond hair and a raspy voice.

"Not a chance," I replied. "But you should feel free to put yours down."

They stood frozen, their guns aimed at my head. I told myself that they had a poor shooting solution: hitting someone in the head isn't as easy as it looks on TV, and if they missed they were perfectly set up to catch each other in crossfire. That was my cerebral assessment of the situation. In my gut, I felt as if their gun barrels were as big as bazookas.

I pushed my gun's barrel end against O'Malley's temple.

"Let's de-escalate. We'll start with your lowering your weapons," I said.

They continued to aim at me.

I pushed my Ruger harder against O'Malley's head. He grunted, probably more of a reflex than pain, but it had the desired effect. The four lowered their weapons.

I glanced over my shoulder at the two white men behind me, a dark-haired man with bad skin and a super-skinny guy with a ridiculously bushy mustache. "You two, Dark Hair and Fu Manchu, come around in front of me. Move very slowly and circle to my right."

They took up positions next to the two men who were in front of O'Malley and me. From my right, it was Fu Manchu, Dark Hair, Pinched Face, and a guy I hadn't bothered to nickname.

"Very good," I said like an approving kindergarten teacher talking to a class of five-year olds. "Now, starting with you, Fu Manchu, crouch down very slowly, place your gun on the ground, and then step back from it. Way back."

He glanced to his right, past Dark Hair, to Pinched Face, who nodded. Fu Manchu complied perfectly and stepped back.

"Go ahead," I said to Dark Hair. He also followed instructions and stepped back.

I turned to Pinched Face. Oh shit, I thought, the guy's got crazy eyes. He was going to shoot me.

He began to crouch down, but as he reached out to put his pistol on the ground, his arm whipped up and in one motion fired. He missed. I fired twice, catching him in the right shoulder, smashing him down onto the plaza.

The guy I hadn't bothered to nickname was swinging his gun up, too. He and I fired almost simultaneously. I'd swear his bullet whizzed right past my ear. Mine caught him in the gut, slamming him backward.

I pivoted slightly to cover Dark Hair and Fu Manchu. They both had their hands up, clearly wanting no part in any more shooting.

Someone was gasping for breath. I saw O'Malley lying on the ground, a gaping wound in his chest, blood flowing from the exit wound in his back onto the plaza. His eyes locked on mine. Pinched Face had shot him not me.

"Help me, please . . ."

"Only God can help you now."

His eyes widen with terror, then he was still.

Dark Hair and Fu Manchu meekly submitted to being cuffed: wrists and ankles. Just to be absolutely sure they wouldn't make an escape, I cuffed them to the wounded Pinched Face and No Nickname. Both of them were alive but unconscious.

I heard police sirens wailing.

"Time for me to go," I said. I walked downhill into Riverside Park toward the Hudson. Once I was out of sight of the plaza, I said, "Harry?"

"Yes."

"You look so much better than I feel."

He smiled. A lingering smile. "I've already taken care of all security cameras, fingerprints in the SUV, and ballistics from your weapon. Do you need anything else?"

I shook my head, "I don't think so."

The police sirens were getting very loud. I peered through the bare trees at the Hudson River.

"Was . . . was O'Malley's getting shot instead of me

. . . was that the Chairman's protecting me?"

"Who else? He probably felt that your getting shot three times in one week was too much."

"Yeah, I'm sure that's the reason." I looked to the sky and said, "Thank you." Then to Harry, "Would you mind taking me home."

"Not at all."

We were in my living room within the tiniest fraction of a second.

"You look tired," Harry said.

"I guess I'm still not 100 percent. Getting justice really takes it out of you. I mean . . . out of me."

"Would you like some cappuccino? I'm going to make myself a cup."

"Yes, thank you."

*   *   *

A week later, on the day after the first day of spring, I treated myself to a cab ride to Kim's apartment. It was a partly cloudy afternoon with the temperature just over the 50-degree mark. The kind of weather that can be handled with a sweater and a windbreaker.

I hadn't heard from Kim since her texted apology for walking out of my apartment. Until this morning, I hadn't reached out to her. But unable to maintain the silence between us any longer, I had called and invited myself over for coffee.

When I reached the lobby of her building, the doorman told me that Kim would meet me on the roof. I thanked him, took the elevator to the top floor, then the stairway up to the rooftop terrace.

Kim was dressed in an off-white, wool turtleneck sweater and blue jeans. Her red hair cascaded gloriously over her shoulders, brilliant against the sweater. She was standing near the western side of the building, looking out over the Hudson River. As I crossed the roof to meet her, I couldn't help but recall that Raymond O'Malley had met his death about a half-mile from where we were.

She smiled. It seemed a tiny bit more robust than the fragile smile she had had the last time I saw her, but only a tiny bit. We hugged, and I kissed her on the cheek.

"Coffee?" she said, pointing to a small table between two patio chairs. "I have mugs and a thermos full of hot coffee."

"Yes, you do," I said, smiling. A smile seemed like a good idea under the circumstances. "And are these biscotti from Café Sabatini?"

"They are."

We sat down, and Kim poured coffee. She offered me a mug with one hand and the plate of biscotti in the other.

"How are you feeling?" she asked. "Better?"

"Pretty much. Harry's taking out my stitches tomorrow. I've taken it easy, rested a lot, read Dick Francis thrillers, and gone to meetings. I even had two sessions with Dr. Hoffman."

"Well, you're just a picture of spiritual, mental, and physical health."

"Getting there."

We sipped coffee, and I took a bite out of my biscotti. All was right with the world. If I could just ignore the elephant in the room. But I couldn't. I was pretty sure that Kim couldn't ignore it either.

"Listen, I . . . , uh, I've come to a decision. I'm retiring as a righter of wrongs—" I held my hand up to stop her from jumping in, "I'm not doing this because of you. Well, not primarily because of you. I'm retiring for me. I can't take this anymore. Getting shot twice in a week is too much of a good thing."

She grinned, but it faded fast.

"Retiring is the main thing I talked about with Dr. Hoffman."

"What did he say?"

"He agreed with you. He said I had to do this for myself and not to make you happy."

"Does he think you're doing it for you and not me?"

"I think he found the shot-twice-in-one-week reasoning persuasive."

"You didn't really answer my question."

"I don't know what he thought. Shrinks are masters of obfuscation."

She nodded. "I guess I'll find that out for myself. I've got an appointment with Dr. Hoffman."

"That's good. I hope . . . I hope you feel that he helps you."

We sat silently for a couple of minutes, drinking coffee and, in my case, eating more biscotti. But I felt uncomfortable in the silence. That damn elephant.

"You're . . . not happy," I said. "Or maybe 'happy' is the wrong word. You're not convinced about my retirement."

"Your calling has defined you. How can you leave it behind?"

"Maybe I feel like it's time for a new definition. There's only so much violence one guy can take. Or at least, there's only so much violence I can take. I've had enough. I want to try something new."

"What about the people you've helped?"

"My last client ended up dead. I wasn't a lot of help to her."

"I'm sure that wasn't your fault."

I shrugged. "It doesn't matter whether it's my fault or not. This last case changed things for me."

She didn't know how to respond to that. After a minute, she asked, "More coffee?"

"Yes, please."

Kim filled my mug from the thermos. "More biscotti?"

"I'm fine, thanks."

She screwed the top back on the thermos and took a sip of her coffee.

I kept my big mouth shut. I was pretty sure there was still an elephant lurking on that rooftop.

Kim sighed, "I don't know where we go from here."

"Are we going from—" I had to swallow before I could finish my thought, "—taking a break to breaking up?"

We were quiet for a long moment. I had an urgent impulse to say something, but I realized that this was one of those moments best served by listening.

Finally, Kim said, "Yes, we are." She stopped and wiped tears from her cheeks. "I'm so sorry. I meant it when I said I wanted to marry you. I wanted to be together and have a family with you. I love you. But, I didn't . . . I didn't know. . . ."

"You didn't know what it would be like to kill somebody. And even though you did it to save my life, killing someone changed everything."

"It does change everything. And this isn't about you. It's me. I don't think I can be with you after what happened . . . after the killing . . . I'm so sorry."

"I know," I said in a husky whisper. My throat was so tight it was a miracle I could speak even in a raspy croak. "I know. Believe me, I know how you feel."

Kim threw her arms around my neck and kissed me as if it was the last kiss we would ever have. I could taste the salt from her tears on her lips. I wanted to hold on forever, to save us from the wasteland of breaking up.

But eventually, we gently pulled away from each other.

"I love you," she said.

"I love you, too." I gave her one final, quick, soft kiss on the lips, turned, and went down the stairs to the top floor.

As I stood waiting for the elevator, I kept hoping Kim would come down the stairs and invite me back to the rooftop terrace. She didn't.

The elevator arrived. Step inside, Tyrrell. Push the button for the lobby.

I nodded to the doorman as I walked out into the late afternoon. I crossed West End Avenue and then across West 81st Street and stood on the southwest corner of the intersection looking up at Kim's windows.

"Harry?"

"I don't mean to add to your pain at this moment," he said, making his usual out-of-nowhere appearance, "but isn't standing here and watching Kim's building—"

"A little stalker-ish? Yeah . . . I should get moving." I began walking downtown on West End Avenue, and Harry fell into step beside me.

"Can you . . . make her forget like all the others?"

"The others?"

"The people I've helped in our other cases. Do any of them still remember me?"

332

"No."

"Okay. Can you do the same thing for Kim? Make her forget me."

"Do you want to make it so that Kim never knew you?"

"Yes, never have known me—without me, she wouldn't have killed anybody, and she wouldn't have suffered that trauma. She wouldn't be hurting the way she is now. I just want her to be happy."

"Do you understand that you'll lose her forever?"

I nodded. "Yes, I do. But I'll love her forever."

Harry stopped at the corner of 79th Street and West End Avenue. "Are you sure?"

"Yes. I'm sure. I want her to be happy."

"I will submit . . . your request to the Chairman." Harry offered me his hand—something he had almost never done in our relationship. We shook.

He disappeared.

It was about 4 miles from Kim's apartment to my place on Grove Street. I walked the whole way, alone.

It would take more than miles to say goodbye to her. To let go of her.

Geoff Loftus is the author of the thrillers *Murderous Spirit*, *Dark Mirage*, *No Traveler Returns*, *Fracture of the Soul*, and *Casual Slaughters* (all Jack Tyrrell novels), as well as the thrillers *Double Blind*, *Engaged to Kill*, and *The Dark Saint*.

Geoff also wrote *Lead Like Ike: Ten Business Strategies from the CEO of D-Day* and was the 2010 Keynote Speaker at the Eisenhower Legacy Dinner at the Eisenhower Presidential Museum and Library. He blogged on leadership for FORBES.com for almost a decade.

He collaborated with John Drimmer on the teleplay *Hero in the Family* for *The Wonderful World of Disney*. He has been a member of the Writers Guild of America, East for more than thirty years.

He lives in Scarsdale, New York with his wife, Margy.

Acknowledgments

I wouldn't be writing about Jack Tyrrell if not for the wonderful work of Charles Dickens, author of *A Christmas Carol*; Philip K. Dick, writer of the short story *Adjustment Team*; and George Nolfi, the writer-director of the terrific movie based on Dick's short story: *The Adjustment Bureau*. I am beyond grateful to them, because without them, there is no Jack Tyrrell.

Thanks to my editors: Alice Siempelkamp and Ted Berk. They've done so much to sharpen my ideas and clean up my many mistakes. Any remaining blunders are my fault. Tom Seligson has been my editor and publisher at Saugatuck Books through the years, and I'm very grateful for his continuing support.

Thank you to the many friends who have helped me through all of my writing and the rest of my life: Tom and Judy Galligan, Erica Fross, Steve Pitts, Katie Ryan, Jill Quist, Marcia Menter, Sal Vitale, and Lindy Sittenfeld.

Special thanks to my son, Greg. Nothing in my life has been as wonderful as being his father.

Finally and especially, thanks to the love of my life, my wife, Margy.

www.ingramcontent.com/pod-product-compliance
Lightning Source LLC
Chambersburg PA
CBHW071045250626
47159CB00002B/371